THIS BOOK WAS W
RANDY FLORES AN
TRUE-LIFE EVENT
ANDREA WE COME .... TOWN SOUTH OF HOUSTON TEXAS CALLED ROSENBERG TEXAS, WE BOTH HAD DIFFERENT LIFE MY PARENTS WERE WONDERFUL PARENTS FULL OF LOVE AND HAPPINESS ON THE OTHER HAND HER PARENTS WERE MEAN TO HER IN THIS STORY I HAVE THE OPPORTUNITY TO SHARE TRUE EVENTS NAMES HAD BEEN CHANGED TO PROTECT THE ACTUAL PERSON THESE THINGS GO ON EVERY DAY IN PEOPLE LIVES BUT NO ONE SPEAKS UP CAUSE THEY ARE TOO SCARED TO OR TOO EMBARRASSED TO BUT I THANK GOD THAT AFTER ALL WE HAD BEEN THREW WE NEVER LOST HOPE OR GAVE UP I WANT TO THANK MY PARENTS FOR ALL THEY HAVE DONE AND I THANK JESUS CHRIST FOR GIVING ME THE KNOWLEDGE TO PUT THIS DOWN ON PAPER WITHOUT OUR LORD AND SAVIOR, WE ARE NOTHING, AND I WANT TO THANK ALL THE PEOPLE IN THIS BOOK FOR BEING A PART OF OUR LIVES FOR YOU ALL ARE THE REASON I WROTE THIS BOOK I HOPE THE READERS OF THIS BOOK ENJOY IT

CHAPTER 1   I WAS ONLY A CHILD

I WAS BORN IN A SMALL TOWN SOUTH OF HOUSTON CALLED ROSENBERG TEXAS I WAS BROUGHT UP IN GOOD STANDARDS WITH LOTS OF WILL UPBRINGING AND HAD GOOD PARENTS WHO ALWAYS PROVIDED AND SHOW LOTS OF LOVE FOR ME AND MY 4 OLDER SIBLINGS, IT'S OCTOBER 1ST 1974 I AM 7 YEARS OLD WHICH WAS THE MOST TRAGIC DAY OF MY LIFE I RECALL WE WERE GOING TO MY AUNT'S HOUSE AND FROM THERE WE WERE GOING TO THE PARK SO AS WE WERE THERE, WE WERE GETTING READY TO GO TO THE PARK, I WAS PLAYING WITH MY COUSINS AND HAVING A GOOD TIME MY MOM AND AUNT WAS INSIDE GETTING FOOD READY FOR US I WAS OUTSIDE PLAYING AROUND THE CARS AND I WAS UNDER THE TRUCK PLAYING WITH MY CARS AND I HEARD THE SOUND I WILL NEVER FORGET THE TRUCK TURNED ON I TRY TO RUSH FROM UNDER THE TRUCK BUT I WAS HALF WAY OUT AND THE TRUCK RAN OVER MY BACK BUSTED MY STOMACH WIDE OPEN I GOT OUT FROM UNDER THE TRUCK HELD MY GUTS THEN I FELL TO THE GROUND MY MOM AND AUNT CAME RUNNING OUT IN TEARS, THEY PICK ME UP AND RUSH ME TO THE HOSPITAL ON THE WAY TO THE HOSPITAL I PASSED OUT SO MY AUNT STARTED GIVING ME CPR TO START THE PROCESS OF SAVING MY LIFE HALFWAY TO THE HOSPITAL THE CAR GOT A FLAT TIRE SO MY MOM GOT OUT OF THE CAR AND WAVE ANOTHER CAR DOWN

WHICH TURNS OUT TO BE A TAXI AND HE RUSHES ME TO THE HOSPITAL I REMEMBER ON MY WAY TO THE HOSPITAL I SAW MY MOM WITH THE SADDEST LOOK IN HER EYES WHEN I GOT TO THE HOSPITAL, THEY RUSHED ME TO THE OPERATING ROOM AND WE GOT

THERE MY MOM RUSHED TO LOOK FOR A PHONE SHE WAS RUNNING DOWN THE HALL LOOKING FOR A PHONE TO CALL MY DAD AT HIS JOB HE WAS WORKING A 12-HOUR SHIFT AS SOON AS MY DAD GOT THE MESSAGE THAT I GOT RAN OVER HE DROPPED THE PHONE AND RUSHED TO THE HOSPITAL AND AS HE SAW ME ON THE OPERATING TABLE FULL OF BLOOD HE DROPPED TO HIS KNEES AND CRIED AND PRAYED TO JESUS TO SAVE ME FROM THIS MISFORTUNE THAT I WAS GOING THREW THIS ACCIDENT CAUSED MANY PEOPLE LOTS OF PAIN AND SUFFERING SO AS MY PARENTS WERE EXPERIENCING WHAT WAS GOING ON THE DR. OPERATING ON ME COULD NOT DO ANYTHING FOR ME MY STOMACH WAS BUSTED OPEN I LOST HALF LIVER WAS FILLED WITH LOTS OF LITTLE ROCK'S AND THEY TRIED AND TRIED BUT COULD NOT HELP ME THEY WORK ON ME FOR LIKE 4 HOURS MAYBE LONGER SO AFTER ALL THIS THEY COULD NOT HELP THE SURGEON IN CHARGE HAD ME ON AN EMERGENCY LIFE FLIGHT TO THE HOUSTON HOSPITAL AND THREW THE WHOLE TIME I DID NOT FEEL ANY PAIN I WAS IN SHOCK SO AT THE HOUSTON HOSPITAL I WAS ON THE OPERATING TABLE I REMEMBER I HAD DIED FOR 2 HOURS AND WHEN I DIED I SAW MY SOUL GOING TO HEAVEN AND HALFWAY THERE AN ANGEL CAME DOWN AND PUT HIS HANDS ON MY SHOULDER AND PUSH MY SPIRIT BACK INTO MY BODY AND BEFORE MY SPIRIT WENT BACK INTO MY BODY THE LORD SPOKE TO ME AND SAID I AM NOT DONE WITH YOU SO THE DR, NEVER GAVE UP

ON ME I REMEMBER THAT DAY AS IF IT HAD HAPPENED A FEW DAYS AGO I WILL NEVER FORGET I LOST 23 PINTS OF BLOOD THERE WAS AN EMERGENCY BROADCAST THAT I NEEDED BLOOD DONATIONS AND PEOPLE FROM ALL OVER CAME TO MY RESCUE I STAYED IN THE HOSPITAL FOR THE TERM OF 2 WEEKS WHICH WAS OK LOTS OF PEOPLE BROUGHT ME GIFTS AND GAVE ME LOTS OF LOVE WITH ALL THE ATTENTION I FELT LOVED, BUT MOST OF ALL OUT OF ALL THAT WAS GOING ON I KNEW GOD'S PRESENCE WAS IN MY LIFE FOR IF IT WAS NOT BY HIS TENDER HANDS LOVE AND MERCY THAN I WOULD NOT SURVIVE THE ACCIDENT, BUT AFTER 2 WEEKS IN THE HOSPITAL I WAS FINALLY RELEASED AND ABLE TO GO HOME, AND THE WEEKS TO FOLLOW WERE A CHALLENGE BEING ABLE TO WALK AND STAND AGAIN, AND BEING ABLE TO EAT AND ABLE TO HOLD FOOD DOWN WITHOUT BRINGING PAIN TO MY STOMACH WHICH WAS HARD CAUSE EVERYTHING I DID OR ATE CAUSED PAIN IT TOOK TIME AND AS TIME WENT ON, I WAS ABLE TO GET OVER THIS SITUATION AND MOVE ON WITH MY LIFE, SO ITS OCTOBER 1, 1975, ITS MY BIRTHDAY I JUST TURNED 8 YEARS OLD MY MOM AND DAD PLANNED A SURPRISE PARTY FOR ME AND IT SURELY WAS A SURPRISING DAY ALL MY FRIENDS AND FAMILY WERE THERE WE HAD MY PARTY AT THE PARK I GOT ALL KINDS OF GIFTS MY DAY WAS A GREAT DAD, AS A CHILD I HAD EXPERIENCED A LOT OF DIFFERENT SITUATIONS SOME GOOD SOME BAD BUT OVERALL, MY LIFE AS A CHILD, WAS EVERYTHING I WANTED IT TO BE I WAS SLOWLY GETTING OVER MY DEADLY ACCIDENT, AND I STILL HAVE FLASHBACKS FROM THAT DAY. I FEEL THAT NO MATTER HOW MANY YEARS PASS, I'LL NEVER FORGET THAT TRAGIC OF THAT DAY. WILL JUST FEW MORE DAYS AND SUMMER IS OVER AND IT'S TIME TO GO BACK TO SCHOOL

THE START OF THE SCHOOL YEAR WAS NOT SO GREAT THERE WERE LOTS OF THINGS GOING ON IN MYLIFE THAT I DID NOT KNOW IF I WAS READY TO START A NEW SCHOOL YEAR WITH ALL THAT HAPPEN 1 ST PERIOD WAS GYM I WAS EMBARRASSED TO TAKE OFF MY SHIRT I DID NOT WANT PEOPLE TO STAIR AT ME OR MAKE FUNNY REMARKS ABOUT MY SCARE, THE WHOLE TIME I KEPT TO MYSELF I WAS CAUGHT UP IN MY PRIVATE WORLD STRUGGLING WITH MY SITUATION WONDERING WHAT WOULD BECOME OF MY LIFE, I WAS STILL AT A YOUNG AGE BUT AFTER THE ACCIDENT MY WHOLE LIFE CHANGED, I LOOKED AT THINGS AT A DIFFERENT WAY THAN OTHER PEOPLE DID, FOR THE FIRST MONTHS I KEPT TO MYSELF WANTING TO HAVE NO CONTACT WITH ANYONE WITH THE SCARY THOUGHT OF SOMEONE ASKING OF MY ACCIDENT, IT WAS AN UNPLEASANT EXPERIENCE EATING LUNCH BY MYSELF KEEPING TO MYSELF AT THE PLAYGROUND, SO MY FIRST YEAR BACK IN SCHOOL WAS AN UNPLEASANT EXPERIENCE AND NOT BECAUSE THE OTHER KIDS TREATED ME BADLY, EVERYONE WAS TRYING TO BE MY FRIEND, BUT INSECURITY OF MY SELF KEPT ME FROM TALKING TO ANYONE AND NOT MAKING ANY FRIENDS, THEN ONE DAY DURING LUNCH I WAS EATING BY MYSELF AND THIS BOY IN MY CLASS CAME UP TO ME AND SPOKE HELLO, I'M TIM, I NOTICE YOU HAVE BEEN KEEPING TO YOURSELF ALL THIS TIME DO YOU MIND IF I SIT WITH YOU, AND I HESITATE FOR A BIT THEN SAID OK THAT'S FINE YOU CAN SIT HERE I AM RANDY HOW ARE YOU I AM OK I WAS JUST WONDERING HOW ARE YOU DOING I'VE SEEN YOU HAVE BEEN BY YOURSELF ALMOST THE WHOLE SCHOOL YEAR MAY I ASK WHY WILL LAST SUMMER I WAS IN A BAD CAR ACCIDENT AND I ALMOST DIED AND IT LEFT AN UGLY SCARE ON MY STOMACH AND I GUESS I AM JUST

EMBARRASSED THAT PEOPLE MAY FIND OUT AND MAKE FUN OF ME, NO RANDY YOU ARE WRONG NO ONE WILL MAKE FUN OF YOU WE HAVE ALL BEEN TRYING TO TALK TO YOU WE WANT TO BE YOUR FRIEND BUT YOU NEVER GAVE ANYONE THE CHANCE TO TALK TO YOU I KNOW TIM I WAS JUST INSECURE ABOUT HOW I LOOK WILL I MEAN HOW MY STOMACH LOOKS IT IS OK RANDY NOW YOU KNOW WE ARE ALL YOUR FRIENDS NO ONE IS HERE TO HURT YOU WE ARE HERE TO MAKE SURE YOU ARE HAPPY THANKS, TIM SO, WE TALKED AND TALKED AND HE BECAME MY BEST FRIEND AFTER THAT DAY MY LIFE STARTED TO CHANGE AND I WAS GETTING OVER BEING IN SECURE AND THE REST OF THE SCHOOL YEAR TURNED OUT GREAT IT WAS AN LIFE-CHANGING AND NEW EXPERIENCE THANKS TO THAT ONE PERSON THAT TOOK THE TIME OUT OF HIS LIFE TO MAKE MY LIFE A BETTER ONE, I LOOK FORWARD TO THE REST OF MY SCHOOL YEAR, THE NEXT DAY I WAS IN THE PLAYGROUND WITH MY FRIEND TIM, WE SAT AND TALKED THEN ONE BY ONE OTHER BOY AND GIRL CAME UP TO ME AND STARTED TALKING TO ME, FROM THAT POINT, I FELT AS IF I HAD A PLACE IN LIFE AND A PLACE IN THAT SCHOOL, AND THEN I STARTED GETTING INVITED TO OTHER BIRTHDAY PARTIES AND SLEEP OVER'S, AND BY THE END OF THE SCHOOL YEAR I HAD MORE FRIENDS THEN I COULD HAVE IMAGINED, AND THIS HOLD TIME BEFORE MY BREAK THREW, I WAS WORRIED OF WHAT PEOPLE WOULD THINK OF ME WHEN THEIR ONLY THOUGHT WAS WHEN WOULD I COME AROUND AND OPEN UP TO THEM AND TALK, AND NO ONE ASK ME ABOUT MY SCARS OR ACCIDENT, IT WAS JUST MY INSECURITY THAT KEPT ME DOWN, THE SCHOOL YEAR IS ALMOST OVER ONLY A FEW MORE WEEKS IT WILL BE SUMMERTIME, I HOPE THIS SUMMER WILL BE BETTER THAN LAST SUMMER

OF 1974 WHICH WILL ALWAYS BE THE SUMMER OF MY LIFE THAT I STORE IN THE BACK OF MY MIND AS A REMINDER OF HOW BLESSED I AM TO BE ALIVE AND ABLE TO ENJOY THE LOVE AND HAPPINESS OF MY FAMILY AND FRIENDS, TODAY I'M GOING BACK TO MY AUNTS HOUSE THE PLACE THAT MY ACCIDENT HAPPENED, I HAVE NOT BEEN TO HER HOUSE SINCE THAT DAY SO I WILL SEE HOW I FEEL THE EXPERIENCE OF GOING BACK TO WHERE MY TRAGEDY HAPPENED IS GOING TO BE A INTERESTING DAY, I AM KINDA OF NERVOUS TO GO BUT IT IS SOMETHING THAT MUST BE DONE SO I CAN GET OVER THIS CHAPTER IN MY LIFE, AS I ARRIVE AT MY AUNT'S HOUSE I START TO GET, NERVOUS AS WE PULL UP AND WHEN I GET OUT OF THE CAR, I FIND MYSELF STANDING IN THE SPOT WHERE I GOT RUN OVER MY WHOLE BODY TREMBLED AS I LOOKED AROUND, I CAUGHT MYSELF LIVING THAT MOMENT AGAIN AND FOR A COUPLE OF MINUTES, I COULD NOT MOVE I CLOSED MY EYES AND THAT DAY WAS FLASHING BEFORE MY EYES, AFTER A SLIGHT PAUSE I WAS ABLE TO ACCEPT THAT DAY AND THEN I WENT TO MY AUNT GAVE HER A BIG HUG AND SAID TO HER THANK YOU FOR BEING THERE FOR ME AND NEVER GAVE UP ON ME BECAUSE OF YOU I MADE IT TO THE HOSPITAL AND WAS ABLE TO LIVE MY LIFE AS GOD HAD PLANNED IT, EVERYTHING IS FALLING INTO PLACE I AM FINDING PEACE IN MY LIFE, IT'S JULY 13, 1976, I HAVE GONE OVER HIGH HURDLES I HAVE BEEN THREW A LOT BUT THREW ALL AND ALL I HAVE OVERCOME, ALL THE OBSTACLES I HAVE FACED, AND NOW IT'S TIME FOR A NEW JOURNEY IT'S TIME TO LEAVE MY AUNT'S HOUSE AND GO HOME, AND PREPARE FOR WHAT I AM ABOUT TO FACE TOMORROW WHICH WILL BE AN INTERESTING DAY I WILL BE ABLE TO TELL MY FRIENDS ABOUT MY VISIT TO MY AUNT'S HOUSE AND WHAT I EXPERIENCED DURING MY VISIT

AND AFTER SCHOOL I HAVE A DR. APPOINTMENT WITH A NEUROLOGIST, I HAVE BEEN EXPERIENCING DRUNK SPILLS AND SEEING THINGS THAT ARE NOT THERE I WOULD WAKE UP AT 1 IN THE MORNING CRYING AND SCARED TO WALK CAUSE I WOULD SEE LOTS AND LOTS OF EYES ALL OVER THE FLOOR AND IN THE AIR SO HOPEFULLY THE DR. CAN HELP AND GIVE ME A RELIEVING ANSWER, I WAS TIRED OF WHAT I EXPERIENCED EVERY DAY, THE DR TOLD ME THAT I HAVE A LOT OF ELECTRICITY IN MY BRAIN DUE TO THE ACCIDENT, AND IT WILL RESOLVED IN THE YEARS TO COME IT TOOK ME YEARS AFTER THE ACCIDENT TO OVERCOME THIS IT'S MORNING TIME TO GO TO SCHOOL, AS I GOT TO SCHOOL, I SAW MY BEST FRIEND AND HE TOLD ME THAT HE HAD SOMETHING VERY IMPORTANT TO TELL ME SOMETHING SERIOUS AND HE WILL TELL ME LATER HE LOOKED AT ME WITH A SAD LOOK AND TEARS IN HIS EYES AND TOLD ME THE MOST HEARTBREAKING NEWS HIS DAD HAD GOT ANOTHER JOB IN A DIFFERENT STATE, SO THIS WILL BE HIS LAST YEAR IN SCHOOL MY HEART DROPPED HE WAS MORE THAN JUST A FRIEND HE WAS LIKE A BROTHER, BUT HE TOLD ME SOMETHING THAT I WILL NEVER FORGET HE SAID THAT IF I EVER FEEL LOST LOOK UP INTO THE SKY AND THERE I WILL FIND THE ANSWER THAT WILL SET ME FREE AT FIRST I DID NOT UNDERSTAND WHAT HE WAS SAYING THEN THE DAY CAME AND I FELT ALONE I REMEMBER WHAT HE SAID TO LOOK UP IN THE SKY AND THEN I SAW MY HAPPINESS ALL I HAD TO DO WAS ASK GOD TO SET ME FREE FROM THIS AND IT MIGHT BE TIM LAST YEAR IN SCHOOL BUT I WILL NEVER FORGET HIM AND THEN I HEARD HIM TALKING TO OTHER FRIENDS AND HE TOLD THEM IF RANDY EVER NEED'S ANYTHING MAKE SURE HE GET'S WHATEVER HE NEEDS I WAS RELIEVED TO KNOW THAT EVEN IF HE WAS NOT GOING TO BE

THEREHIS LOVE FOR ME AS A FRIEND AND A BROTHER WILL ALWAYS BE I FEEL IN MY HEART THAT I WILL ALWAYS BE HAPPY NO MATTER WHAT HAPPENS IN LIFE HIS FRIENDSHIP WILL ALWAYS BE WITH ME THE SCHOOL YEAR IS OVER AND I WILL SEE WHAT MY PARENTS PLAN I WILL SEE WHAT WE DO THIS SUMMER, I KNOW THAT WHATEVER WE DO IT WILL BE GREAT FOR OUR LIFE AS A FAMILY IS FULL OF LOVE AS I SIT HERE AND THINK ABOUT MY FAMILY, I ALSO THINK ABOUT ALL THE OTHER FAMILIES OUT THERE THE CHILDREN THAT ARE NOT AS BLESSED AS I AM TO HAVE WONDERFUL PARENTS THAT WILL CARE FOR THEM AND LOVE THEM AS MY PARENTS HAVE SHOWN SO MUCH LOVE AND HAPPINESS TO ME, NOT A DAY HAS GONE BY

CHAPTER 2 THE TRAGIC TRUTH

MY PARENTS WERE NOT THERE FOR ME THEY ALWAYS SHOWED ME THAT A PARENT LOVE IS FOREVER, AS I THINK ABOUT EVERYTHING, I AM ALSO NERVOUS ABOUT MY FIRST SCHOOL YEAR NEXT YEAR I DO NOT KNOW HOW I AM GOING TO SURVIVE WITHOUT MY BEST FRIEND TIM,HE WAS ALWAYS THERE FOR ME AND SHOWED ME THAT I COULD MAKE IT NO MATTER WHAT THE TIME IS NEAR FOR THE NEW SCHOOL YEAR IT'S FEBRUARY 23, 1981, I AM STARTING MY FIRST

YEAR OF SCHOOL I'VE FINALLY MADE IT TO THE 8TH GRADE, BUT I DON'T KNOW IF I AM READY TO FACE MY NEW SCHOOL WITH NEW PEOPL I FEEL LIKE I'M BACK IN THE 6TH GRADE ALL OVER AGAIN ALL ALONE NO ONE TO TALK TO, THERE WILL NEVER BE A FRIEND LIKE MY BEST FRIEND MY BROTHER, TOMORROW I WILL BE GOING TO SCHOOL AT LEAST THIS TIME I DO NOT HAVE GYM 1ST PERIOD. BUT ONE THING THAT WILL ALWAYS KEEPING ME STRONG AND KEEP ME GOING IS PUTTING GOD FIRST IN EVERYTHING I DO, AND I HAVE MY BEST FRIEND TO THANK FOR INTRODUCING ME TO OUR LORD AND SAVIOR I'M GOING TO GET MY REST GONNA NEED IT FOR WHAT I AM ABOUT TO FACE TOMORROW, MOM ALWAYS TOLD ME SON ALWAYS EXPECT THE UNEXPECTED FOR ONLY THEN YOU WILL SEE WHAT LIFE IS ALL ABOUT, MY MOM ALWAYS HAD A SPECIAL WAY OF PUTTING THINGS SO I COULD UNDERSTAND WHAT SHE WAS TELLING ME, IT'S TIME TO REST MORNING WILL BE HERE SOON, AS RANDY TRIED TO SLEEP THAT NIGHT, HE COULD NOT HE JUST KEPT WAKING UP THINKING ABOUT HIS FIRST DAY OF SCHOOL, HE STARTED THINKING ABOUT HIS BEST FRIEND TIM, FOR ONE MOMENT HE WISHES THAT TIM WAS THERE WITH HIM, AS HE WAS IN THE PAST BUT RANDY KNEW, HE HAD TO FACE THIS ALONE, LET'S SEE HOW RANDY WILL MANAGE TO START A NEW SCHOOL YEAR. AS RANDY WAKES UP, HE NOTICE IT IS 7 AM. AS I GET UP, I SEE IT IS TIME TO GET READY FOR SCHOOL I FEEL NERVOUS EVERYTHING WILL BE OK; I JUST FEEL SO INSECURE AND ALONE KNOWING I'M GOING TO START A NEW SCHOOL ALL ALONE, AS I ARRIVED AT SCHOOL, I SEE LOT'S OF NEW FACES I DID NOT SEE LAST YEAR AND PEOPLE THAT I SPENT TIME IN THE PAST WITH SO THIS NEW START MIGHT NOT BE THAT BAD I JUST HAVE TO MOVE FORWARD LEAVE THE PAST IN THE PAST AND

CONTINUE MY LIFE AS GOD HAS INTENDED ME, ME TO DO AS I GET OUT OF THE CAR, I START WALKING TOWARDS THE OFFICE TO GET TO MY CLASSROOM SCHEDULE, I HEAR A FAMILIAR VOICE AS I TURN AND LOOK IT IS TIM'S OTHER FRIEND, WHO STARTED TO BE A GOOD FRIEND TO ME ALSO, IT WAS A RELIEF TO HEAR HIS VOICE HE ASKED ME HOW I WAS DOING AND WITH A SURPRISED LOOK ON MY FACE I TOLD HIM I WAS OK AND STILL A LITTLE BIT NERVOUS ABOUT MY NEW YEAR IN SCHOOL, HE LOOKED AT ME AND PUT HIS HAND ON MY SHOULDER, AND SAID TO ME MY FRIEND YOU HAVE NOTHING TO FEAR, I AM HERE BY YOUR SIDE, AND I WILL MAKE SURE THAT EVERYTHING WILL BE GREAT FOR YOU, SO PUT ALL FEARS AND DOUBTS OUT OF YOUR HEAD AND ENJOY YOUR NEW SCHOOL YEAR, IT IS MUCH DIFFERENT THAN WHERE YOU COME FROM, AND YOU WILL SEE HERE YOU WILL FIND A NEW START AND CREATE NEW MEMORIES THAT YOU WILL ALWAYS REMEMBER AND USE IN YOUR LIFE AHEAD IT IS NEVER TOO LATE FOR A GREAT START I WAS SET AT EASE TO HEAR THOSE WORDS, I TOLD HIM THANKS LET ME GO TO THE OFFICE TO GET MY SCHEDULE I WILL TALK TO YOU LATER TODAY AS I GET TO THE OFFICE, I SEE THE MOST BEAUTIFUL VISION THE GIRL I USED TO GO TO SCHOOL WITH WHEN WE WERE IN THE 6TH GRADE, I NEVER GOT A CHANCE TO TALK TO HER BECAUSE SHE HAD MOVED OUT OF TOWN BEFORE THE SCHOOL YEAR WAS OVER AND NOW SHE IS BACK, AND SHE JUST GOT TRANSFERRED BACK TO OUR SCHOOL BECAUSE HER FAMILY HAD MOVED OUT OF TOWN, WHEN WE WERE IN THE 6TH GRADE SO I NEVER REALLY GOT A CHANCE TO TALK TO HER, BUT NOW THAT SHE HAS RETURN I WILL DO MY BEST TO TALK TO HER AND HOPEFULLY MAKE HER MY GIRLFRIEND, I AM FINISHING UP IN THE OFFICE

AS I WALK OUT, OF THE OFFICE WE GLANCE AT EACH OTHER I LOOK AT HER, AND AS SHE WALKS INTO THE OFFICE I STAND OUTSIDE AND AM IN A DAZE JUST LOOKING AT HER THROUGH THE GLASS AND WAITING FOR HER IN THE HALL HOPEFULLY, I WILL HAVE MY OPPORTUNITY TO TALK TO HER WHEN SHE COMES AS I SAY HI TO HER, THE THOUGHTS THAT I HAD IN MY MIND THAT I WOULD TELL HER IF I EVER GOT A CHANCE TO TALK TO HER, ESCAPE ME AND I FORGOT EVERYTHING I WAITED AND WANTED TO TELL HER FOR SO MANY YEARS THE MOMENT SHE CAME OUT OF THE OFFICE AT THIS POINT I WAS KIND OF NERVOUS AND SILENT, AS SHE CAME AND LOOKED AT ME, SHE STOOD WITHOUT SAYING A WORD AS IF SHE WAS TRYING TO REMEMBER ME, SO AS SHE STOOD THERE IN FRONT OF ME SILENT FOR A MOMENT THEN FINALLY SHE SPOKE WITH THE MOST BEAUTIFUL VOICE AND SAYS HI YOUR RANDY RIGHT FROM MY 6TH GRADE CLASS, AND I KINDA HESITATE FOR A MOMENT BEFORE I SPOKE AND THEN I SAID IN A SOFT VOICE YES THAT'S ME, I ASK HER I THOUGHT YOU AND YOUR FAMILY MOVED OUT OF TOWN WHAT HAPPEN, AND HER RESPONSE WAS MY DAD'S JOB HAD ENDED SO WE HAD NO CHOICE BUT TO MOVE BACK INTO TOWN SO HERE I AM, THEN I SAID TO HER THANK GOD MY PRAYER HAS BEEN ANSWERED I PRAYED AND HOPED YOU WOULD COME BACK AND YOU HAVE COME BACK I HAVE SOMETHING I NEED TO TELL YOU; SHE LOOKED AT ME PUZZLED AND ASK WHAT IS IT, I CLEARED MY THROAT AND SAID IN A LOW VOICE I HAVE HAD AND STILL HAVE A BIG CRUSH ON YOU, BUT I ALWAYS WAS TOO SCARED TO SAY ANYTHING AND I DID NOT WANT TO BE TURN DOWN OR TURN AWAY SO I STAYED SILENT AND KEPT IT TO MYSELF SO MANY TIMES I JUST WANTED TO GO UP TO YOU AND SAY ANDREA I LIKE YOU A LOT AND I WANT

US TO BE TOGETHER AND LOTS OF TIMES I CAME CLOSE TO DOING IT BUT EVERY TIME I SAW YOU, I FROZE NOW I AM SAYING IT ANDREA, I LIKE YOU A LOT I HAVE ALWAYS LIKED YOU AND I ALWAYS WILL AFTER I TOLD HER THIS, SHE WAS SHOCKED AND STAYE SILENT AFTER THAT I LOOKED AT HER AND SAID OK, I SHOULD HAVE NOT SAID ANYTHING I WILL LET YOU GET TO CLASS AND LEAVE YOU ALONE AS I WAS WALKING AWAY, SHE SAID NO STOP AND I SAID WHAT IS IT AND THEN SHE SURPRISE ME WHEN SHE SAID TO ME A PERSON WHO THOUGHT I WAS NOBODY THAT NO ONE WOULD BE WITH ME HER WORDS MADE ME SO HAPPY WHEN SHE TOLD ME, FOR MANY YEARS I HAVE CAUGHT MYSELF THINKING ABOUT YOU, I NEVER KNEW WHY I WOULD BUT I WOULD MORE THAN NORMAL I ASKED HER TO TELL ME EXACTLY WHAT IS IT AND I PRAY YOU ARE TELLING ME WHAT I THINK YOU SO WHAT ARE YOU TRYING TO TELL ME, SHE LOOKED INTO MY EYES AND SAID WHAT DO YOU THINK I AM SAYING, I AM TELLING YOU THAT I LIKE YOU MORE THAN YOU CAN IMAGINE, THAT DAY I ASK HER TO BE MY GIRLFRIEND AND SHE SAID YES AND THAT DAY WAS THE START OF ALL THE HAPPINESS IN MY LIFE AT LEAST I THOUGHT IT WAS I DID NOT EXPECT WHAT THE NEAR FUTURE WOULD BRING THAT WILL CHANGED EVERYTHING AND HOW I LOOK AT LIFE, WE WENT ON WITH OUR DAY I WAS SO HAPPY I INTRODUCED HER TO ALL MY FRIENDS, AND THERE WAS NOTHING THAT I WOULD NOT DO FOR HER, ALL SHE HAD TO DO WAS JUST ASK, AND I WOULD GIVE HER EVERYTHING SHE WANTED OR I WOULD JUST GIVE HER GIFTS AND GIVE HER ROSES, AND TELL HER I'M GIVING YOU THESE ROSES BECAUSE YOU ARE MORE BEAUTIFUL THEN ALL THE ROSES IN THE WORLD, WE ARE IN THE LAST PERIOD AND I HAVE HER FOR MY LAST CLASS THE WHOLE

TIME IN CLASS WE DID NOT PAY ATTENTION TO THE TEACHER WE WOULD SEND EACH OTHER NOTES AND JUST GIGGLE AT EACH OTHER IT WAS THE TIME OF OUR LIVES SO AFTER SCHOOL, SHE ASKED ME WHAT WAS I DOING TODAY AND I SAID TO HER I DON'T KNOW JUST GO AND HANG OUT AND I'M NOT DOING ANYTHING SHE ASKS ME WOULD YOU LIKE TO COME OVER TO MY HOUSE I HAVE A FEW FRIENDS COMING OVER JUST TO HANG OUT I WOULD LIKE TO INTRODUCE YOU TO MY FRIENDS, SO I THOUGHT ABOUT IT AND I SAID OK THAT WOULD BE OK I WILL GO OVER THERE IN A WHILE HAVE TO GO HOME AND DO SOMETHING FIRST I WILL MEET YOU AT YOUR HOUSE, SHE SAID OK GREAT WE ARE GOING TO HAVE LOTS OF FUN, AS SHE LEFT ALL KINDS OF THOUGHTS WERE GOING THREW MY HEAD WHAT KIND OF FUN IS SHE TALKING ABOUT WHAT ARE WE GOING TO DO I HOPE IT IS NOTHING BAD OR ILLEGAL I GUESS I AM JUST OVERTHINKING THINGS; I KNOW SHE IS A GOOD PERSON SHE NEVER SHOWED ANYTHING OUT OF THE ORDINARY, AS I AM WALKING HOME, I SEE HER TALKING TO OTHER BOYS AND GIRLS AND THEY ARE ALL LAUGHING AND ACTING NOT SO NORMAL, SO I JUST LOOKED AND WALKED ON WITHOUT LOOKING BACK, I GOT HOME AND WENT TO MY ROOM I SAT ON MY BED AND STARTED THINKING ABOUT EVERYTHING SHE HAD TOLD ME ABOUT THE GET-TOGETHER AT HER HOUSE AND ALSO STARTED THINKING ABOUT OUR FIRST CONVERSATION IN SCHOOL, SO I SAID TO MYSELF HOW CAN SOMEONE SO SWEET AND BEAUTIFUL DO ANYTHING WRONG THAT WOULD CAUSE HURT AND PAIN TO HERSELF OR A LOVED ONE AT THAT POINT I FELT THAT I HAD NOTHING TO WORRY ABOUT, I PUT IT OUT OF MY MIND AND STARTED GETTING READY TO GO OVER TO MY GIRLFRIEND HOUSE, THEN AS I WAS LEAVING MY FRIEND CAME

OVER TO MY HOUSE HEY WHAT'S UP AND WHERE ARE YOU GOING, WHERE DO YOU THINK I AM GOING OVER TO MY GIRLFRIEND'S HOUSE SHE HAS SOME OF HER FRIENDS OVER AND HE LOOKED AT ME AND SAID YES, I KNOW THEY TOLD ME EVERYTHING THEY HAD INVITED ME TO GO BUT I TURNED THEM DOWN I SAID NO THANK YOU I PASSED, THEN HE HAD LOOKED AT ME WITH A WORRIED LOOK ON HIS FACE LOOK RANDY WE NEED TO TALK I HAVE TO TELL YOU SOMETHING ABOUT YOUR GIRLFRIEND ANDREA THAT I HAVE KNOWN FOR MANY YEARS AND IT'S BEEN A BIG SECRET IN MY LIFE AND I AM TIRED OF HOLDING THIS IN IT'S TIME I SPEAK OUT SO MY FRIEND HERE IT GOES SEE YOUR GIRLFRIEND ANDREA; HAS HAD A BAD LIFE HER PARENT WERE NOT SUCH GOOD PARENT'S THEY HAD MANY PROBLEMS AND WOULD SOMETIMES TAKE IT OUT ON ANDREA, THEY HAD GOT REPORTED TO THE AUTHORITY SO WHEN THEY FOUND OUT THEY WERE GETTING IN TROUBLE WITH THE LAW THEY DECIDED TO MOVE OUT OF TOWN, HERE WE GO A FEW YEARS LATER THEY ARE BACK, THEN I ASK HIM TO TELL ME EVERYTHING PLEASE TELL ME EVERYTHING YOU KNOW WHAT HAPPEN TO HER AND HOW DO YOU KNOW ABOUT THIS WITH TEARS IN MY EYES I ASK HIM TO LET ME KNOW ALL HE KNOWS, SO HE PAUSES FOR A MINUTE AND SAID OK HERE IS THE WHOLE STORY BUT BEFORE I TELL YOU I ASK YOU TO BE STRONG, AND WHAT I AM ABOUT TO TELL SAY I KNOW ALL OF THIS BECAUSE SHE USED TO BE TOGETHER WITH MY BEST FRIEND WHEN HE SAW THIS HE LOST HIS MIND AND ALMOST PUT HIS SOUL TO REST, I AM SAYING THAT BEFORE I TELL YOU THIS PLEASE ASSURE ME THAT YOU WILL NOT DO ANYTHING CRAZY AND TRY TO END YOUR LIFE I WON'T DO ANYTHING CRAZY YOU HAVE MY WORD; OK SIT DOWN LET'S DISCUSS THIS IT STARTED WHEN

SHE JUST TURNED 9 YEARS OLD SHE STAYED WITH HER MOM AND DAD AND LITTLE BROTHER THINGS SEEMED OK ON THE OUTSIDE BUT ON THE INSIDE SHE EXPERIENCED TORTURE AND PAIN IN THE MORNING SHE WOULD WAKE UP TO YELLING AND GETTING HIT WITH THE BELT OR WHATEVER THEY HAD IN THEIR HAND FOR NO REASON AND WOULD TELL HER ALL KINDS OF BAD THINGS LIKE YOU UGLY YOU ARE NOT MY CHILD WHY DON'T YOU RUN AWAY OR KILL YOURSELF SELF DO US ALL A FAVOR AND HURRY AND GET OUT OF THIS HOUSE YOU ARE A WASTE OF SPACE THEN THEY WOULD SLAP HER IN HER FACE AND THE OTHER KID THEY WOULD HUG HIM AND SHOW HIM LOVE AND HAPPINESS, THEN WHEN HER FATHER WOULD GET HOME FROM WORK THE FIRST THING HE WOULD DO IS GO TO HER ROOM AND HE SPANKED HER AND SHE WOULD CRY AND BEG HIM TO STOP BUT HE WOULD JUST LAUGH AND HIT HER HARDER, BUT THE MOST TERRIBLE PART OF ALL OF THIS THEY WOULD DRINK A LOT, AND RANDY WHEN HE SAID MY NAME HE PAUSED AND LOOKED AT ME AND I SAID WHAT IS IT TELL ME, SO HE TOOK A DEEP BREATH AND SAID WHEN HER DAD WOULD GET DRUNK, HE WOULD HAVE HIS WAY WITH HER HE TOOK HER INNOCENCE, AND THAT WEEK THAT IT HAPPENED SHE WAS NOWHERE TO BE FOUND THE WHOLE WEEK WE LOOK FOR HER BUT SHE WAS NOT THERE, HER PARENTS SENT HER AWAY FOR THE WEEK TO GO STAY WITH A FAMILY MEMBER, SO I ASK HIM BUT DID SHE TELL HER MOM WHAT HAPPENED THAT NIGHT AND WHAT HAPPENED WITH HER DAD AND WHAT HE DONE TO HER, YES, SHE DID AND HER MOM SLAPPED HER AND SAID STOP YOUR LYING YOU KNOW WHAT THE TRUTH IS YOU LAY WITH A BOY AND NOW YOU'RE BLAMING YOUR DAD FOR WHAT YOU DID YOU KNOW IT'S NOT RIGHT I CAN NOT STAND YOU I AM SENDING YOU AWAY FOR THE

WEEK GO OVER TO MY SISTER'S HOUSE AND LET HER DEAL WITH YOUR LIE I'M DONE, SO THEY SENT HER OFF FOR THE WEEK, WHEN SHE CAME BACK TO SCHOOL THE FOLLOWING WEEK, SHE WAS A TOTALLY DIFFERENT PERSON, I ASK WHAT DO YOU MEAN, AT THIS POINT I'M IN TEARS FROM EVERYTHING HE WAS TELLING ME ABOUT HER, SO HE SAID SHE USED TO BE ALIVE AND TALKATIVE WITH EVERYONE IT LOOKS LIKE SHE WAS ENJOYING LIFE SHE HID HER PAIN VERY WELL, BUT THIS TIME YOU COULD SEE IT WAS IN HER FACE AND THE WAY SHE WAS ACTING SOMETHING WAS NOT RIGHT, WE WENT ON WITH THE DAY THROUGHOUT THE DAY WE WERE CONFUSED AND WONDERING WHAT HAPPENED TO HER LAST WEEK, WHICH HAD HER ACTING THE WAY SHE WAS AND THEN DURING OUR LAST CLASS I SAW HER BY HER LOCKER SHE WAS JUST CRYING AND BANGING HER HANDS AGAINST THE LOCKER AND SAYING IN A SOFT VOICE WAY IS THIS HAPPENING TO ME I HAVE NOT DONE ANYTHING WRONG I AM A GOOD DAUGHTER A GOOD PERSON WHO NEVER GETS IN TROUBLE AND STILL ALL THIS HAPPENS TO ME, AND I FEEL LIKE I AM NOT WORTH ANYTHING, AND AFTER WHAT MY DAD DID TO ME I CAN NOT BELIEVE I AM STILL HERE LORD, PLEASE HELP ME FIND A WAY OUT BUT NO ONE LISTENS TO ME NO ONE CARES ABOUT ME, AT THAT POINT I WALKED UP TO HER AND SPOKE TO HER AND SAID ARE YOU, OK SHE LOOKED AT ME WITH TEARS IN HER EYES AND REPLIED AND SAID YES, I AM FINE I JUST REMEMBER SOME STUFF FROM THE PAST BUT I PROMISE EVERYTHING IS OK, I DID NOT BELIEVE HER BUT I DID NOT QUESTION HER I FEEL SHE WILL TALK WHEN SHE IS READY. ALL I COULD DO WAS JUST BE THERE FOR HER AND BE HER FRIEND AND NOT TALK ABOUT ANYTHING NEGATIVE, SO WEEKS PASSED THE BEATING HAD STOPPED AND THEY HAD STOP

YELLING AT HER, AND HER DAD WAS KEEPING HIS HANDS OFF HER SHE SEEMED TO START COMING AROUND SLOWLY, I STARTED TALKING TO HER MORE AND MORE AS FRIENDS ALWAYS AS FRIENDS NOTHING MORE, SO HER LIFE WAS GETTING BACK TOGETHER AT LESS SHE THOUGHT IT WAS, SHE DID NOT EXPECT WHAT SHE HAD IN STORE FOR HER WHEN SHE GOT HOME, AFTER SCHOOL THAT DAY SHE SAID TO ME THANKS FOR BEING THERE FOR ME AND BEING A GOOD FRIEND AND I TOLD HER YES IT'S NOT A PROBLEM I AM ALWAYS HERE FOR YOU SO SHE WALKS AWAY AND WALKS HOME FROM SCHOOL, WHEN SHE GOT HOME, THE TORTURE STARTED HER MOM SLAPPED HER AS SOON AS SHE WALKED IN THE DOOR, AND SHE STARTED CRYING AND HER MOM TOLD HER WHERE YOU HAVE BEEN YOUR LATE, AND SHE LOOKED TOWARDS THE TABLE AND SAW HER DAD AND TWO OF HIS FRIENDS, SITTING THERE WITH HIM DRINKING AND THEY ALL LOOK AT HER UP AND DOWN, SO HER MOM PULLS HER HAIR AND TELLS HER GO TO YOUR ROOM AND WAIT FOR WHAT YOU HAVE COMING TO YOU, SHE WAS IN HER ROOM SCARED BECAUSE SHE REMEMBERS EVERYTHING HER DAD DID TO HER NOW, SHE IS IN TEARS THINKING WHAT WAS GOING TO HAPPEN, AND HER DAD'S FRIENDS PAID HIM TO BE WITH HER, THE FIRST MAN WALKED IN AND SAID TO HER, OK YOU MIND FOR 1 HOUR AND HE HAD HIS WAY WITH HER, AND THEN AFTER HE WAS DONE THE NEXT MAN WALKED IN AND TOLD HER TO CLEAN UP, I GOT YOU FOR AN HOUR, SHE WAS CRYING AND PLEADING WITH HIM TO STOP AND SHE LOOKED OUT THE DOOR AND SAW HER DAD AND MOM STANDING THERE LAUGHING AT WHAT WAS HAPPENING TO HER AFTER THE OTHER THE MAN, FINISH WITH HER HE WALKED OUT AND SHE JUST WANTED TO KILL HERSELF SHE WAS GETTING READY TO GO SHOWER WHEN IT HAPPENED HER DAD WALKED

IN AND SAID OK IT'S MY TIME MAKE YOUR DADDY HAPPY, HE DID WHAT HE WANTED TO DO TO HER AND BOTH OF THEM WERE JUST LAUGHING AT HER AND HER MOM TELLING HER YOU NO-GOOD NOBODY WANTS YOU THEN AS HE LEFT THE ROOM, SHE WAS IN SHOCK SHE JUST WANTED TO KILL HERSELF SHE WAS IN PAIN SHE HAD TO GO TO THE HOSPITAL THAT NIGHT BECAUSE SHE WAS SICK AND IN LOTS OF PAIN AND HER PARENTS TOLD YOU BETTER NOT SAY NOT ONE WORD IF YOU DO, WE WILL BLAME YOUR BOYFRIEND AND HE BE THE ONE GOING TO JAIL, ANDREA LIED AT THE HOSPITAL SAYING SHE GOT RAPED BUT DID NOT KNOW WHO WERE THE BOYS THAT DID IT, SHE WAS RELEASED FROM THE HOSPITAL AND HAD NO CHOICE BUT TO GO BACK HOME SHE WAS ONLY 12 YEARS OLD AND WAS GOING THREW ALL THIS TORMENT AFTER THAT THERE WAS ONLY A FEW MORE WEEK BEFORE SCHOOL WAS OVER IT'S MONDAY AND SHE DID NOT COME TO SCHOOL, AT THAT POINT I KNEW IT HAPPEN AGAIN, BUT WHEN SHE CAME TO SCHOOL THE FOLLOWING DAY SHE SEEMED DIFFERENT SHE WAS ALWAYS HAPPY AND I DID NOT QUESTION HER HAPPINESS AT FIRST, BUT THEN I SAW HER MOOD SWING SHE WOULD BE HAPPY THEN SAD THEN ONE DAY I WAS PASSING BY AND I SAW HER AT HER LOCKER AND SHE WAS TAKING SOME KIND OF PILLS SHE HAD GOTTEN FROM THIS PERSON IN SCHOOL SO FROM THAT DAY FORWARD SHE WAS HOOKED ON THOSE DRUGS, SHE HAS FOUND A WAY TO DEAL WITH THE LIFE THAT WAS HANDED TO HER BY HER PARENTS AND THE ABUSE CONTINUED TO HAPPEN FOR A FEW MORE YEARS THEN FINALLY ALL THE TORTURE AND TORMENT SHE HAD EXPERIENCED FINALLY ENDED WHEN SHE TURNED 14 YEARS OLD ONE THING THAT STILL CONTINUES UP TO THIS DAY IS HER USE OF DRUGS SHE IS STILL HOOKED ON THE DRUGS, I

SAID TO HIM WAIT I WAS SO CONFUSED AND LOST WHEN I SAW HER THAT DAY IN SCHOOL, SHE DID NOT SEEM LIKE SOMEONE THAT HAS GONE THREW ANYTHING LIKE THAT SHE LOOKED HAPPY WITHOUT A CARE IN THE WORLD, SO HOW CAN THAT BE, HE TELLS ME YES CAUSE EVERY MORNING SHE TAKES HER PILLS TO COPE WITH HER DAILY ACTIVITIES. AFTER MY FRIEND TOLD ME ALL OF THIS ABOUT MY BEAUTIFUL GIRLFRIEND ALL I COULD DO WAS JUST SIT THERE ON MY BED AND CRY LIKE A BABY, I DID NOT KNOW WHAT TO DO BUT I KNEW I COULD NOT GIVE UP ON HER, SO I WIPE MY TEARS AND GOT READY AND STARTED GOING TO HER HOUSE AS I GOT THERE I PAUSED AND JUST LOOKED AT WHAT WAS GOING ON, THE FRIENDS THAT SHE WAS TALKING TO AFTER SCHOOL WERE SITTING IN THE FRONT YARD A FEW OF THEM WERE DRINKING, AND THE OTHERS WERE TAKING SOME KIND OF DRUGS, THEY LOOKED LIKE THEY WERE IN A TRANS, I WALKED UP TO THEM, AND I ASK THEM WHERE IS ANDREA, AND THEY SAID WHO, WHAT ARE YOU TALKING ABOUT WHO IS THAT AND I SAID ANDREA THE GIRL THAT LIVES HERE WHERE IS SHE, AND THEY SAID HMMM GOOD QUESTION FIRST OF ALL WHO ARE YOU AND WHY ARE YOU LOOKING FOR OUR GIRLFRIEND, I PAUSE FOR A BIT AND SAID WHAT DO YOU MEAN YOUR GIRLFRIEND SHE IS MY GIRLFRIEND, AND THEY LAUGH AND SAID OH YOU MUST BE RANDY, I SAID WHAT YOU MEAN I MUST BE RANDY, THEY PAUSED AND RESPONDED SAYING YES, SHE LET US KNOW WHEN SHE GETS A NEW BOYFRIEND OR GIRLFRIEND, I GUESS YOU DID NOT KNOW SHE GOES BOTH WAYS BUT HEY IT'S OK WE ALL SHARE HER SO TO YOUR QUESTION YOU ASK WHERE SHE IS, I THINK IT'S JOSIE'S TURN SHE IS IN THE ROOM WITH HER BUT DON'T WORRY AFTER YALL ARE TOGETHER FOR A FEW WEEKS YOU WILL GET YOUR WEEKLY

TURN WITH HER BUT HEADS UP YOU HAVE TO SUPPLY HER WITH WHAT SHE NEEDS WEEKLY OR SHE WILL STOP BEING WITH YOU AND LET YOU GO, AT THAT POINT I HAD TEARS IN MY EYES AND I ASK HOW LONG THIS HAD BEEN GOING ON, THEY SAID IT HAD BEEN GOING ON FOR A WHILE IT WAS HER IDEA THIS STARTED LIKE A YEAR AGO AND WE HAVE BEEN DOING THIS EVER SINCE THEN, SHE SAID I DO NOT CARE ABOUT NOTHING JUST KEEP GIVING ME MY PILLS AND YOU ALL CAN HAVE ME ALL YOU WANT, AFTER HE TOLD ME THIS, I JUST LOOK DOWN AND COULD NOT BELIEVE WHAT I WAS HEARING, WITH TEARS COMING OUT I SAID TO MYSELF I CAN NOT GIVE UP ON HER I LOVE HER TOO MUCH TO LET HER GO LIKE THIS SO I WIPED THE TEARS FROM MY EYES AND WENT INSIDE HER HOUSE TO LOOK FOR HER I CALLED HER NAME AND THERE WAS NO RESPONSE, THEN I HEARD CRYING COMING OUT FROM THE FRONT ROOM I WALKED IN AND I COULD NOT BELIEVE WHAT I SAW, MY GIRLFRIEND ON THE FLOOR, I ASKED HER FRIEND WHAT HAPPENED WHAT DID YOU DO TO HER TELL ME, I HAD RAGE AND TEARS COMING OUT SHE SAID I DID NOT DO ANYTHING SHE JUST LOST IT, AND STARTED CRYING SAYING I AM DONE I AM TIRED OF MY LIFE I JUST WANT IT ALL TO END TODAY SO SHE TOOK A HAND OF THOSE DRUGS ON THE TABLE I CAN NOT BELIEVE THAT MY GIRLFRIEND WOULD DO SOMETHING LIKE THIS SHE WAS SO FULL OF LOVE, I GUESS ALL THE ABUSE SHE HAS EXPERIENCED IN HER LIFE FINALLY TRIGGER A PART OF HER OF NO RETURN, I RUSHED TO HER AND I DROPPED TO MY KNEES CALLING OUT HER NAME AND SHE WAS PASSED OUT I CRIED TO HER AND SAID PLEASE DON'T DIE I LOVE YOU I STAYED BY HER SIDE TO TRY TO WAKE HER UP I CALLED OUT TO GOD TO PLEASE HELP HER, AND NOT TAKE HER FROM ME I TRIED AGAIN SHE WAS NOT RESPONDING

SO I CALLED 911 AND THE AMBULANCE GOT TO HER HOUSE WITHIN MINUTES PARAMEDICS STARTED WORKING ON HER IN THE ROOM THEY SAW THAT THEY HAD TO RUSH HER, AT THE HOSPITAL, AS THE PARAMEDICS PUT ANDREA INTO THE AMBULANCE, I GOT IN WITH HER AND AS WE GOT TO THE HOSPITAL, THEY PLACED HER IN ONE OF THE OBSERVATION ROOMS, THEY RAN A TEST AND PUMP, THE PILLS OUT OF HER STOMACH BUT DURING THE OBSERVATIONS THEY NOTICE ALL THE ABUSE ON HER BODY AND HOW SHE HAS BEEN VIOLATED SO THEY CALLED THE COPS AND WITHIN AN HOUR THEY SHOWED UP, FIRST THEY QUESTIONED ME IF I KNEW WHAT HAD HAPPENED AND I LOOKED AT THEM AND SAID NO SIR I DO NOT KNOW STILL TRYING TO FIND OUT MYSELF, SO THEY ASK ME TO STEP OUT OF THE ROOM FOR A BIT, AS I WAS IN THE WAITING ROOM, I SAW HER PARENTS ARRIVED IN A RAGE DEMANDING TO TAKE HER HOME AND THAT THEY WOULD TAKE CARE OF HER, BUT THE STAFF REFUSED TO RELEASE HER SO BACK IN THE ROOM THE POLICE ASKED HER VARIOUS QUESTIONS FIRST, THEY ASK HER FOR HER NAME, AND SHE REPLIES AM I IN TROUBLE WITH THE LAW, AND THEY SAID NO YOU'RE NOT WE ARE HERE TO HELP YOU THE DOCTOR NOTICED ALL THE ABUSE YOU HAVE BEEN IN AND WE KNOW YOU ARE SCARED TO SPEAK RIGHT NOW BUT WE PROMISE YOU WE WILL HELP NOW WHO DID THIS TO YOU, IT'S OK TELL US YOU ARE SAFE WITH US SHE DID NOT WANT TO SAY NOTHING AS SHE STARTED TO SPEAK, SHE HEARD HER PARENTS IN THE HALL SCREAMING, SO SHE CHANGE HER MIND AND DID NOT TELL THE POLICE, WHAT HAPPENED TO HER SHE LIED ABOUT EVERYTHING SO, AFTER A WHILE THE POLICE STOPPED ASKING HER QUESTIONS AND LEFT SO I WENT BACK INTO THE ROOM AND I LOOKED AT ANDREA AND

ASKED WHAT HAPPENED, WHAT DID YOU SAY AND SHE STARTED CRYING AND SAID I DID NOT SAY ANYTHING THEN SHE PAUSED AND ASKED WHAT ARE YOU DOING HERE AND WHY AM I HERE WHAT HAPPENED, SO I ASK HER WAIT YOU DO NOT REMEMBER WHAT HAS HAPPEN TO YOU, WHY YOU ARE HERE AND SHE SAID NO I DON'T SO I TOLD HER EVERYTHING THAT HAS HAPPEN WHY SHE LANDED IN THE HOSPITAL AFTER I TOLD HER SHE SAID I DO NOT REMEMBER NOTHING, THEN I STARTED TO TELL HER THAT I KNEW WHAT HAD HAPPENED TO HER IN THE PAST, AS I STARTED TO SPEAK HER PARENTS WALKED IN ACTING AS IF THEY CARED, AND THEY TOLD ME YOU CAN GO NOW, WE WILL TAKE CARE OF HER IT IS YOUR FAULT SHE IS LIKE THIS GET OUT OF HERE, AND ANDREA SAID NO IT IS NOT HIS FAULT HE SAVED MY LIFE, AND THEY LOOKED AT ME AND SAID YES EXACTLY IT'S HIS FAULT YOU ARE STILL ALIVE HE RUINED EVERYTHING, SO I LEFT BUT DID NOT GIVE UP ON HER I'M ALWAYS BY HER SIDE, NEVER STOP CARING FOR HER, AND WILL NEVER STOP SEARCHING FOR A WAY TO GET HER OUT OF THIS SITUATION THAT SHE IS IN, SO THE FOLLOWING DAY SHE GOT OUT OF THE HOSPITAL I WENT TO GO SEE HOW SHE WAS DOING, AND SHE CAME OUT OF THE HOUSE IN TEARS AND I ASKED HER WHAT WAS WRONG, AND SHE SAID MY PARENTS ARE SENDING ME OFF TO GO STAY WITH MY AUNT WHICH I HAD NEVER MET NEVER KNEW SHE EXISTED AND I WAS IN SHOCK I SAID SO I AM LOOSENING YOU FOR GOOD SHE LOOKED AT ME WITH THE SADDEST EYES. AND SAID NO YOU WILL NEVER LOSE ME I WILL JUST BE GONE FOR A WHILE BUT THE CRAZY THING ABOUT THIS MY PARENTS SAID DO NOT BELIEVE WHAT MY GRANDMA TELL'S ME THAT SHE LIKES TO LIE A LOT SO WHEN IT COMES TO US IT WILL BE NOTHING BUT LIES, SO I TOLD HER WOW THAT

IS CRAZY SO WHEN ARE YOU LEAVING TO YOUR AUNT'S HOUSE AND SHE SAID I WILL BE GOING THIS WEEKEND THEY ARE GOING TO DRIVE ME TO MY GRANDMA'S HOUSE YOU KNOW RANDY I NEVER THOUGHT I WOULD FINALLY MAKE IT OUT OF THIS HOUSE BUT I PRAYED AND PRAYED AND HOPE THAT GOD WOULD ANSWER MY PRAYER AND TAKE ME OUT OF THIS HOUSE AND MY PRAYER WAS ANSWER

CHAPTER 3   DEEP SECRETS

IT IS GOING TO BE A RELIEF TO GET AWAY FROM THIS, AS SHE TURNS AND STOPS ON THE WAY BACK TO HER HOUSE, SHE STAND'S ON HER PORCH WITH TEARS IN HER EYES NOT SAYING A WORD JUST LOOKING DOWN THEN SHE SAY'S RANDY DO YOU KNOW HOW IT FEELS TO GET ABUSED EVERY DAY OF YOUR LIFE FOR NO REASON JUST CAUSE YOU'RE THERE WAKING UP TO BEATINGS IN THE MORNING AND THEN AT NIGHT HAVING YOUR DAD AND HIS FRIENDS ALL OVER YOU MY DAD TOOK MY INNOCENCE AWAY FROM ME THAT IS SOMETHING I CAN NEVER GET BACK SHE WAS IN TEARS AND SAID I WAS ONLY A LITTLE GIRL HOW CAN THE PARENTS OF A LITTLE GIRL BRING SO MUCH PAIN AND SUFFERING FOR THEIR CHILD I THOUGHT PARENTS ARE SUPPOSED TO BE

LOVING AND CARING AND BRING HAPPINESS TO THERE CHILDREN NOT PAIN AND SUFFERING, I DO NOT UNDERSTAND THIS DID I DO SOMETHING WRONG WAS I NOT SUPPOSED HAVE BEEN BORN, I LOOK AROUND AND SEE ALL THE OTHER KIDS MY AGE THEY ARE HAPPY WITH THEIR PARENTS AT THE MALL, AT THE MOVIES OUT TO EAT I SEE THERE PARENTS BUYING THEM GIFT'S JUST HAPPY FAMILIES, BUT MY PARENTS ALL THEY DO IS BUY DRUGS AND ALCOHOL, AND IF THEY RUN OUT OF MONEY THEN MY DAD SALES ME TO HIS FRIENDS, AND THEY ALL JUST SIT THERE AND USE ME AND ABUSE ME AND LAUGH RANDY ONE DAY I WILL GET MY REDEMPTION I HAVE TO GO I WILL TALK TO YOU LATER I LOVE YOU AS SHE WALKED INSIDE ALL I COULD DO WAS STAND THERE SPEECHLESS WITH TEARS IN MY EYES WITHOUT A WORD TO SAY AND LOTS OF PAIN IN MY HEART FOR HER ALL I COULD DO WAS JUST THINK ABOUT ALL SHE HAD BEEN THROUGH, THERE HAS TO BE MORE THAN WHAT IS GOING ON HOW COULD SOMEONE TREAT THEIR CHILD LIKE THAT FOR NO REASON, I WILL DO WHATEVER I CAN AND I WILL DO MY BEST TO FIND A WAY OUT FOR ANDREA TOMORROW IS SATURDAY AND SHE WILL BE GOING TO HER AUNT'S HOUSE WHICH SHE HAD NEVER MET OR KNOWN ABOUT, SO WE WILL SEE HOW THAT VISIT GOES, I WILL PRAY FOR HER. AS I GET HOME, I AM JUST THINKING ABOUT EVERYTHING THAT WAS REVIEW TO ME, AND ALL THAT HAPPENED TO ANDREA SO TONIGHT I WILL JUST WAIT AND HOPE FOR A SOLUTION FOR HER SHE DOES NOT DESERVE THIS I WILL GO SEE HER EARLY IN THE MORNING BEFORE SHE LEAVES, I WILL LAY FOR THE NIGHT AND WAKE UP EARLY IN THE MORNING, AND GET READY AND GO SEE ANDREA, FOR THE LAST TIME UNTIL I DO NOT KNOW WHEN AS I SLEEP, I FOUND MYSELF IN A

DREAM ABOUT HER IN MY DREAMS WE WERE AS HAPPY AS WE COULD BE NOT A WORRY FOR EVERYTHING WAS GREAT, AS RANDY LAY IN HIS BED TO SLEEP ALL HE COULD THINK ABOUT AND DREAM OF HIS TRUE LOVE ANDREA, HE WOULD SEE THE PAIN THAT SHE HAS BEEN GOING THREW, AT THAT POINT RANDY DID NOT UNDERSTAND EVERYTHING THAT WAS GOING ON BUT HE NEW THAT SOMETHING GOOD WILL BE COMING OUT OF ALL OF THIS, MORNING IS NEAR, LETS SEE HOW RANDY WILL RESPOND AS HE WAKES UP TO GO TO ANDREA HOUSE FOR THE LAST TIME, HE IS IN A LOT OF PAIN FROM KNOWING HE WILL NOT SEE ANDREA AGAIN AFTER TODAY AS I WOKE UP THIS MORNING I WAS BROUGHT BACK INTO REALITY THAT IS HAPPENING, I'M GOING TO START GETTING READY TO GO TO ANDREA AS I GET CLOSE TO HER HOUSE, I AM NERVOUS I DO NOT KNOW HOW I WILL RESPOND KNOWING THIS WILL BE THE LAST TIME THAT I SEE HER UNTIL SHE RETURNS ALL I KNOW IS THAT I WILL MISS HER DEARLY AND WILL ALWAYS BE THINKING ABOUT HER, AS I AM WALKING TO HER HOUSE EVERY STEP, I TAKE REMINDS ME OF HOW WE USED TO WALK DOWN THOSE STREETS EVERY DAY, AND NOW I WILL BE WALKING THE STREETS BY MYSELF WELL, HERE I AM AT HER HOUSE, I AM NOT READY FOR THIS, AS I TAKE A DEEP BREATH AS SHE WALKS OUT OF HER FRONT DOOR LOOKING AS BEAUTIFUL AS ALWAYS, SHE SLOWLY WALKS DOWN THE STEPS, SHE STOPS ON THE LAST STEP WITH TEARS IN HER EYES AND SHE PAUSES THERE FOR A BIT JUST LOOKS AT ME AND THEN SLOWLY WALKS TOWARD ME AND AS SHE STANDS IN FRONT OF ME I HOLD HER IN MY ARMS AND SAY TO HER I WILL ALWAYS BE HERE FOR YOU I LOVE YOU, AND SHE SAY'S TO ME I LOVE YOU I DO NOT WANT TO LEAVE YOU, BUT I MUST GO FOR A WHILE I HAVE TO FIND WHO I

AM I HAVE BEEN LOST ALL OF THESE YEARS; I NEED A NEW START BUT I PROMISE YOU THAT WILL ONLY BE SEPARATED A FEW MONTHS I HAVE TO GO NOW BUT I WILL ALWAYS HAVE YOU IN MY HEART AND I WILL ALWAYS LOVE YOU AND KEEP YOU IN MY PRAYERS, I LOVE YOU FOR YOU ARE MY LIFE AND I WILL NEVER LET YOU GO I TOLD HER MY LAST GOODBYE AND LEFT HER HOUSE AND I DID NOT LOOK BACK I JUST KEPT WALKING IN A DAZE I COULD NOT BELIEVE WHAT WAS HAPPENING AT THE MOMENT SO AS I STOOD AT THE END OF HER BLOCK I SAW HER DRIVING BY SHE SAW ME AND THREW ME A GOING AWAY KISS AND THAT WAS IT FOR IT WAS THE LAST TIME THAT I SAW HER, AS SHE LEFT, SHE SAID I HATED TO LEAVE, RANDY LIKE THIS IT BROKE MY HEART TO SEE THE SAD LOOK ON HIS FACE AS WE DROVE OFF, WILL IN A FEW HOURS I WILL BE AT MY AUNT'S HOUSE THEN MAYBE SHE CAN TELL ME WHAT'S GOING ON WITH MY FAMILY WHY THEY ARE TREATING ME LIKE THIS, AND WHY DID I HAVE TO GO THREW ALL THIS PAIN FOR ALL THESE YEARS, IT WAS A LONG RIDE TO MY AUNT'S HOUSE AS WE WERE ON THAT LONELY ROAD I LOOK OUT THE WINDOW, AT ALL THE MOUNTAINS AROUND ME I WAS JUST THINKING AND SAYING TO MYSELF I WISH I COULD JUST DISAPPEAR INTO THOSE MOUNTAINS, BUT OVERALL AND ALL IT WAS A VERY BEAUTIFUL SCENERY, THERE WERE NO CARS OR ANYBODY FOR MILES AND MILES, AS I LOOKED AT THESE TREES, I CLOSED MY EYES AND IMAGINE BEING AS FREE AS THOSE TREES I GUESS THE WHOLE TRIP, I WAS TRYING TO FIND MY INNER PEACE, BUT IT IS SO HARD WHEN I HAVE MORE TRAUMA THAN PEACE, I HAVE COME TO REALIZE THAT I NEED A NEW START IN MY LIFE I MUST START THE RECOVERY PHASE OF MY LIFE, A FEW MORE HOURS AND

WE WILL ARRIVE AT MY AUNT'S HOUSE, NOW THAT I THINK ABOUT IT, I AM GLAD I AM FINALL GOING TO GET TO KNOW HER I ALWAYS WANTED TO KNOW ALL MY FAMILY, BUT UNFORTUNATELY, ALL I KNEW IN MY LIFE WAS THE TORTURE AND THE THAT PART OF MY LIFE WHICH WAS FULL OF PAIN AND SUFFERING, WAS HANDED TO ME BY MY PARENTS BUT THOSE DAYS ARE OVER WITH, THE SCARES ARE STILL THERE IN MY HEAD AND IN MY HEART THE INNER PART OF ME WILL REGROW TO BE A STRONGER AND BETTER PERSON FULL OF LOVE AND HAPPINESS, WE WILL BE TO MY AUNT'S HOUSE IN LIKE AN HOUR, AS WE APPROACH HER HOUSE CLOSER AND CLOSER, I SAT BACK AND CLOSED MY EYES FOR A BIT MY WHOLE LIFE WAS FLASHING IN MY MIND AND I DID NOT LIKE WHAT I WAS LOOKING AT I THANK GOD FOR TAKING ME OUT OF THE SITUATION I WAS IN AND I FEEL THIS WILL BE JUST WHAT I NEED TO HELP WITH MY RECOVERY, AS WE ARRIVE AT MY AUNT'S HOUSE, I LOOK OUT THE WINDOW, SEE MY AUNT STANDING ON THE PORCH, AND LOOKING AT HER WAS LIKE LOOKING AT MY MOM, AND THIS OTHER LADY THAT WAS STANDING NEXT TO HER, I ASKED MY SO-CALLED MOM WHO SHE WAS AND SHE STAY SILENT THEN THE MAN SHE WAS WITH SAID THAT IS YOUR GRANDMA, I GOT OUT OF THE CAR AND STOOD THERE FOR A BIT JUST THINKING AM I GOING TO GET ABUSED HERE OR WHAT SO I JUST I WALKED TOWARDS THEM AND STOOD THERE IN FRONT OF THEM BOTH AND MY AUNT SAID YOU JUST A BABY, AS SHE SAID THIS, SHE STARTED WALKING OFF THE PORCH GIVING ME A BIG HUG AND TELLING ME I HAVE BEEN WANTING TO MEET YOU FOR A LONG TIME, BUT YOUR MOM NEVER BROUGHT YOU AROUND, AS I GO ONTO THE PORCH I ASKED THE LADY STANDING THERE ARE YOU, MY GRANDMA, SHE SMILED AS SHE HUGGED ME

AND SAID WITH A BIG SMILE SAYS I WAITED FOR THIS DAY AND SAID YES, MIJA I AM YOUR GRANDMA, AS I WAS STANDING THERE TALKING TO THEM, I TURNED BACK AND SAW MRS. GARCIA AND HER HUSBAND DRIVE OFF, AND I JUST SAID TO MYSELF FINALLY THEY ARE GONE, NOW IT IS TIME TO REST AND FIND OUT THE TRUTH ABOUT EVERYTHING, WHICH WILL HAPPEN AT THE RIGHT TIME, SO MY AUNT ASKED ME ARE YOU HUNGRY DO YOU NEED ANYTHING LET US KNOW WHAT WILL MAKE YOU HAPPY, THEN SHE LOOKED AT ME AND SAID THERE IS MUCH I HAVE TO TELL YOU ABOUT YOUR PARENT BUT I WILL SAVE THAT CONVERSATION FOR ANOTHER DAY, RIGHT NOW I WANT YOU TO GO TO YOUR ROOM AND SEE WHAT WE GOT YOU, AS I WALKED AWAY, I HAD TEARS IN MY EYES AND STOPPED AND LOOKED AT MY AUNT CONFUSE AND ASKED MY AUNT WHY SHE WAS BEING SO NICE TO ME NOT EVEN KNOWING ME AND SHE AND SHE SMILED AND SAID YOU ARE FAMILY; YOU ALWAYS TREAT FAMILY RIGHT AND SHOW THEM ALL LOVE AND HAPPINESS WHEN SHE SAID THAT I COULD NOT HELP IT I STARTED CRYING, AND MY AUNT ASK WHAT WAS WRONG AND WHY ARE CRYING AND I TOLD HER IT WAS A MIX OF HAPPY TEARS AND SAD TEARS SHE ASK WHAT DO YOU MEAN SAD AND HAPPY TEARS PLEASE EXPLAIN, I TOLD HER SEE MY SO CALL MOM AND DAD WERE NOT EXACTLY THE BEST PARENTS THEY NEVER SHOWED ME, LOVE, ALL THEY SHOWED WAS PAIN AND SUFFERING, THEY NEVER TOLD ME THEY LOVED ME THEY NEVER DID ANYTHING NICE FOR ME ALL THEY DID WAS USE ME AND ABUSE ME AND LAUGH AT ALL MY PAIN AND SUFFERING, WHEN I TOLD HER THIS, I COULD SEE TEARS COMING OUT OF HER EYES AND SHE SAID, MY POOR CHILD I KNEW SOMETHING WAS NOT RIGHT WITH THEM, ONCE YOU ARE SETTLED IN GOOD THEN WE ARE GOING

TO HAVE A LONG TALK ABOUT YOUR PARENTS, AND I LOOKED AT HER FOR A SECOND. AND TOLD HER YES, I HAVE LOTS OF QUESTIONS I AM NOT READY FOR THIS RIGHT NOW I WILL LET YOU KNOW WHEN I AM READY TO TALK ABOUT MR. AND MRS. GARCIA THEN MY AUNT SAID OK ME AND YOUR GRANDMOTHER ARE HERE FOR YOU, YOU ARE HOME AFTER, SHE TOLD ME THAT I FELT A BURDEN LIFT FROM MY HEART A RELIEVED THAT I HAVE BEEN SEARCHING FOR ALL THESE YEARS, BUT THE ONLY THING THAT IS STILL DEEP IN MY HEART IS THE FACT THAT I STILL HAVE NOT SPOKEN TO RANDY, I HAVE BEEN HERE A WEEK ALREADY, AND ME RANDY HAS NOT SPOKEN I HOPE HE IS OK I KNOW HE MISSES ME AS MUCH AS I MISS HIM, AND I HOPE I CAN GO BACK TO HIM SOON, AS I WALK INTO THE KITCHEN, I SEE MY AUNT JOSIE AND MY GRANDMA IS SITTING AT THE TABLE DRINKING A CUP OF COFFEE AND TALKING AS THEY SEE I WALKED IN THEY PAUSED AND ASKED ME IF EVERYTHING WAS OK, I TOLD THEM YES EVERYTHING IS GREAT, I JUST WANTED TO LET YOU KNOW THAT I AM READY TO TALK ABOUT MR. AND MRS. GRACIA AND THEY LOOKED AT EACH OTHER THEN THEY LOOKED AT ME AND SAID OK MIJA LET ME MAKE YOU SOMETHING TO EAT THEN WE WILL TALK, THEN I TOOK A DEEP BREATH AND SAID OK SO I SAT DOWN AT THE TABLE AND THEY STARTED TELLING ME EVERYTHING, MY GRANDMA STARTED TELLING ME SHE SAID, MIJA I REMEMBER WHEN YOUR DAD FIRST CAME TO THE HOUSE, HE WAS DATING MY DAUGHTER SANDRA, AND THEN I SAID WAIT THAT IS NOT MY MOM'S NAME HER NAME IS YVETTE, AND THEN SHE SAID YES, I KNOW THERE IS LOT'S MORE TO SAY THEN I SAID OK TELL ME, THEN SHE TOLD ME SEE YOUR DAD AND MY DAUGHTER HAD JUST GOT MARRIED AND THEY TRY AND TRY TO HAVE

KID'S, BUT MY DAUGHTER COULD NOT HAVE KID'S SO HE LEFT HER AND GOT TOGETHER WITH ANOTHER WOMAN AND HE HAD A GIRL WITH HER, AND I ASKED IF IT WAS ME AND SHE SAID NO THAT WAS YOUR OLDER SISTER, AND SHE STAYED WITH HER UNTIL YOUR SISTER TURNED 15 THEN HE LEFT HER ANDREA LOOKS AT ME WITH THE SADDEST EYES, AND I ASK WHAT IS IT GRANDMA TELL ME SHE LOOKED AT ME AND SAID YOUR MOM IS YOUR OLDER SISTER WHEN SHE TOLD ME THIS I WAS IN THE WORST SHOCK EVER, AND I SAID WAIT HOW CAN THIS BE, THEY NEVER TOLD ME ANYTHING, AND WHAT ABOUT MY BROTHER, SHE SAID SEE YOUR DAD IS AN EVIL PERSON AND HE TURNED YOUR SISTER INTO AN EVIL PERSON TOO, SHE IS FULL OF HATE AND LOVES TO SEE PEOPLE GET HURT, THAT IS WHY THEY TREATED YOU THE WAY THEY DID, SO I SAID WHAT ABOUT MY BROTHER AND MY AUNT SAID WILL YOUR BROTHER IS YOUR COUSIN'S SON YOUR DAD GOT YOUR COUSIN DRUNK AND GOT HER WHEN SHE PASS OUT AND A FEW MONTHS LATER YOUR BROTHER WAS BORN, I ASKED MY AUNT WHICH COUSIN IS SHE SAID YOUR COUSIN SANDRA, AND I SAID WOW SHE IS ONLY 17 YEARS OLD, AND MY AUNT SAID SHE WAS ONLY 14 YEARS OLD WHEN SHE HAD YOUR BROTHER, AND YOUR DAD SAID I WILL TAKE THE BOY WITH ME AND RAISE HIM, AFTER I HEARD ALL OF THIS, I DID NOT WANT TO HEAR NO MORE I GOT UP FROM THE TABLE AND RAN TO MY ROOM IN TEARS I CLOSED MY EYES AND LOOK FOR RANDY IN MY THOUGHTS FOR HE IS THE ONLY ONE THAT CAN MAKE ME FEEL BETTER I CRY MY HEART OUT ALL NIGHT, THIS TORE ME UP I AM READY TO GO BACK HOME I NEED TO LEAVE I WILL REST TONIGHT AND GO EARLY IN THE MORNING I MISS MY FRIENDS AND RANDY I NEED TO GO TO MY HOMETOWN I NEED TO TALK TO RANDY AND LET HIM KNOW ABOUT ALL THAT I HEARD, AS I

AM HEADING TOWARDS THE KITCHEN TO TELL THE BOTH OF THEM, I MUST GO BACK HOME, AND THE FIRST THING I AM GOING TO DO IS FILE CHARGES AGAINST MY DAD FOR EVERYTHING HE DID TO ME AND ON MY MOM FOR LETTING HIM DO THESE THINGS TO ME, AS I GET TO THE KITCHEN MY AUNT AND GRANDMA WAS TALKING ABOUT EVERYTHING THEY HAD TOLD ME AND I SAW MY AUNT CRYING I WALKED IN AND THEY LOOK AT ME AND SAID WHAT IS IT AND I SIT THERE AT THE TABLE AND I TOLD THEN, LOOK I ENJOY BEING HERE WITH BOTH OF YOU I FEEL ALL THE LOVE FROM THE BOTH OF YALL, THE DAYS I HAVE BEEN HERE YOU BOTH HAVE SHOWN ME MORE LOVE AND HAPPINESS THEN THEY SHOW ME ALL MY LIFE AND I WANT TO SAY THANK YOU BOTH FOR EVERYTHING, BUT I MUST GO BACK HOME, FIRST THING I AM GOING TO DO IS FILE CHARGES AGAINST MY PARENTS FOR ALL THEY HAVE DONE TO ME, AND I HAVE TO SEE MY BOYFRIEND I KNOW HE IS WORRIED ABOUT ME, BUT I PROMISE YOU WHEN I GET EVERYTHING SETTLE, I WILL COME BACK TO STAY WITH THE BOTH OF YOU WILL TOMORROW I WILL BE GOING BACK HOME, AS I WALK OUT OF THE KITCHEN I STOP AT THE DOOR WAY, I SAID YOU KNOW WHAT AND THEY BOTH SAID WHAT IS IT, I SAID YOU KNOW FOR YEARS I WOULD ASK THE QUESTION WHY DO I GET TREATED LIKE THIS WHY DON'T THEY LOVE ME, THEY LOOK AT ME WITH A LOT OF HATE, AND I ALWAYS THOUGHT IT WAS MY FAULT, THAT I ALWAYS DID SOMETHING WRONG, BUT THE WHOLE TIME IT WAS THEM THAT WAS IN THE WRONG, I HATE THEM I NEVER WANT TO SEE THEM AGAIN; THEY STAYED SILENT AFTER I SAID THAT THEN I JUST PUT MY HEAD DOWN AND WALK TOWARDS MY ROOM, WILL TOMORROW IS ALMOST HERE TIME TO TRY AND SLEEP. I WILL LAY TO REST AND DREAM OF RANDY AND HOW

GREAT IT WILL BE WHEN I GET BACK TO TOWN TO SEE HIM AND TELL HIM EVERYTHING THAT IS GOING ON, I LAY TO SLEEP NOW AND HOPEFULLY WAKE UP TO A BETTER DAY, AS I WAS FALLING ASLEEP, I HEARD MY AUNT AND GRANDMA TALKING IN THE KITCHEN AS THEY WERE TALKING, I HEARD FOOTSTEPS IN THE HALL AND THEN MY DOOR OPENED SLOWLY, AS I SAW MY DOOR OPENING, I GOT SCARED IT BROUGHT BACK MEMORIES OF HOW MY PARENTS WOULD COME INTO MY ROOM, AND ABUSE ME, BUT IT WAS NOT THEM IT WAS MY PRECIOUS GRANDMA, JUST STOOD THERE AND SAID, SHE IS SO BEAUTIFUL AND SHE IS JUST A BABY, MY HEART GOES OUT TO HER SHE DOES NOT DESERVE THIS TREATMENT, I LOVE HER AS MY OWN DAUGHTER, AND I HOPE SHE DOES COME BACK AFTER ALL IS DONE AS SHE PROMISED SHE WOULD, THEN THE DOOR CLOSED SHE STARTED WALKING BACK TO THE KITCHEN, I HEARD MY GRANDMA TELL MY AUNT I AM GOING TO MISS HER SO MUCH I ALWAYS WANTED A DAUGHTER SHE IS SUCH A PRECIOUS PERSON AND FOR HER TO SUFFER AS SHE DID IS NOT RIGHT, I HOPE WHEN SHE GET'S BACK SHE MAKES THEM PAY FOR ALL THE PAIN THEY HAD CAUSED HER, AND MY AUNT TELLS MY GRANDMA YES, MAMA, THEY DESERVE TO PAY FOR THIS AND I AM GOING TO SEE TO IT MYSELF THAT JUSTICE IS BROUGHT FOR ANDREA, IT IS ALMOST MORNING AND ANDREA WILL BE LEAVING US, AS SHE CAME TO US LIKE A GIFT FROM THE SKY THAT WE WERE ABLE TO CHRISE FOR A WHILE, WILL GOOD NIGHT YES, GOOD NIGHT SARA YES GOOD NIGHT GRANDMA, AS EVERYONE LAY IN A DEEP SLEEP MORNING CAME SOONER THAN THEY EXPECTED, GOOD MORNING ANDREA HOW YOU SLEEP MIJA GRANDMA WAS ASKING ME AND I SAID I SLEPT WELL GRANDMA HOW WAS YOUR NIGHT GRANDMA LOOKED

AT ME AND SAID NOT SO GOOD WAS JUST THINKING ABOUT YOU LEAVING US TODAY, OH GRANDMA DON'T WORRY I WILL BE BACK BEFORE YOU KNOW IT, I JUST HAVE TO GO BACK AND TAKE CARE OF WHAT NEEDS TO BE TAKEN CARE OF AND WHEN I COME BACK CAN I BRING RANDY BACK WITH ME HE IS MY BOYFRIEND AND HE IS VERY NICE AND YOU WILL LOVE HIM, YES MIJA HE CAN COME TO STAY WITH US ARE YOUR MOM AND DAD GOING TO COME TO PICK YOU UP, AND I SAID OH NO IT IS A SURPRISE VISIT THEY NOT EXPECTING ME BACK AND WHEN THEY SEE ME, I WILL BE WITH THE COPS AND I WILL STAND THERE, AND GET THE LAST LAUGH AS I SEE THE COPS TAKE THEM TO JAIL, THEN HOW ARE YOU GOING BACK HOME, I TOLD HER I WAS TAKING THE BUS BACK I SHOULD BE BACK TO ROSENBERG IN LIKE 4 HOURS, MY BUS WILL LEAVE IN 2 HOURS AS I WAS GOING TO PACK, I TURNED BACK TO LOOK AT GRANDMA'S AND I SAW TEARS IN MY AND THE HURT THAT MY GRANDMA WAS EXPERIENCING I WALKED AWAY AS I WAS GOING TO MY ROOM, I WAS TELLING MY GRANDMA AND MY AUNT SARA, I LOVE YOU BOTH VERY MUCH AND I WILL MISS YOU BOTH BUT I WILL BE BACK SOONER THAN YALL THINK, MINUTES LATER I COME OUT OF THE ROOM WITH MY SUITCASE AS I STAND BY THE FRONT DOOR I LOOK AT THEM FOR THE LAST TIME I TELL THEM AGAIN I LOVE THEM, AND THEY BOTH CAME UP TO ME AND GAVE ME A BIG HUG AND KISSED AND SAID I LOVE YOU HURRY BACK, I TOLD THEM I PROMISED I WOULD, AS I WALKED OUT OF THE HOUSE AND TO THE BUS STOP WHICH WAS A FEW BLOCKS AWAY ALL I COULD DO WAS THINK ABOUT MY BOYFRIEND AND HOW MUCH I MISSED HIM AND I KNOW HE MISSES ME MORE THAN I MISS HIM I AM SO BLESSED TO HAVE A HIM BY MY SIDE. I LOVE HIM, I AM HERE AT THE BUS STOP AS I GO IN TO GET MY TICKET, I AM EXCITED TO GO

HOME TO HIM I STOP AT THE ENTRANCE TO THE BUS STATION WITH MY HAND ON THE DOOR HANDLE I SIT THERE AND THINK FOR A BIT, I STARTED THINKING WHAT IF HE LEFT ME AND FOUND ANOTHER GIRL, OR WHEN I GET BACK HE TELLS ME HE DOESN'T LOVE ME NO MORE THAT I HAVE BEEN GONE SO LONG THAT HE LOST THE LOVE HE HAD FOR ME, NO I CAN NOT LOSE HIM I NEED TO HURRY UP AND GET BACK HOME AND TELL HIM HOW I LOVE HIM AND MISS HIM, BUT I KNOW EVERYTHING WILL BE OK I AM JUST OVER THINKING ABOUT EVERYTHING, NOW I WILL GO INSIDE AND GET MY TICKET. AS I GET TO THE COUNTER THE MAN, THERE ASK WHERE WILL YOU BE GOING AND I SMILED AND SAID ONE WAY TO ROSENBERG TEXAS HE SAID OK THAT WILL BE $28.50 I GAVE HIM THE MONEY AND HE TOLD ME YOU JUST IN TIME THE BUS WILL BE HERE IN A LITTLE BIT, AND WILL REACH ROSENBERG TEXAS BY 4:30 I LOOKED AT THE CLOCK ON THE WALL READ 12:30 I THEN GOT MY BAGS AND WAITED FOR THE BUS TO GET THERE THAT WAS THE LONGEST WAIT I EVER WAITED I WAS IN A HURRY TO GET BACK HOME I NEED TO LEAVE THIS TOWN FOR A LITTLE WHILE BUT I WILL RETURN, I THINK I SEE THE BUS COMING YES, IT IS THE BUS. I STOOD THERE FOR A BIT JUST LOOKING INTO MY PAST AND ALL I COULD DO WAS CRY INSIDE WITH A BROKEN HEART AND BROKEN DREAMS, I DID NOT KNOW WHAT MY LIFE WAS GOING TO BE FROM THAT DAY FORWARD ALL I KNEW AS LONG AS I HAD RANDY IN MY LIFE, I WOULD BE OK, I JUST PRAY THAT WHEN I GET BACK, HE WILL BE THERE WAITING FOR ME, I KNOW I DID NOT CALL HIM OR TALK TO HIM FOR ALMOST 6 MONTHS I JUST HOPE HE IS STILL WAITING FOR ME, BUT IF HE LEAVES IT WILL NOT BE THE FIRST TIME I LOSE SOMEONE; I HAVE BEEN LOOSENING PEOPLE MY WHOLE LIFE SO

I AM USED TO IT, I AM A BIG LOOSER, AS I STOOD THERE, I LOOKED AROUND ME AND SAW ALL THESE HAPPY FAMILIES JUST SMILING AND HUGGING EACH OTHER SAYING I LOVE YOU I MISS YOU I AM GLAD YOU CAME BACK HOME, WHY CAN'T I GET THAT KIND OF RESPONSE WHY DO PEOPLE HATE ME I ALWAYS GET THE WORST OUT OF EVERYONE, AND THAT IS WHY I CAN NOT LOSE RANDY HE IS THE ONLY ONE BESIDES MY AUNT AND GRANDMA THAT SHOWED ME TRUE LOVE AND HAPPINESS, I KNOW WHEN I GET BACK, I HAVE A LOT OF EXPLAINING TO DO, I JUST HOPE RANDY BELIEVES ME WHEN I TELL HIM WHAT I NEED TO TELL HIM, IT HAPPENED TO ME AND I STILL DON'T BELIEVE IT SO HOW CAN I EXPECT SOMEONE ELSE TO BELIEVE ME, I NEVER LIED TO RANDY SO I HOPE IT ALL GOES WELL, I KNOW THAT WHATEVER HAPPENS, I WILL ALWAYS LOVE HIM AND SHOW HIM, LOVE, AS THESE PEOPLE SHOWED EACH OTHER HER AT THIS STATION WILL IT IS TIME TO GO I SEE MY TRIP HOME PULLING UP, ANDREA WAS FIXING TO BOARD THE BUS TO GO BACK TO HER HOMETOWN ROSENBERG, WHERE SHE GREW UP IN A VIOLENT HOME, SHE KNEW WHEN SHE GOT HOME THAT SHE WAS GOING TO GO THREW A LOT SO AT THAT POINT SHE WAS SCARED AND WORRY, ABOUT THE OUTCOME OF EVERYTHING THAT WAS GOING ON WITHIN A MATTER OF HOURS SHE WILL BE HOME AND SHE STILL DOES NOT KNOW THAT RANDY IS IN THE HOSPITAL IN A COMA HOW WILL SHE REACT KNOWING HER LOVE IS IN THE HOSPITAL HOW WILL SHE REACT KNOWING SHE HAS NOT SEEN RANDY IN A LONG TIME AND NOW WHEN SHE SEES HIM FOR THE FIRST TIME, HE WILL BE IN THE HOSPITAL IN A COMA SO WHEN SHE GET'S HOME WHAT WILL BE HER NEXT MOVE? BEFORE SHE GOT ON THE BUS, SHE HEARD HER NAME CALLED ON THE LOUDSPEAKER, TO COME TO THE DESK THERE WAS A

CALL FOR HER, SO SHE WENT TO THE DESK AND SAID I AM ANDREA, THEY HANDED THE PHONE TO HER IT WAS JUDY ON THE LINE, AND SHE SAID ANDREA IS THAT YOU, ANDREA SAID YES WHO IS THIS AND THE REPLY WAS IT IS ME JUDY, I HEARD YOU WILL BE RETURNING HOME TODAY, AND I WAS SHOCKED THAT SHE KNEW THAT I TOLD HER YES, I AM, HOW DO YOU KNOW JUDY REPLIED, " I HAVE WAYS OF FINDING OUT BUT THE REASON I CALLED YOU IS WE NEED TO TALK WHEN YOU GET HOME I WILL BE AT THE BUS STATION WAITING FOR YOU WHEN YOU GET HOME, AND ASK HER ABOUT WHAT AND SHE SAID I WILL TELL YOU WHEN YOU GET HOME HAVE A SAFE TRIP BACK HOME SEE YOU IN A FEW. AS ANDREA WENT BACK TO HER SEAT SHE SAT THERE UNTIL THE BUS ARRIVED, SHE WAS SPEECHLESS, DID NOT KNOW WHAT TO THINK, THEN SHE SMILED AND SAID SOMEONE ELSE BESIDES RANDY CARES ABOUT ME AND LOVES ME, I CAN NOT WAIT TO GET BACK HOME, AT THIS POINT ANDREA WAS HAPPY FOR A FEW HOURS SHE KNEW THAT WHATEVER HAD HAPPENED IN THE PAST WILL NOT HAPPEN NO MORE SHE HAS FRIENDS AND A BOYFRIEND THAT LOVE HER AND CARE ABOUT HER AND WILL TAKE CARE OF HER, ANDREA STANDS UP AND WALKS TOWARDS THE WINDOW AT THE BUS STATION AND SHE SEES THE BUS COMING, SHE RUNS AND GETS A DRINK TO TAKE WITH HER ON HER LONG TRIP BACK HOME, AS SHE LOOKED UP, SHE SAW THAT IT WAS HERE COMING AROUND THE CORNER, AS I STOOD THERE AND WAITED FOR THE BUS TO ARRIVE I STILL CAN NOT BELIEVE EVERYTHING THAT HAS HAPPENED TO ME I HAVE BEEN THREW SO MUCH IN MY LIFE I SUFFERED SO MUCH IN THE HANDS OF MY PARENTS AND FINALLY I CAN SAY IT IS GOING TO BE OVER REAL SOON I SEE THE BUS JUST PULLED INTO THE BUS STATION AND I CAN NOT STOP WONDERING HOW

CHAPTER 4   MY HOMETOWN

THINGS WOULD HAVE BEEN IF I HAD NEVER COME TO STAY WITH MY AUNT AND GRANDMA, I WOULD HEVE NEVER KNEW THE TRUTH ABOUT MY PATENTS AND THE TRUE EVIL PEOPLE THAT THEY ARE I NEVER NEW THAT MY MOM WAS MY OLDER SISTER, AND MY BROTHER WAS MY STEPBROTHER MY PARENTS ARE SO TWISTED AS THE BUS WAS PULLING UP, I GOT MY SUITCASE AND TICKET READY TO BOARD THE BUS, I SEE A DISTURBING NEWS ON TV OF HOW A BOY MY AGE WAS ENGAGED IN A HIT-AND-RUN, AND THEY **HAVE NO SUSPECTS AND STILL DON'T KNOW WHO THE** BOY IS THAT GOT HIT, I HOPE HE IS DOINGGOOD PRAYERS GO OUT TO HIM AND HIS FAMILY. WAIT NO IT CAN NOT BE BUT WHAT IF IT IS RANDY NO, IT IS NOT HIM, IF IT WAS HIM, I WOULD LOSE IT, HE PROMISE HE WOULD NEVER LEAVEME, BUT I KNOW WHEN I GET HOME, HE WILL BE AT HIS HOUSE WAITING FOR ME TO GET HOME AND I AM GOING TO GIVE HIM THE BIGGEST HUG AND KISS THAT I EVER GAVE HIM, HE IS MY LIFE PARTNERTHERE IS NO ONE ELSE FOR HIM AND NO ONE ELSE FOR ME WILL WE ARE TAKING OFF TO GO BACK TOMY SMALL HOMETOWN ROSENBERG, AS I AM HEADING BACK TO ROSENBERG, I SEE ALL THE SITES I SAW ON MY WAY TO MY GRANDMA AND AUNT, I STARTED THINKING OF HOW I WAS HEART BROKEN, AND BROKEN INTO LITTLE PIECES, WHEN I GOT THERE, I SAW LOTS OF LOVE AND HAPPINESS IN THERE EYES I NEEDED TO FIND MYSELF AND COME BACK TO HAPPINESS, THE WONDERFUL PERSON I WAS BEFORE ALL THE ABUSE STARTED A

FEW YEARS AGO, THANK GOD AND THANK FAMILY MEMBERS THAT REALLY CARE AND WERE THERE FOR ME WHEN I NEEDED SOMEONE TO BE WHEN MY BOYFRIEND COULD NOT BE THERE FOR ME THEY WERE, BUT HE NEVER STOPPED BEING BY MY SIDE I LOVE HIM WE ARE PASSING THE CURVE WHERE I HAD SAID I WISH COULD DISAPPEAR INTO THOSE MOUNTAINSTHOSE TREES NOW AS I SEE THEM, I SAY I AM BLESSED TO BE PASSING THESE BEAUTIFUL TREES ON MYWAY BACK HOME WILL A FEW MORE HOURS AND I WILL BE BACK THERE SO MUCH THAT I MUST DO WHEN I GET BACK HOME, I WILL CLOSE MY EYES AND THINK ABOUT EVERYTHING THAT I HAVE TO DO WHEN I GET HOME, ANDREA CLOSES HER EYES AND THINKS ABOUT EVERYTHING THAT HAS HAPPENED TO HER AND WHAT SHE HAS TO DO WHEN SHE GETS BACK HOME; SHE IS HAPPY SHE IS GOING TO SEE HER BOYFRIEND WHOM SHE HAS NOT SEEN OR TALKED TO FOR 6 MONTHS BUT LITTLE DOES SHE KNOW THAT HE IS IN THE HOSPITAL IN A COMA AND HAS BEEN FOR 2 WEEKS ALREADY AND HER PARENTS ARE STILL UP TO NO GOOD DRINKING AND DOING DRUGS, AND NOW THEY HAVE A YOUNG GIRL STAYING WITH THEM, SHE IS ONLY 13 YEARS OLD BUT THIS GIRL IS NOT THEIR FAMILY MEMBER THEY KIDNAP HER FROM THE PARK AND THEY ARE DOING THE SAME TO HER AS THEY DID TO ANDREA, LETS'S **SEE WHATHAPPENS NEXT WHEN ANDREA GET'S HOME** AND SURPRISE THEM WITH THE COPS AND HOW ANDREAWILL FEEL WHEN SHE FINDS OUT HER BOYFRIEND IS IN THE HOSPITAL, I AM FINALLY HOME FIRST THINGI NEED TO DO IS GO SEE RANDY BUT I ALSO NEED TO GO TO THE COPS AND I NEED TO TALK TO SARA I MUST GO TO THE COPS FIRST AND FILE CHARGES ON MY PARENTS. THEN I WILL GO TO RANDY HOUSE I KNOW HE IS

GOING TO BE SURPRISED TO SEE ME, AS I GRAB MY BAGS FROM THE BUS STATION, I SEE MY OLD FRIEND LOOKING AT ME WITH THE SADDEST LOOK ON HER FACE, WHAT IS WRONG I WILL TELL
YOU ARE LATER I KNOW YOU HAVE MUCH TO TAKE CARE OF RIGHT NOW BUT DO NOT FORGET I HAVE TO TALK TO YOU SO PLEASE CALL ME THIS IS VERY IMPORTANT SO, CALL ME WHEN YOU ARE DONE AND I WILL TELL YOU, I WILL CALL YOU AFTER I GO TO THE POLICE STATION AND GO SEE RANDY OK KAREN IF THIS IS FIND, I WILL CALL YOU LATER TODAY, AS I WALKED AWAY, I WAS PUZZLED ABOUT WHAT COULD HAVE HAPPENED THAT COULD OF BEEN SO DISTURBING THAT SHE COULD NOT TELL ME, I WONDER IF IT HAD ANYTHING TO DO WITH THE ACCIDENT THAT OCCURRED WHEN I WAS OUT OF TOWN, I GUESS I WILL FIND OUT SOON ENOUGH, I JUST HOPE IT IS NOTHING TO SERIOUS, AS I AM WALKING TO THE POLICE STATION WITH MY SUITCASEIN MY HAND, I COULD NOT HELP BUT THINK ABOUT ALL THE ABUSE I SUFFERED AT THE HANDS OF MYPARENTS IT IS SO SAD A CHILD IS SUPPOSED TO FEEL SAFE AND LOVED AND TAKEN CARE OF BY GOOD PARENTS AND NOT ABUSE AND TREAT THEM LIKE A DOG, THE WAY, THEY TREATED ME TO STAND THERE ANDLAUGH AT ME WHILE I WAS IN PAIN AND SUFFERING WHEN THESE GROWN MAN WERE ON TOP OF MEWAS MORE THAN ANY 12-YEAR-OLD CHILD WOULD BE ABLE TO TAKE, I THANK GOD, HE GAVE ME THESTRENGTH TO OVERCOME ALL I HAVE BEEN THREW AND TODAY IS THE DAY THAT I WILL GET JUSTICE FOR WHATTHEY DID TO ME AND IT WILL BE ME LAUGHING AT THE END THEY WILL FINALLY SEE WHAT IT FEELS LIKE TO BE IN THE HANDS OF OTHER PEOPLE AND TO SUFFER IN THEIR HANDS, I HAVE ARRIVED AT THE POLICE STATION AS I GET HERE, I PAUSED

FOR A BIT ON THE FIRST STEP, KINDA SCARED AND NERVOUS, AND WHAT IF THEY DIDN'T BELIEVE ME WHAT IF THEY THINK I AM MAKING ALL OF THIS UP, NO, I HAVE TO GO IN AND REPORT AM GREETED BY THE COP AT THE DESK AND HE ASKS ME HOW CAN WE HELP YOU; I STAYED QUIET HE ASKED ME AGAIN SAYING MAMA HOW CAN WE HELP YOU WHAT'S GOING ON AND THEN I OPENED UP AND SAID I, I, I, I WANT TO REPORT ABUSE AND THEN I BUSTED OUT CRYING THE COP CAME FROM BEHIND THE COUNTER GAVE ME A TISSUE AND SPOKE COME WITH ME LET'S GO TO THE DETECTIVE, AS I WALK INTO THE ROOM, I SEE TWO DETECTIVES SITTING AT THEIR DESK THEY ASK THE COP WHAT IS GOING ON AND HE SAYS WITH A SURPRISED LOOK ON HIS FACE SHE WANTS TO REPORT ABUSE BY HER PARENTS, THEY LOOKED AT ME PUZZLE AND THEN ONE OF THE DETECTIVES GRAB A CHAIR AND PLACED IT NEXT TO HER DESK AND SAID COME SIT DOWN I WILL TAKE YOUR STATEMENT; SHE ASKED ME WHAT IS YOUR NAME I TOLD HER I AM ANDREA GARCIA AND SHE SAID MY NAME IS DETECTIVE RODRIGUEZ THIS IS MY PARTNER AND HIS DETECTIVE MORALES WE ARE GOING TO HELP YOU, NOW TELL US ALL THAT HAPPEN TO YOU, I STARTED SPEAKING, I SAID OK I AM 16 NOW AND THIS STARTED WHEN I HAD JUST TURNED 9 YEARS OLD WHAT HAPPENED TO YOU? THE ABUSIVE PARENTS WERE NOT SUCH GOOD PARENTS THEY DRANK A LOT AND WOULD ALWAYS HIT ME, AT FIRST I FIGURED THAT I WAS DOING SOMETHING WRONG THAT IS WHY THEY ABUSED ME, BUT IT WAS NOT ME IT WAS ALL OF THEM THEY HATED THEIR LIVES AND TOOK IT OUT ON ME, THE DETECTIVE STOPPED ME AND ASKED WAIT YOU ARE REPORTING YOUR PARENTS FOR HITTING YOU, AND I LOOKED AT HER AND STARTED CRYING AND SAID NO MAMA I AM REPORTING THEM CAUSE

MY DAD WOULD COME INTO MY ROOM AT NIGHT AND DO THINGS TO ME HE TOOK ADVANTAGE OF ME HE TOOK MY INNOCENCE, AND THEN HE WOULD SALE ME TO HIS FRIENDS I COULD NOT BELIEVE THIS WAS HAPPENING TO ME HE DID IT SO HE COULD BUY MORE DRUGS, THE DETECTIVE WAS SHOCKED WHEN I TOLD THEM THIS, AND SHE ASKED ME YOU HAVE PROOF AND I SAID YES MAMA I DID THAT NIGHT AFTER MY DAD AND BOTH OF HIS FRIENDS HAD THEIR WAY WITH ME I WAS IN A LOT OF PAIN I HAD TO BE RUSHED TO THE HOSPITAL, AND AS I WAS THERE THEY NOTICED THE ABUSE, THEY CALLED THE COPS THERE IS A REPORT ON THIS, AND THE DETECTIVE LOOKED AT THE REPORT ON FILE AND SAID OH MY GOD SHE LOOKED AT ME WITH TEARS IN HER EYES HUGGED ME AND SAID I AM SO SORRY, THIS HAPPENED TO YOU, I STARTED CRYING I TOLD THE DETECTIVES I BEGGED THEM TO STOP I TOLD THEM THEY WERE HURTING ME MY DAD SAID, GOOD GIRL AND THEY LAUGHED AT ME, WHY DID THEY DO THIS TO, ME WHY **DON'T THEY LOVE ME, WHY, AFTER** I GAVE MY REPORT, THEY SENT COPS TO MY PARENTS' HOUSE AND HAD THEM BOTH ARRESTED FOR CHILD ABUSE AND ASSAULT CAUSING INJURY TO MY BODY ENDANGERMENT TO A CHILD SO THAT DAY MY PARENTS GOT ARRESTED AND BOTH OF MY DAD FRIENDS WERE NOWHERE TO BE FOUND, AS I WAS LEAVING THE POLICE STATION THE DETECTIVE SAID YOU ARE A VERY BRAVE YOUNG LADY A STRONG GIRL TO STEP FORWARD LIKE THIS AGAINST YOUR PARENTS I WILL KEEP IN CONTACT WITH YOU TO LET YOU KNOW THE COURT DATE, AS I WAS LEAVING THE STATION, I SAW THE COPS BRINGING MY PARENTS IN THAT WAS THE HAPPIEST DAY OF MY LIFE, NOW THAT I AM DONE HERE, I CAN GO SEE RANDY MY BOYFRIEND AND GIVE HIM THE

GOOD NEWS, ON MY WAY TO HIS HOUSE I SEE HIS OLD FRIEND TIM COMING UP THE ROAD, I HAVE NOT SEEN HIM IN YEARS I WONDER WHAT HE IS DOING HERE, HE NOTICE ME, HE STOPPED AND ASKED HOW IS RANDY DOING, AND I SAID OK I AM GOING TO HIS HOUSE RIGHT NOW, HE LOOKED AT ME SAYING SO YOU DON'T KNOW AND I LOOKED AT TIM AND ASKED HIM KNOW WHAT TELL ME, HE SAID COME ON GET IN I WILL TELL YOU ON THE WAY TO THE HOSPITAL, WHEN HE SAID THAT MY HEART DROPPED I JUMPED IN THE CAR AS FAST AS I COULD AND I ASKED TIM AGAIN, OK NOW TELL ME WHAT HAPPEN, HE SAID DID YOU HEAR IN THE NEWS ABOUT THE BOY THAT WAS IN A HIT AND RUN, WHEN HE SAID THIS, I SCREAMED OUT AS LOUD AS I COULD SAYING NO IT CAN NOT BE TRUE NOT MY RANDY THIS IS A LIE HE CAN NOT BE IN THE HOSPITAL TELL ME YOU'RE PLAYING A GAME HE IS OK, HE PROMISED HE WOULD NEVER LEAVE ME, STOP PLAYING WHERE IS HE FOR REAL PLEASE SAY THIS IS NOT TRUE; I CAN NOT LOSE HIM I LOVE HIM SO MUCH AND HE PROMISED ME WE WOULD ALWAYS BE TOGETHER; I KNOW HE IS DOING THIS TO PAY ME BACK FOR BEING GONE ALL THESE MONTHS AND NOT TALKING TO HIM, OK I LEARNED MY LESSON NOW TAKE ME BACK TO HIS HOUSE, THIS IS NOT FUNNY TIM AS I SAID THIS, HE LOOKED AT ME WITH TEARS IN HIS EYES AND SAID ANDREA I PROMISE YOU I AM TELLING YOU THE TRUTH HE IS HERE IN THE HOSPITAL, AS WE GOT TO THE HOSPITAL, I DID NOT EVEN LET THE CAR STOP COMPLETELY I JUMPED OUT AND RAN INSIDE THE BUILDING, AND I ASKED THE LADY AT THE FRONT DESK WHAT ROOM IS RANDY GARCIA IN, THEY LOOKED IN THEIR RECORDS AND SAID HE IS IN THE SECOND FLOOR IN ROOM 223, BUT MAMA RANDY IS STILL IN A COMA, AS THEY TOLD ME THIS I WANTED TO FAINT RIGHT THERE BUT I

STAYED STRONG FOR HIM, AS I GOT TO THE SECOND FLOOR, I SLOWLY WALKED TO HIS ROOM I COULD NOT BELIEVE WHAT I WAS LOOKING AT IT WAS LIKE I WAS IN A BAD DREAM TEARS FAILI WAS SCARED TO SEE HIM LIKE THAT, I PAUSED AT THE DOOR FOR A BIT THEN I WALKED IN AS I SAW HIM LAYING IN THAT BED WITH ALL THE TUBES ALL OVER HIS BODY I BUSTED OUT CRYING AND I WENT UP TO HIM I STOOD BY HIS BED AND HELD HIS HAND, AND I TOLD HIM I AM HERE RANDY, I MADE IT BACK AS PROMISE I TOLD YOU I WOULD NEVER LEAVE YOU, AND YOU PROMISE ME YOU WOULD NEVER LEAVE MEI WILL BE HERE BY YOUR SIDE UNTIL YOU ARE READY TO GO HOME AND WE WILL LEAVE TOGETHER I WAITED MANY MONTHS TO SEE YOU AS I WAS TALKING TO HIM TEARS WERE COMING OUT OF MY EYES I TOLD HIM RANDY; I LOVE YOU PLEASE WAKE UP DON'T LEAVE ME I NEED YOU I NOTICED AS I WAS TALKING TEARS WERE COMING OUT OF HIS EYES WHEN I SAW THAT THERE WAS RELIEF IN MY HEART, AS I WAS TALKING TO HIM, I SAW TIM STANDING AT THE DOORWAY WITH TEARS IN HIS EYES AND I TOLD TIM, IT'S OK HE IS JUST RESTING RIGHT NOW HE WILL WAKE UP SOON, TIM STAYED AT THE HOSPITAL WITH US FOR A FEW DAYS THEN HE HAD TO GO BACK HOME AS HE WAS LEAVING HE SAID I WILL BE BACK IN A WEEK TELL RANDY I WAS HERE AND I WILL BE BACK AND DON'T FORGET TO LOOK UP IN THE SKY FOR THERE HE WILL FIND THE HAPPINESS AND JOY HE NEEDS TO MAKE IT OUT OF THIS SITUATION, AS TIM WALK AWAY I HEARD HIM PRAY TO GOD AS HE PRAYED; HE SAID LORD PLEASE HELP RANDY OUT OF THIS TRAUMA HE IS IN ONLY YOUR MERCIFUL HANDS CAN HELP HIM I LEAVE HIS LIFE IN YOUR HANDS AMAN, AS HE WAS PRAYING, I STOOD THERE WITH TEARS IN MY EYES PRAYING THAT GOD

ANSWER HIS PRAYERS, AFTER TIM LEFT, I STOOD THERE IN A DAZE THEN I WAS BROUGHT OUT OF MY DAZE BY THE MOST WONDERFUL VOICE I EVER HEARD, AS I LOOKED AT RANDY, HE HAD FINALLY OPENED HIS EYES, THE THE FIRST WORDS HE SAID WERE ANDREA ARE YOU HERE, AND I HELD HIS HAND AND SAID YES, MY LOVE I AM HERE FOR YOU, TRY NOT TO TALK GET YOUR REST; I PROMISE YOU I WILL NEVER LEAVE YOU AND I WILL BE BY YOUR SIDE, THE WHOLE TIME YOU ARE HERE IN THIS HOSPITAL, AND WHEN YOU GO HOME, I WILL BE THERE WITH YOU TO TAKE CARE OF YOU, AND GIVE YOU EVERYTHING YOU NEED TO MAKE IT, I MISS YOU SO MUCH, AS I SAID ALL OF THIS, HE LOOKED AT ME WITH TEARS IN HIS EYES AND I ASKED HIM WHAT DID IT TELL ME, HE SAID I ALMOST LOST MY LIFE, BUT I KNEW I COULD NOT LEAVE YOU, I FOUGHT TO STAY ALIVE, YOUR LOVE FOR ME KEPT ME ALIVE, AS HE LOOKED AT ME, HE SAID ANDREA THERE IS SOMETHING I HAVE TO TELL YOU, AND I ASKED HIM WHAT IS IT, HE SAID THIS WAS NOT JUST A HIT AND RUN, THE CAR THAT HIT ME, JOEL WAS DRIVING IT, AND AFTER HE HIT ME, HE GOT OUT OF THE CAR AND SAID, IF I CAN NOT HAVE ANDREA NOBODY CAN, HE TRIED TO KILL ME, BUT HE DID NOT AND I KNOW WHEN HE FINDS OUT HE DID NOT ACCOMPLISH WHAT HE PLANNED TO DO HE WILL TRY AGAIN, **I TOLD HIM NO HE WON'T CAUSE WE ARE GOING TO CALL THE COP'S ON HIM AND HAVE** HIM ARRESTED, AS I HAD MY PARENTS ARRESTED, HE LOOKED AT ME WHEN I SAID THIS, AND HE STOPPED ME AND ASKED ME TO WAIT WHAT DO YOU MEAN, YOU HAD THEM ARRESTED, YES, I WENT TO THE POLICE STATION THE OTHER DAY BEFORE I CAME TO THE HOSPITAL AND I MADE THE POLICE REPORT AND I TOLD **THE COP'S EVERYTHING MY PARENTS DID TO ME, FROM THE TIME WAS 9 YEARS**

OLD, AS I FINISHED TELLING THEM WHAT THEY DID, A FEW COPS WENT TO PICK THEM UP, JOEL WILL JOIN MY PARENTS IN JAIL, NOW GET YOUR REST MY LOVE DON'T WORRY I AM HERE WITH YOU, AS I SAID THIS RANDY LOOKED AT ME AND STARTED SPEAKING, HE WAS TELLING ME YOU KNOW THE DAY WHEN WE FIRST GOT TOGETHER I NEVER KNEW OUR LOVE WOULD GROW AS STRONG AS IT DID, WE HAD FOUGHT TO THE DEPTH OF BEING TOGETHER, IT HAS COME TO THE POINT IN OUR LIVES THAT IT DOESN'T MATTER WHAT PEOPLE TRY TO KEEP US APART WE GROW CLOSER TOGETHER, NOW JOEL TOLD ME THAT DAY WHEN YOU BECAME MY GIRLFRIEND, HE WOULD NOT STOP TRYING TO MAKE YOU HIS GIRLFRIEND BUT, I KNOW YOU WOULD NEVER BE HAPPY WITH HIM FOR YOU ARE MY GIRLFRIEND, MY FUTURE WIFEWHEN HE TOLD ME I WAS GOING TO BE HIS FUTURE WIFE MY HEART FELT A SING OF THAT I HAVE NOT FELT IN MY LIFE BESIDES MY AUNT AND GRANDMA I HAVE SOMEONE THAT LOVES MEAND CARE SO MUCH FOR ME THAT THEY ARE WILLING TO SPEND THE REST OF THEIR LIVES MAKEME HAPPY AND TAKE CARE OF ME, AND ALWAYS BE THERE FOR ME NOW THE FIRST WE MUST DO IS GETOUT OF THIS HOSPITAL, I TOLD RANDY I LOVE YOU SO MUCH AND I WOULD BE HAPPY TO BE YOUR WIFE WHEN THE TIME IS RIGHT, I WILL BE RIGHT BACK I'M GOING TO TALK TO THE DR. SEE HOW MUCH LONGER YOU ARE GOING TO BE IN THIS HOSPITAL I NEED YOU HOME WITH ME, AS I WALK OUT THE DOOR RANDY SAID ANDREA, I LOVE YOU SO MUCH AND I THANK GOD EVERY DAY FOR HAVING YOU IN MY LIFE, AND I PROMISE YOU I WILL NEVER HURT YOU OR LEAVE YOU, AS HE SAID THIS HAPPY TEARS CAME OUT OF MY EYES, I CLOSE THE DOOR BEHIND ME AS I GO UP TO TALK TO THE DR, I AM HOPING FOR GOOD NEWS THE DR. LOOKS AT

ME AND ASKS MAY I HELP YOU I CLEAR MY THROAT AND ASK HOW MUCH LONGER RANDY WOULD HAVE TO STAY IN THE HOSPITAL, AND HE SAID RANDY SUFFERED A BAD ACCIDENT HE WILL HAVE TO STAY HERE FOR THERAPY THE DR. SAID THE THERAPY WOULD LAST 1 OR 2 WEEKS DEPENDING ON HOW RANDY RESPONDED TO THE TREATMENT; THE DR. ASK ME WHAT WAS MY RELATIONSHIP TO I PAUSED AND WITH A SMILE ON MY FACE I SAID I WAS HIS FUTURE WIFE, THE DR. SMILE, AND SPOKE **OK MRS. GARCIA LET'S GET YOUR HUSBAND BETTER SO HE** CAN GO HOME WITH YOU, AS WE WENT BACK IN THE ROOM THE DOCTOR SAID I NEED YOU TO STAND BY RANDY AND SUPPORT HIM IN THIS, I TOLD THE DR.I PROMISE RANDY, I WILL NEVER LEAVE HIM AND I AM BY HIS SIDE, THREW THIS WE ARE GOING THREW **THIS TOGETHER, THAT IS GOOD TO HEAR OK LET'S GET** HIM BETTER, THANK YOU DR. AS WE WALK INTO THE ROOM RANDY LOOK AT US THINKING THE WORST, THEN I TOLD RANDY THE DR. SAID YOU HAVE TO TAKE THERAPY FOR A FEW DAYS THEN YOU CAN GO HOME, WHEN I SAID THIS, HE OUT OF BED, AND WE BOTH SAID WAIT WHERE ARE YOU GOING RANDY SAID I AM READY FOR THE THERAPY LET'S DO THIS, I TOLD RANDY THE THERAPY WILL START TOMORROW YOU ARE SOMETHING SPECIAL, I LOVE YOU RANDY LOOKED AT ME AND **SAID I LOVE YOU TOO LET'S GO HOME DR. SAID THIS IS SO SWEET** I HARDLY EVER SEE TWO PEOPLE MORE IN LOVE THAN THE BOTH OF YOU OK I WILL LEAVE FOR NOW AND WE WILL START YOUR RECOVERY FIRST THING IN THE MORNING AS HE

CHAPTER 5   THE RECOVERY

WAS WALKING OUT THE DOOR, AND WE BOTH SAID AT THE SAME TIME THANK YOU, DOCTOR. FOR ALL YOU HAVE DONE HE STOOD AT THE DBACK WITH JUST LOOKED AT RANDY AND ANDREA SPEECHLESS AND JUST SMILED AND LEAVES AS RANDY AND ANDREA SAT IN THE HOSPITAL ROOM THEY WERE SILENT AND DID NOT SAY ONE WORD, ALL THEY COULD DO WAS JUST THINK ABOUT THE FOLLOWING DAY, THE DAY WHICH THEY HAD HOPED FOR WHERE RANDY WOULD GET THE HELP HE NEEDED, TO RECOVER FROM THE ACCIDENT THAT HE WENT THREW, NOW WE WILL SEE HOW THAT DAY TURNS OUT, AS RANDY SPEAKS, HE TOLD HER I NEED TO TELL YOU SOMETHING ANDREA WHAT IS IT RANDY, A LOT HAS HAPPENED IN MY LIFE, BUT THE MOST SPECIAL PART OF MY LIFE WAS WHEN YOU CAME INTO MY LIFE A DREAM COME TRUE DOESN'T MATTER WHAT HAPPENS FROM THIS DAY FORWARD I KNOW EVERYTHING WILL BE GREAT MY LOVE I ASSURE YOU WHEN I GET OUT OF THIS HOSPITAL, I WILL DO MY BEST AND MAKE YOU THE HAPPIEST PERSON IN THE WORLD, SHE LOOKED AT ME AND SHE ASK ME DO YOU PROMISE, AND I TOLD HER YES, I PROMISE AFTER I SAID THAT SHE SAID THERE IS SOMETHING I NEED TO TELL YOU WHEN I WENT TO STAY WITH MY AUNT AND GRANDMA, THEY SHOWED ME MORE LOVE IN ONE DAY THAN I COULD IMAGINE THEY WERE MORE OF A FAMILY, THEN MY PARENTS WERE ALL MY LIFE, SO I TOLD THEM THAT WHEN I WAS DONE, DOING WHAT I NEED TO ACCOMPLISH HERE, I

WILL RETURN AND STAY WITH THEM WHEN I SAID THIS RANDY LOOK HURT AND BEFORE HE SAID ANYTHING I TOLD HIM; WAIT I AM NOT FINISHED TELLING YOU WHAT ELSE HAPPENED, AND HE JUST LOOKED AT ME WITH THE SADDEST LOOK, I TOLD HIM I ASKED MY AUNT AND GRANDMA, IF YOU COULD COME BACK WITH ME AND STAY WITH US AT THEIR HOUSE, THEY BOTH SAID YES, THEY WOULD LOVE TO MEET YOU, AND THEY WOULD BE HAPPY TO HAVE YOU STAY, WITH US SO MY LOVE WHEN I BACK IF YOU WANT YOU CAN GO BACK WITH ME, SO WHAT YOU THINK I WAITED FOR AN ANSWER AND HE DID NOT SAY ANYTHING FOR A BIT, THEN HE SAID YES, I WILL BE HAPPY GO BACK TO YOUR AUNT'S HOUSE WITH YOU AFTER ALL, YOU ARE MY FUTURE WIFE WE WILL SPEND OUR LIVES TOGETHER, AFTER HE SAID THAT I WAS PLEASED AND RELIEVED KNOWING THAT WE WILL BE TOGETHER FOREVER, OK RANDY IT IS GETTING LATE IT IS TIME WE GET SOME REST I WILL SLEEP ON THE COUCH I AM HERE FOR YOU IF YOU NEED ANYTHING, I GAVE RANDY A GOOD NIGHT KISS AND WE BOTH FAIL INTO A DEEP SLEEP, THEY BOTH FELL ASLEEP FAST THAT NIGHT AND ALL THEY COULD DO WAS DREAM ABOUT THEIR LIVES TOGETHER, AND SOON MORNING WILL BE HERE AND THEN EVERYTHING THEY BEEN PRAYING FOR WILL BE, THE START OF A NEW LIFE, WITH NEW HOPES AND PROMISES, BOTH ANDREA RANDY HAS BEEN SUFFERING A LOT IN THEIR LIFE NOW IT IS TIME FOR HEALING AND RECOVERY. GOOD MORNING RANDY ANDREA SPEAKS IN A LOW VOICE, AS RANDY TURNS HIS HEAD TOWARDS HER AND **SAY'S GOOD MORNING MY LOVE HOW WAS YOUR NIGHT, WITH** A SMILE ON HER FACE SHE **SAY'S IT WAS** THE BEST NIGHT I HAD IN A LONG TIME HOW WAS YOURS I LAY THERE AND THOUGHT ABOUT IT AND SAID IT WAS A BLESSING I LAID HERE IN THIS BED MANY NIGHTS ASLEEP AND NO MATTER HOW HARD I TRIED I COULD NOT I WOULD WAKE UP

IN MY SLEEP SCREAMING AND TRYING TO KICK AND DOING EVERYTHING POSSIBLE BUT COULD NOT WAKE UP, SO YES, IT IS A BLESSING TO BE ABLE TO WAKE UP AFTER A GREAT SLEEP THEY WILL BE HERE SOON TO START MY THERAPY, I AM NERVOUS AND SCARED, ANDREA ASKED ME WHY WAS I FELT THAT WAY I SAID BECAUSE I HAD BEEN IN THIS BED FOR ALMOST 2 MONTHS WHAT IF WHEN I GET UP I FALL OR LOSE **MY BALANCE, RANDY DON'T WORRY WE WILL BE THERE BY YOUR SIDE AND I WON'T LET YOU GET HURT, AS ANDREA** LOOKED UP THE DOOR SLOWLY OPENED IT WAS DR. GOOD MORNING DR. WE ARE READY TO GO, THE DR SMILE AND SAID WILL FIRST WE GOING TO START, HERE IN THE ROOM I NEED TO SEE IF RANDY CAN STAND ON HIS OWN BUT FIRST, I AM GOING TO SEE IF HE CAN SIT UP STRAIGHT, RANDY PULLED HIS SHEETS OFF HIM AND SAID OK I AM READY THE DOCTOR WENT UP TO HIM AND SAID OK GRAB MY ARM AND PULL YOURSELF UP, AS THE DR. TOLD RANDY THAT I SAID COME ON RANDY YOU CAN DO IT I BELIEVE YOU CAN SHOW US HOW MUCH YOU WANT THIS, IT IS UP TO YOU HOW LONG TREATMENT LAST, AS I LOOKED AT RANDY PULL HIMSELF UP, I WAS SO PROUD OF HIM HE DID IT, YES RANDY **THAT'S IT AS HE SIT'S ON THE BED, THE DR.** ASKED HIM HOW ARE YOU ARE FEELING ARE YOU IN PAIN RANDY RESPONDED AND SAID NO **DR. I DON'T FEEL ANY PAIN, THE DR. SAID OK THAT'S GREAT I AM GETTING YOUA BED LIFE ROPE AND YOU'RE GOING TO BE DOING** LIFT EXERCISES AS PART OF YOUR TREATMENT, I WILL HAVING THE NURSE COME GET YOU AFTER BREAKFAST TO TAKE YOU TO THE TREATMENT ROOM ANDSTART YOUR REHABILITATION, OK DR THAT SOUNDS GREAT AS THE DOCTOR WALK OUT OF THE ROOM RANDY LOOKED AT ANDREA AND SAID THAT FELT GREAT I DID NOT FEEL ANY PAIN, AND I HOPED THE REST OF THE THERAPY, GOES AS SMOOTHLY AS THIS DID, ANDREA RESPONDED TO RANDY AND SAID YES, MY LOVE I KNOW YOU ARE A STRONG PERSON AND YOU HAVE THE

WILL AND WILL DO GREAT AND GET THREW YOUR THERAPY SOONER THAN YOU THINK, AS ANDREA WAS SPEAKING TO RANDY SHE HEARD HER NAME CALLED OUT ON THE INTERCOM, RANDY AND ANDREA LOOKED AT EACH ANOTHER PUZZLE WONDERING WHO IT COULD BE THAT NEEDED TO TALK TO HER, SO ANDREA TELLS RANDY I WILL BE BACK, LET ME GO SEE, WHO IS CALLING ME, AS I WALKED OUT THE DOOR RANDY LOOKED AT ME WITH A CONFUSED LOOK ON HIS FACE, I WENT TO THE PHONE AS I SAID HELLO, I HEARD A LOT OF TALKING IN THE BACKGROUND I SPOKE AND SAID THIS IS ANDREA, THE PERSON ON THE OTHER SIDE OF THE PHONE WAS THE DETECTIVE THAT IS ON MY CASE, HELLO ANDREA THIS IS DETECTIVE RODRIGUEZ I AM CALLING YOU TO INFORM YOU THAT THE TRIAL STARTS NEXT WEEK AND WE ARE GOING TO NEED YOU THERE TO SPEAK ON YOUR BEHALF ABOUT WHAT YOUR PARENTS DID TO YOU, NOW IT IS GOING TO BE THE HARDEST THING YOU WILL HAVE TO DO YOUR WHOLE LIFE WHEN THE DETECTIVE SAID THAT I SO NO YOU KNOW REALLY WHAT THE HARDEST THING TO DO WAS, AND THE DETECTIVE ASKED WHAT WAS THAT, AND ANDREA SAID IT WAS STAYING IN THE SAME HOUSE WITH TWO MONSTERS AND GETTING ABUSED EVERYDAY OF YOUR LIFE SO YES WHERE YOUR PARENTS ABUSE YOU AND YOUR DAD COMES INTO YOUR ROOM AT NIGHT AND HAS HIS WAY WITH YOU AND IT DOESN'T MATTER HOW MUCH YOU CRY AND BEG HIM TO STOP HE WON'T HE WOULD JUST LAUGH AND DID NOT GET OFF YOU AND YOUR MOM IN THE NEXT ROOM LAUGHING AT YOUR PAIN THE WHOLE TIME, WHICH IS THE HARDEST THING ONE WOULD HAVE TO DO THEIR WHOLE LIFE, THIS IS A PIECE OF CAKE AFTER THAT I TOLD THE DETECTIVE I WOULD BE THERE NEXT WEEK, AND AFTER THAT WE BOTH HUNG UP, I STOOD WITH MY HAND ON THE PHONE AND WAS JUST THERE AT THE NURSE'S DESK SILENT I COULD NOT SAY A WORD, THE NURSE IN

CHARGE LOOKED AT ME AND ASKED ARE YOU OK, I SAID WITH A SMILE ON MY FACE YES, I AM GREAT, I HAVE TO GO TO COURT NEXT WEEK, THINGS ARE FALLING INTO PLACE AS I SAID I STARTED BACK TOWARD THE, ROOM, I WALKED IN AND RANDY WAS JUST FOCUSED ON ME, I LOOKED AT HIM AND HE ASKED WHO WAS IT ON THE PHONE, **THAT CALLED YOU I LOOKED INTO RANDY'S EYES** SMILED AND SAID TO HIM IT WAS THE DETECTIVE, HE TOLD ME THAT THEY WERE TAKING MY PARENTS TO TRIAL NEXT WEEK, AND I NEED TO BE THERE TO TESTIFY AGAINST THEM AND LET THE WHOLE WORLD KNOW THE MONSTERS THAT MY PARENTS ARE AND HOW THEY HURT AND ABUSED **ME, AS I SAT BY RANDY'S SIDE** HE REACH OUT AND HELD MY HAND AND ASK ARE YOU READY FOR THIS YOU KNOW IT IS GOING TO BE ROUGH IN THAT COURTROOM, I KNOW IT IS BUT I NEED TO DO THIS THEY CAN NOT GET AWAY FROM THIS, THEY REALLY DESTROYED ME TOOK MY CHILDHOOD AWAY THE THINGS THEY TOOK AWAY FROM ME I CAN NEVER GET BACK. I AM SUPPOSED TO HAVE GOOD MEMORIES AS A CHILD I AM SUPPOSED TO BE ABLE TO TELL GOOD STORIES OF HOW IT WAS GROWING UP IN THAT HOUSE, BUT ALL I HAVE IS BAD MEMORIES, THAT ARE STILL HUNTING ME EVERY DAY, I WAKE UP CRYING AND SCARED FROM THE AWFUL TORTURE MY DAD PUT ME THREW, I STILL FEEL ALL THOSE MEN ON ME I STILL SEE MY DAD AS HE WALK INTO MY ROOM AT NIGHT, LOOKING AT ME SAYING IT IS TIME TO PLEASE YOUR DAD AGAIN, AND ALL I COULD DO WAS JUST LAY THERE AND CRY, NO RANDY I AM GOING THREW THIS NOTHING IS GOING TO STOP ME FROM GETTING JUSTICE FOR WHAT I HAVE BEEN THREW, BUT WAIT THIS IS YOUR MOMENT WE NEED TO GET YOU READY FOR YOUR TREATMENT THE NURSE WILL BE HERE SOON TO TAKE YOU TO THERAPY, AFTER A WHILE, THE NURSE CAME TO TAKE RANDY TO HIS TREATMENT, AS THEY WERE LEAVING, HE LOOK BACK AND ME AND ASKED ARE YOU

COMING WITH US, AND I SPOKE YES, I AM IT IS OKAY WITH THE NURSE THAT I GO WITH YOU, THE NURSE SAID YES IT BE FINE FOR YOUR SISTER TO COME WITH US AND RANDY RESPONDED SHE IS NOT MY SISTER, SHE IS MY FIANCE WHEN HE SAID THAT I FELT THE LOVE HE HAS FOR ME THEN THE NURSE SAID OK SHE SMILED **AND SAID WILL LET'S GO** MRS. GARCIA AS WE WALKED DOWN THE HALL TO THE THERAPY, I WAS JUST PRAYING THAT HIS THERAPY WOULD GO GREAT AND WE COULD GO HOME BY THE END OF THE WEEK, AS WE GOT TO THE ROOM WHERE RANDY WAS GOING TO DO HIS TREATMENT HE LOOKED AT ME SMILE AND SAID OK MY LOVE THIS IS THE START OF MY RECOVERY, AND I AM READY FOR THIS, AS RANDY WAS SITTING IN MY CHAIR THE THERAPIST CAME TO HIM AND SAID OK MR. GARCIA **LET'S** SEE HOW STRONG YOUR LEGS ARE TRY TO STAND UP, ON MY FIRST ATTEMPT I FAILED TO BACK DOWN, THE **THERAPIST SAID IT'S OK WE JUST HAD TO WORK** HARD TO GET YOU ON YOUR FEET WHEN SHE SAID THAT I FELT DEFEATED, AND BOTH ANDREA AND THE THERAPIST TURNED AROUND TO TALK WHEN THEY DID I TOOK A DEEP BREATH AND TRIED TO STAND UP AGAIN AND THIS TIME I ACCOMPLISHED IT, STANDING THERE ON MY TWO FEET WITHOUT HOLDING ONTO ANYTHING, I SPOKE OUT AND SAID OUR WORK IS NOT GOING TO BE THAT HARD AND THEY BOTH TURNED AROUND AND SAW ME STANDING ON MY TWO FEET, ANDREA WAS CRYING HAPPY TEARS AND THE THERAPISTS SAID THAT IT WAS AMAZING AND WITH THAT KIND OF DETERMINATION AND I KNOW YOU WILL MAKE GOOD PROGRESS SO YOU WILL BE GOING HOME SOONER THAN YOU THINK, WHEN THE NURSE SAID THIS, I SAW A LOOK OF RELIEF **ON RANDY'S FACE AND I WAS FULL OF JOY WITHIN MY** SOUL, I KNEW IT WAS BY THE HEALING HAND OF OUR LORD AND SAVIOR THAT HE IS GETTING BETTER SO MUCH FASTER THAN WE HAD IMAGINE, RANDY FINISHED HIS

THERAPY FOR THAT DAY, THEN WE STARTED GOING BACK TO HIS ROOM AND HALFWAY THERE WE SAW HIS FRIEND TIM, STANDING AT THE DOOR OF HIS ROOM AS WE GOT CLOSER, HE WAS JUST SMILING; RANDY ASKED WHAT ARE YOU DOING HERE I CAME BACK TO SEE HOW YOU ARE DOING WHEN YOU WERE IN A COMA, I WAS HERE WITH YOU FOR A WEEK AND I TOLD ANDREA THAT I HAD TO LEAVE TO GO BACK TO WORK BUT I WILL RETURN SO HERE AS I SAID THIS, I SAW TEARS IN RANDY EYES AS HE SAID WOW MY BEST FRIEND TOOK TIME OUT OF HIS LIFE TO COME SPEND TIME WITH ME, JUST AS HE DID BACK IN THE 6TH GRADE, HE TOOK TIME TO MAKE ME FEEL BETTER AND TIM, I CAN NOT BELIEVE YOU DROVE ALL THIS WAY TO COME TO SEE ME AND CHECK UP ON ME I SAY THAT YOU TRULY ARE A FRIEND A BROTHER, HE JUST SMILED AND SAID I LOVE YOU, MY BROTHER, SO WHAT DID THEY SAY ABOUT HOW THINGS ARE GOING I LOOKED AT TIM AND SAID THE DOCTOR TOLD ME THAT AS SOON AS I FINISH MY THERAPY I WILL BE ABLE TO GO HOME AND I STARTED MY THERAPY TODAY, AND THEY SAID I DID GREAT IF I KEEP IT UP, I CAN LEAVE AND GO HOME BY THIS WEEKEND, THAT IS THE GOOD NEWS NOW THE BAD NEWS, AND TIM HAD A LOOK AS IF HE WAS CONFUSED AND SAID WHAT IS THAT I LOOKED AT ANDREA AND SHE PUT HER HEAD DOWN AND SAID THE DETECTIVE CALL ME THE HERE AT THE HOSPITAL AND SAID NEXT WEEK I HAVE TO APPEAR IN COURT TO TESTIFY AGAINST MY PARENTS FOR WHAT THEY DID TO ME FOR SO MANY YEARS, AND I WAS KINDA SCARED TO SEE THEM, THEN TIM TOLD ME LOOK THEY WERE NOT SCARED OR HAD NO HEART TO DO TO YOU WHAT THEY DID, YOU SHOULD NOT BE SCARED TO RETURN TO THEM THE PAIN, THEY IMPOSED ON YOU FOR SO MANY YEARS, AFTER HE SAID THAT RANDY GRABBED MY HAND AND SPOKE LOOKED ANDERA YOU MUST DO **THIS, DON'T WORRY** I WILL BE BY YOUR SIDE THE WHOLE TIME, AND AFTER ALL IS SAID AND

DONE THEN WE CAN MAKE PLANS FOR OUR FUTURE, AND AS YOU PROMISE YOUR AUNT AND GRANDMA, WE WILL BE GOING BACK TO STAY WITH THEM, AND WHEN THE TIME IS RIGHT TO GET MARRIED AND RAISE A FAMILY, AS I SAID THIS ANDREA STAYED SILENT AND LOOKED INTO SPACE NOT A WORD TO SAY, I WAS LOST FOR WORDS AND I ASKED HER WHAT SHE WAS THINKING, AND SHE SAID, YOU KNOW FOR YEARS **LOT'S THINGS** HAVE HAPPENED TO THE BOTH OF US AND NO ONE WAS THERE TO HELP US OR LISTEN TO US OR BELIEVE WHAT WE WERE GOING THROUGH ONLY IF THERE WAS ONLY ONE PERSON THAT WE COULD HAVE GONE TO, SOMEONE THAT WOULD HAVE BEEN THERE FOR US TO BELIEVE WHAT WE HAVE TO SAY AND WHAT WE FEEL IN OUR HEARTS AND WITH A VERY OPEN MIND BUT MOST IMPORTANTLY AN UNDERSTANDING OF OUR ABUSE AND FEAR, I REPLIED AND SAID YES THAT WOULD HAVE BEEN GREAT BUT WHO, WOULD THAT PERSON BE THAT WE CAN TURN TO SHE SAID IT WOULD BE ME, AND I LOOKED CONFUSED AND ASKED WHAT DO YOU MEAN I WAS CONFUSED YES, I WILL BE THE ONE TO DEFEND ALL THESE KIDS THAT ARE BEING ABUSED AND MISTREATED BY THERE PARENTS NO ONE COULD HELP US SO NOW I WILL HELP THESE KIDS I AM GOING BACK TO SCHOOL AND FINISH AT THE TOP OF MY CLASS AND GO TO COLLEGE AND STUDY CRIMINAL JUSTICE, SEE RANDY PEOPLE THEY NEED SOMEONE TO HELP THEM ALL THE TIME BUT A LOT OF KIDS ARE SCARED TO SAY ANYTHING CAUSE THEY THINK NO ONE WILL BELIEVE THEM, OR THEY WILL NOT SAY ANYTHING BECAUSE THEY ARE TO EMBARRASS TO SAY ANYTHING, WILL I AM GOING TO HELP EVERYONE I CAN, AS ANDREA TOLD ME THIS, I LAY IN MY BED AND SAID IF YOU CAN DO IT, THEN I WILL GO BACK WITH YOU AND WE BOTH WILL GO TO COLLEGE AND STUDY LAW AND GET OUR DEGREE IN CRIMINAL JUSTICE, AFTER WE BOTH AGREED ON OUR FUTURE, IT WAS TIME FOR ME TO GET

READY FOR MY MEAL AND THE REST OF THE DAY, MY THERAPY WAS COMING OUT WELL I CAN NOT IMAGINE THE PAIN THAT RANDY HAS BEEN GOING THREW FROM THE START OF HIS TERRIBLE ACCIDENT THAT WAS CAUSED BY A PERSON WITH NO HEART BUT HIS DAY **WILL COME WHEN RANDY GET'S OUT OF THIS HOSPITAL RIGHT** NOW THE MOST IMPORTANT THING IS FOR RANDY TO GET BETTER AND BE READY FOR HIS RELEASE FOR THIS WEEK IS ALMOST OVER **JUST A FEW MORE DAYS FOR IT TO BE OVER WITH I LOOKED AT** RANDY AND THINK TO MYSELF WHERE WOULD I HAVE BEEN IF RANDY WOULD OF NEVER CAME INTO MY LIFE I WOULD NOT BE HERE RIGHT NOW I WOULD OF PROBABLY BE DEAD RIGHT NOW BUT I GIVE RANDY MORE THAN JUST MY LIFE I GIVE HIM THE WORLD HE HAS SAVED ME AS I HAVE SAVED HIM THANK YOU JESUS CHRIST FOR SAVING THE BOTH OF US FROM ALL THE PAIN AND SUFFERING THAT WE BEEN THREW AND WHATEVER HAPPENS IN OUR LIFE I KNOW YOU ARE IN CONTROL OUR LORD AND SAVIOR, I LOVE YOU AND MAY YOUR HAND ALWAYS BE IN OUR LIVES AS I SIT HERE AND LOOK AT RANDY LAYING THERE IN HIS BED I CLOSE MY EYES AND REMEMBER THE VERY FIRST DAY I TALKED TO HIM BACK IN SCHOOL WE WERE SO HAPPY AND DEEPLY IN LOVE THERE WAS NOTHING THAT MEANT MORE TO ME THAN THAT DAY WHEN OUR HEARTS BOUNDED AS ONE AND I THANK JESUS CHRIST FOR BRINGING US TOGETHER I PRAY EVERYDAY FOR RANDY THAT ALL WILL TURN OUT WILL BUT I KNOW GOD IS IN CONTROL AND AS LONG AS GOD HAS HIS HANDS ON US EVERYTHING WILL BE GREAT I HAVE BEEN THREW SO MUCH WITH RANDY AND THREW EVERYTHING THAT WE EXPERIENCE TOGETHER WE ARE STILL IN LOVE AS WE COULD EVER BE THE TIME IS NEAR FOR RANDY TO LEAVE THIS HOSPITAL **AS I LOOK I SEE THAT THERE IS ONLY A FEW MORE DAY'S LEFT** TO BE EXACT THERE IS ONLY, THREE DAY'S LEFT SO MUCH IS GOING THREW MY HEAD RIGHT NOW WITH MY TRAIL COMING UP

THEN RANDY HAS TO GO TO COURT ALSO WHEN WILL IT ALL END I NEED RANDY TO GET BETTER REAL SOON SO I CAN TAKE HIM HOME AND TAKE CARE OF HIM I JUST PRAY THAT EVERYTHING WILL TURN OUT WILL AND LIKE I SAID THERE IS ONLY 3 MORE DAY'S FOR THIS WEEK TO OVER WITH AND THEN WE WILL SEE WHAT THE DOCTOR TELL'S RANDY YES LORD ONLY

CHAPTER 6   LOVE CONQUERS ALL

 3 MORE DAYS LEFT FOR THIS WEEK TO BE OVER I HOPE HE CAN GO HOME BY THE END OF THE WEEK WE WILL SEE I PRAY. AS RANDY FINISHES HIS DINNER THE DOCTOR COMES INTO THE **ROOM AND SAYS'S RANDY I AM PROUD OF YOU I AM HAPPY TO** SAY THAT YOU WILL BE GOING HOME BY THE END OF THE WEEK AS RANDY, ANDREA, AND TIM SIT IN THE ROOM SPEECHLESS OF EVERYTHING THAT IS HAPPENING AND EVERYTHING THAT IS ABOUT TO HAPPEN WITH ANDREA HAVING TO GO TO COURT, TO GET HER JUSTICE, **AND RANDY'S THERAPY FALLING IN PLACE** THEY BOTH HAVE A LOT OF MEMORIES OF THERE LIVES THAT THEY DO NOT WANT TO REMEMBER AND PARTS OF THEIR LIVES THAT THEY WISH WOULD NEVER END, RANDY'S THERAPY IS ALMOST OVER WE

WILL SEE WHAT HAPPENS NEXT, AS ANDREA LOOKING AT RANDY, SHE SAYS YOU KNOW RANDY LOVE IS JUST A NOUN, WELL THAT'S WHAT IT'S BEEN ALL MY LIFE JUST A NOUN PEOPLE WOULD TELL ME THEY LOVED ME BUT NEVER SHOWED ME, BUT WHAT WAS SHOWN IN MY LIFE WAS ACTION VERBS BY MY PARENTS, WITH ALL THE HATE THEY SHOWED ME, BUT YOU RANDY ONLY YOU SHOWED ME WHAT TRUE LOVE IS YOU WERE THERE FOR ME WHEN NOBODY ELSE WAS YOU STAYED BY MY BEDSIDE WHEN I ALMOST DIED, AND YOU ENCOURAGED ME WHEN OTHERS LET ME DOWN YOUR LOVE FOR ME IS MORE THAN JUST AN ACTION VERB IT IS ETERNITY, AS I TOLD RANDY THIS HE LOOKED AT ME AND SAID AS LONG AS WE HAVE EACH OTHER WE HAVE THE WORLD AND WITH THAT NOTHING IS IMPOSSIBLE, AFTER RANDY TOLD ANDREA THAT THEY BOTH

LOOKED AT TIM HE HAD TEARS IN HIS EYES AND THEY ASKED HIM WHAT WAS GOING ON HE SAID I NEVER KNEW TWO PEOPLE MORE IN LOVE THAN THE BOTH OF YALL MY BEST FRIENDS DEEPLY IN LOVE THAT IS GREAT I AM VERY HAPPY FOR BOTH OF YALL, AFTER TIM SAID THAT RANDY GRABBED ANDREA'S HAND AND SAID OK MY LOVE. IT IS ALMOST TIME FOR ME TO GO TO MY THERAPY, I FEEL THAT AFTER TODAY I SHOULD BE GOING HOME REAL SOON AS I SAID THIS ANDREA WAS LOOKING AT ME AND TEARS CAME OUT OF HER EYES, I ASK HER WHY SHE WAS CRYING AND SHE SAID LOOK RANDY I ALMOST LOST YOU, AND I CAN NOT LOSE YOU SO, PROMISE ME THAT YOU WILL BE MORE CAREFUL OUT THERE, WE NEED TO GET THE COPS TO COME TO THE HOSPITAL AND YOU CAN FILE CHARGES ON JOEL FOR WHAT HE DID TO YOU, JUSTICE WILL BE SERVED FOR YOU AS IT HAS BEEN FOR ME, I AM STILL KIND OF SCARED TO GO TO THE COURTHOUSE NEXT

WEEK BUT IT IS SOMETHING THAT MUST BE DONE, THEY CAN NOT GO FREE AND HURT OTHER KIDS, AS I TOLD RANDY THIS HE THOUGHT ABOUT IT FOR A LITTLE WHILE, OK YOU KNOW YOU ARE RIGHT MY LOVE WE DO NEED TO GET THE COPS INVOLVED IN THIS AND JOEL CAN SHARE A CELL WITH THEM YOUR DAD AND MOM AFTER RANDY TOLD ME THIS, I WENT TO USE THE PHONE AND CALLED THE POLICE STATION AND I TOLD THE COP THAT ANSWERED THE PHONE SHE SAID ROSENBERG POLICE DEPT. HOW CAN I HELP YOU I RESPONDED RIGHT AWAY AND SAID YES, I WANT TO REPORT AN ATTEMPTED MURDER ON MY FIANCE RANDY GARCIA AND SHE ASK ME WHEN THIS HAPPENED WHERE IS HE, I TOLD HER IT HAPPENED WEEKS AGO, RANDY JUST CAME OUT OF A COMA A FEW DAYS AGO AND HE IS READY TO PRESS CHARGES, HE KNOWS WHO HIT HIM WITH THE CAR AFTER I TOLD THE OFFICER THIS, SHE ASKED FOR DETAILS OF WHERE RANDY WAS AND WHAT HOSPITAL WE WERE AT I TOLD HER AT THE MEMORIAL HOSPITAL IN ROOM 237, THEN SHE SAID OK I AM SENDING AN OFFICER TO GET A STATEMENT AFTER THAT WE HUNG UP AND AS I WALKED BACK TOWARDS THE ROOM, I WAS JUST THINKING IT FELT LIKE IT WAS HAPPENING ALL OVER AGAIN AS IT DID THE FIRST TIME WITH MY PARENTS FIRST ME, NOW RANDY THIS IS A CRAZY WORLD WE LIVE IN THANKS TO OUR LORD AND SAVIOR JESUS CHRIST WE HAVE BEEN ABLE TO OVERCOME EVERYTHING THAT WE BEEN GOING THREW, AS I WALKED INTO THE ROOM, I TOLD RANDY I JUST CALLED THE POLICE THEY ARE SENDING AN OFFICER OVER TO GET A STATEMENT, RANDY LOOKED AT ME AND DID NOT SAY A WORD I WAS CONFUSED HE HAD LOOKED AS IF I DID SOMETHING WRONG AND I SAID IN A SOFT VOICE ARE YOU UPSET WITH ME THAT I DID THAT, THEN HE SAID NO

MY LOVE I AM GLAD YOU DID, IT IS JUST THAT SPEAKING ABOUT IT IS GOING TO BRING BACK MEMORIES FROM THAT DAY, BUT IF YOU CAN DO IT, I KNOW I CAN TOO, AFTER HE SAID THAT THE NURSE CAME IN AND SAID OK MR. RANDY ARE YOU READY TO GO FOR YOUR THERAPY IF YOU DO GOOD TODAY, I WILL RECOMMEND THAT YOU GO HOME TOMORROW, WHEN THE NURSE SAID THAT TEARS OF JOY FILLED BOTH OF OUR EYES, WE WENT TO THE THERAPY ROOM I JUMPED OUT OF MY WHEELCHAIR AND ASKED **THE THERAPIST OK WHAT'S** FIRST, I GOT THIS, SHE SMILED AND SAID OK FIRST SIT HERE AND LIFT 20 LBS WITH YOUR LEGS **LET'S SEE HOW MANY** TIMES YOU CAN, LIFT THEM I SAID OK IT IS A PIECE OF CAKE I SAT DOWN AND LIFTED THE WEIGHTS 20 TIMES WITHOUT A PROBLEM, I LOOKED AS ANDREA WAS JUST LOOKING AT ME WITH JOY IN HER EYES, THE THERAPIST SAID VERY WELL, NOW COME AND STAND HERE SO, I DID AS SHE ASKED AND THEN SHE ASKED ME TO SQUAD 20 TIMES WITH MY ARMS EXTENDED IN FRONT OF ME, I TOOK A DEEP BREATH AND SAID OK HERE IT GOES, SHE ASKED FOR 20 I GAVE HER 25 AND SHE LOOKED SURPRISED AND SAID WILL RANDY YOU ARE DOING VERY WELL NOW ONE LAST TEST AND THIS IS THE MOST IMPORTANT TEST OF THEM ALL, I TOOK ANOTHER DEEP BREATH I LOOKED AT ANDREA AND SHE SHOOK HER HEAD AS IF SAYING YOU GOT THIS, I BELIEVE IN YOU, I TOLD THE THERAPIST OK, I AM READY FOR ANYTHING, AND SHE SAID OK GRAB THESE 15LBS WEIGHTS AND FOLLOW ME, WE ALL WALK OUT TO THE HALL AND WENT TO THE STAIRS ON THE OTHER SIDE OF THE HALL, SHE OPENED THE DOOR AND SAID OK ANDREA YOU STAND IN FRONT OF HIM AND I WILL STAND BEHIND HIM, NOW RANDY IF YOU NEED TO TAKE YOUR TIME; I WANT YOU TO WALK DOWN 2 FLIGHTS OF STAIRS AND BACK UP WITH

THESE WEIGHTS BY YOUR SIDE, AS SHE SAID THIS, I STOOD AT THE EDGE OF THE FIRST STEP WITH ANDREA IN FRONT OF ME SHE TOLD ME I GOT YOU AND WORDS I NEEDED TO HEAR I STARTED GOING DOWN THE STAIRS AND TO MY SURPRISE THERE WAS NO PAIN, I WAS ABLE TO WALK BOTH FLIGHTS OF STAIRS WHEN WE WERE DONE, THE NURSE TOOK ME BACK TO MY ROOM AND SAID OK THE DR. WILL BE IN LATER TO TALK TO YOU, AND HE WILL HAVE A FULL THERAPY REPORT OF WHAT HAPPENED, AS I WAS GETTING INTO MY BED THE OFFICER ARRIVED AT MY ROOM, HE STOOD AT THE DOOR SILENT, AS HE STOOD THERE ANDREA AND RANDY TALKED ABOUT THEIR LIVES AS IT HAS BEEN UP TO THAT POINT, HOW THEY HAD TO SUFFER AT THE HANDS OF OTHER PEOPLE THEY WERE BOTH IN TEARS BUT NEVER GIVING UP HOPE OF WHAT IS TO COME, THE POLICE LISTEN TO IT ALL AND COULD NOT HELP IT TEARS CAME TO HIS EYES HE WAS TOUCHED BY WHAT THEY WERE SAYING HOW THEY CARED FOR EACH OTHER AND HOW MUCH LOVE THEY SHOW, NOW THE POLICE WILL TALK TO RANDY AND ANDREA, AS RANDY LOOKED UP, HE SAW THE POLICEMAN AT THE DOOR BOTH RANDY AND ANDREA SAID HELLO TO THE COP AND INVITED HIM TO SIT DOWN HE TOLD RANDY THE STATEMENT THAT YOU GIVE ME TODAY WILL PUT THIS PERSON AWAY, AND I ASSURE YOU, I WILL TRUST AND BELIEVE ALL YOU TELL ME WHEN HE SAID THIS ANDREA WAS RELIEVED TO HEAR THAT, AFTER THAT RANDY STARTED TALKING HE TOLD THE POLICEMAN EVERYTHING ABOUT HOW JOEL PLANNED TO RUN OVER RANDY AND KILL HIM, HE GAVE THE POLICEMAN THE LOCATION OF THE ACCIDENT AND DESCRIBED THE TRUCK JOEL WAS DRIVING AND WHEN IT HAPPENED, AS SOON AS RANDY FINISHED THE POLICE REPORT THE POLICE LEFT THE ROOM AND

WENT TO LOOK FOR JOEL, AS HE WAS LEAVING, TURNED AND SAID TO RANDY YOU ARE BLESSED AND STRONG ENOUGH TO WITHSTAND WHAT YOU ARE GOING THREW AND YOU HAVE A WONDERFUL PERSON BY YOUR SIDE TO HELP YOU I WILL KEEP IN TOUCH AND LET YOU KNOW HOW THE SEARCH IS GOING, AS HE LEFT THE DOCTOR CAME IN BOTH RANDY AND ANDREA LOOKED AT HIM NERVOUS ABOUT WHAT DR. WAS GOING TO SAY, AS THE DR. WALK UP TO ANDREA ASKED THE DOCTOR IF RANDY GOING HOME SOON THE DOCTOR SMILED AND SAID WE WILL SEE; HE ASKED RANDY TO LIFT HIS LEG THE DR. PUT HIS HANDS **ON THE HEELS OF RANDY LEG'S AND** THEN THE DR. SAID OK RANDY PUSH AS HARD AS YOU CAN, RANDY TOOK A DEEP BREATH AND PUSHED SO HARD HE ALMOST KNOCKED THE DOCTOR DOWN THE DR. SAID OK GREAT IT IS OFFICIAL, RANDY ASKED WHAT WAS OFFICIAL THE DOCTOR SAID TOMORROW YOU WILL BE GOING HOME, AS HE LEFT THE ROOM, BOTH ANDREA AND RANDY WERE IN TEARS BUT TEARS OF HAPPINESS, THEN ANDREA LOOKED AT RANDY AND SAID YOU KNOW TOMORROW IS SATURDAY, YES, I KNOW AND YOU HAVE **COURT MONDAY, BUT DON'T WORRY I WILL BE RIGHT THERE** BY YOUR SIDE THE WHOLE TIME I WILL NEVER LEAVE YOU ALONE I PROMISE, LOOK RANDY I AM NOT WORRIED I AM CONTENT THAT I AM DOING THIS, ALL THE PAIN, THEY HAD PUT ME THREW ALL THESE YEARS AND I HAD NO ONE ON MY SIDE, NOW IT'S **THEIR** TURN TO BE ON THEIR OWN WITH NO ONE ON THEIR SIDE, AFTER ANDREA SAID THIS, THEY BOTH STAYED SILENT AND JUST THOUGHT ABOUT WHAT WAS FIXING TO HAPPEN IN THE WEEK TO COME THIS WILL BE ONE TRAIL THAT WILL NEVER BE FORGOTTEN, THIS WILL STAY IN ANDREA'S HEART AND MIND, **FOR A LONG TIME, NOW IT'S**

TIME FOR RANDY TO GO HOME LET'S SEE WHERE THIS JOURNEY WILL TAKE THEM, AS RANDY AND ANDREA WERE LEAVING THE HOSPITAL THE DETECTIVE SHOWED UP TO THE HOSPITAL AND HE MET RANDY AND ANDREA AT THE FRONT DOOR, WILL RANDY, I SEE YOU FINALLY GOING HOME, YES, I AM AND WHY ARE YOU HERE, RANDY I GOT GOOD NEWS FOR YOU, THE POLICE ARRESTED JOEL LAST NIGHT AND WE CHARGED HIM WITH ATTEMPTED MURDER, NOW RANDY WHEN IT IS TIME FOR HIM TO GO TO COURT, WE NEED YOU THERE TO TESTIFY ON WHAT HAPPENED, I WILL BE THERE, AS RANDY AND THE DETECTIVES WERE TALKING ANDREA WAS JUST LOOKING WITH A BLANK LOOK ON HER FACE, AND THEN SHE SAID WOW I CAN NOT BELIEVE ALL OF THIS IS HAPPENING SO QUICKLY, THEN SHE PAUSED AND SAID WILL FIRST I FIND OUT THE TRUTH ABOUT MY PARENTS AFTER ALL THAT HAS HAPPENED AS I GET BACK IN TOWN, I FOUND MY BOYFRIEND HERE AT THE HOSPITAL CAUSE THIS BOY TRIED TO BE WITH ME AND I TURNED HIM AWAY SO I COULD BE WITH THE ONE PERSON THAT I LOVE, AND I HAVE TO GO TO COURT NEXT WEEK AND NOW RANDY IS GOING TO HAVE TO GO TO COURT REAL SOON, WHEN IS ALL OF THIS GOING TO END WHEN ARE WE GOING TO FINALLY BE HAPPY WHEN LORD I TURNED AND SAID TO ANDREA LET US GO HOME, I GRABBED HER HAND AND WE LEFT THE HOSPITAL THE REST OF THE WEEKEND WE STAYED SILENT WE DID NOT TALK, ALL WE COULD THINK ABOUT WAS WHAT WOULD HAPPEN NEXT WEEK, WILL HER PARENTS GO TO PRISON, OR WILL THEY BE SET FREE, WHAT WILL HAPPEN IN MY CASE WILL JOEY GO TO PRISON OR WHAT WILL HAPPEN, ONLY TIME WILL TELL, AS I SIT THERE ANDREA CAME INTO THE ROOM AND I STARTED THINKING ABOUT WHAT HAPPENED AT HER HOUSE THE TORTURE AND SUFFERING AND

THE DAY SHE ALMOST DIED, WHAT THEY HAD TOLD ME ABOUT HER SO IT WAS TIME TO ASK HER ABOUT IT I TURNED TO ANDREA AND ASK HER TO COME AND SIT NEXT TO ME THERE IS SOMETHING, VERY IMPORTANT THAT I HAVE TO ASK HER, SHE SAID OK WHAT IS IT AND I LOOKED HER IN THE EYES AND SPOKE **IT'S ABOUT THAT DAY THAT YOU WENT TO THE HOSPITAL, SHE** LOOKED PUZZLED AND SAID OOK WHAT ABOUT THAT DAY, WILL WHEN I GOT TO YOUR HOUSE YOU WERE INSIDE, AND WHEN I ASKED FOR YOU ONE OF THE BOYS ASKED WHO I WAS, AND I SAID RANDY AND SAID OR YA SHE TOLD US ABOUT YOU, AND THEN HE SAID WE ARE ALL WITH HER SHE IS INSIDE THE HOUSE WITH ANOTHER GIRL, SHE GOES BOTH WAYS WE ALL HAD HER AND YOU WILL GET YOUR TURN AFTER YOU GIVE HER ENOUGH DRUGS, SO I AM ASKING YOU WHAT HE MEANS ABOUT THAT, SHE LOOKED AT ME WITH TEARS IN HER EYES AND SPOKE LOOK RANDY, I HAVE BEEN SUFFERING ALL MY LIFE I KEPT THE PAIN INSIDE OF ME AND LOTS OF SECRETS I HAVE SEEN AND EXPERIENCED NOW THEY WERE JUST FRIENDS NOTHING MORE, YES, WE DID DRUGS TOGETHER I WAS NEVER INVOLVED WITH YES, WE HUNG OUT BUT I ASSURE YOU I WAS NEVER WITH ANY OF THEM, HE WAS PLAYING WITH YOUR **EMOTIONS, YOU'RE** THE ONLY ONE FOR ME I PROMISE AFTER I FELT RELIEF, WE CONTINUED THE REST OF THE NIGHT NERVOUSE FOR NO REASON, BUT WE KNEW WE HAD A LONG WEEK AHEAD OF US I HOPE ANDREA IS PREPARED FOR WHAT SHE IS GOING TO FACE, I HAD TO BE PREPARED FOR WHAT I WAS GOING TO FACE, SOON BUT I KNOW THAT IT DOES**N'T MATTER WHAT** WE WENT THREW IN THE PAST AND THE FUTURE, WE HAVE EACH OTHER, AND AS LONG AS WE HAVE EACH OTHER EVERYTHING ELSE DOES NOT MATTER AFTER RANDY SAID THIS, THEY BOTH

JUST SAT THERE ATE THEIR DINNER AND JUST STARED INTO THE NIGHT, WITH TEARS IN THEIR EYES THEY SPOKE NOT ONE WORD, THEY FINALLY WENT TO BED IT WERE HAPPY TEARS AND AT ONE POINT SAD TEARS, THEY WOULD SOON BE MORNING AND ANDREA WILL HAVE TO GET READY TO GO TO THE ATTORNEY'S IN THE MORNING IT'S SUNDAY HE MADE A SPECIAL TRIP TO HIS OFFICE TO MAKE SURE ANDREA IS READY AND PREPARED FOR WHAT IS GOING TO HAPPEN MONDAY THERE ARE LOTS OF THINGS THEY MUST GO THREW TO BE READY FOR WHAT ANDREA IS ABOUT TO FACE, AS SHE WALKS INTO THE ATTORNEY'S OFFICE HE SAID HELLO, I AM ATTORNEY ANDREW MARTINEZ I WILL BE MANAGING THE CASE AGAINST YOUR PARENTS, I HAVE TO ASK YOU, ARE YOU TELLING THE TRUTH ABOUT EVERYTHING YOU STATED WHAT YOUR PARENTS DID TO YOU, ANDREA LOOKED AT HIM WITH FEAR IN HER EYES AND SAID PLEASE BELIEVE ME, DO NOT BE LIKE THE REST OF THE WORLD THAT DID NOT TRUST ME WHEN I WAS CRYING OUT, SO YES, I ASSURE YOU EVERYTHING IN THAT STATEMENT IS TRUE, THE ATTORNEY LOOKED AT ANDREA AND HIS HEAD DROPPED AS HE COULD NOT BELIEVE WHAT HE WAS READING IN THE STATEMENT AND WHAT ANDREA WAS TELLING HIM HE COULD NOT SAY A WORD THEN HE LOOKED OUT THE WINDOW AND JUST STOOD THERE WITH A LOOK ON HIS FACE OF SADNESS AND THEN HE LOOK AT ANDREA AND HE WAS SILENT, THEN I ASKED HIM ARE YOU OK AND CAN YOU HELP ANDREA GET JUSTICE YES, I CAN HELP HER, IT IS JUST THAT I NEVER KNEW A PARENT COULD TREAT THEIR CHILDREN LIKE THIS I ASSURE YOU ANDREA YOU WILL GET JUSTICE AND I WILL GIVE YOUR PARENTS THE MAXIMA TIME IN PRISON THAT THE LAW ALLOWS NOW YOU, HAVE TO JUST BE STRONG AND TELL THE TRUTH THE WHOLE TIME, IT IS

GOING TO BE ROUGH IN THE COURTROOM THE ATTORNEY IS GOING TO TRY AND PROVE THAT IT WAS YOUR FAULT THAT THEY NEVER HURT YOU, THAT THEY SHOWED YOU NOTHING BUT LOVE, AND **YOU'RE DOING THIS BECAUSE THEY DISCIPLINE YOU TO DO** RIGHT, NOW WE ALL KNOW THEY WILL TRY TO CONVINCE THE JURY THEY ARE INNOCENT, BUT I WILL PROVE THEIR GUILT, I HAVE THE PROOF THAT THEY HURT YOU AFTER THE ATTORNEY SAID THAT THEN HE PUT HIS HAND ON ANDREA SHOULDER LOOKED **HER IN THE EYE AND SAID DON'T WORRY WE ARE** BY YOUR SIDE AND WE WILL NOT LET YOU DOWN NOW GO HOME AND GET YOUR REST AND I WILL SEE YOU, EARLY IN THE MORNING, AS THEY LEFT THE ATTORNEY'S OFFICE ANDREA STOPPED AND SAID OH NO I FORGOT HOW CAN I FORGET; SHE IS GOING TO BE UPSET WITH ME, WHO IS GOING TO BE UPSET WITH YOU WHAT ARE TALKING ABOUT, SARA, SHE CALLED ME WHEN I WAS AT THE BUT STOP AND SAID SHE NEEDED TO TELL ME SOMETHING IMPORTANT, AND WITH EVERYTHING THAT HAS BEEN GOING ON I FORGOT TO GO TALK TO HER, WE NEED TO GO TO HER HOUSE RIGHT NOW, AND SEE WHAT SHE **NEEDED TO TELL ME, LET'S GO,** AS THEY WERE GOING TO SARA HOUSE ANDREA COULD JUST THINK AND WONDERED WHAT SARA HAD TO SAY SHE WAS HOPING IT WAS NOT MORE BAD NEWS, AS THEY GOT TO HER HOUSE ANDERA COULD NOT MOVE THEN FINALLY SHE WALKED UP TO SARA DOOR, AND BEFORE SHE HAD A CHANCE TO KNOCK SARA OPENED THE DOOR, AND SAID FINALLY YOU CAME TO SEE ME WHAT'S GOING ON WHAT DO YOU NEED TO TELL ME, LOOK ANDREA, I KNOW YOU ARE GOING TO COURT TOMORROW, I WANT TO LET YOU KNOW THAT I WILL BE THERE TO TESTIFY ON YOUR BEHALF, BUT HOW DO YOU KNOW

WHAT HAPPENED TO ME, WILL YOUR OLD FRIEND OPEN UP TO ME ON EVERYTHING, AND HE SHOWED ME THE LETTERS THAT YOU WROTE TO HIM EXPLAINING WHAT HAS HAPPENED TO YOU, HE GAVE ME ALL THE LETTERS AND TOOK THEM TO THE ATTORNEY SO THAT IS WHY THE ATTORNEY TOLD ME HE HAD ALL THE PROOF HE NEEDED TO PUT THEM AWAY FOR A LONG TIME, THANK YOU SO TELL ME WHO ALL READ THESE LETTERS YOU KNOW WHEN I WROTE THEM, I WAS IN SO MUCH PAIN I WAS HURTING ALL OVER MY BODY IT FELT AS IF MY BODY WAS TURNED INSIDE OUT ANDREA I HAVE YOU KNOW THAT NO ONE READ YOUR LETTERS I KEPT THEM HERE IN MY CLOSET THANK YOU AGAIN FOR SAVING THEM FOR ME THEY ARE GOING TO BE A BIG HELP IN COURT BUT I HAVE A

CHAPTER 7   JUSTICE FOR ALL

QUESTION DID YOU EVER PLAN ON GIVING ME THESE LETTERS, YES, I WAS JUST HOLDING ONTO THEM FOR YOU I FELT IF I HAD GIVEN THEM TO YOU AT THE WRONG TIME YOU MIGHT HAVE DESTROYED THEM TO GET REID OF THE MEMORIES OF THAT TERRIBLE TIME IN YOUR LIFE YES YOU ARE RIGHT I WOULD HAVE TORN THEM UP AND BURNED THEM, IT WAS A GREAT IDEA THAT YOU KEPT THEM FROM ME SO TELL

ME WHEN YOU READ THEM WHAT DID YOU THINK AND WHAT DID YOU FEEL THE FIRST THOUGHT THAT CAME TO MIND I SHOULD GO TO THE COPS THEN I DECIDED I WANTED TO JUST GET SOME FRIENDS AND GO TO YOUR HOUSE AND KILL YOUR PARENTS FOR DOING THAT TO YOU AND HURTING YOU THEY DO KNOW THAT YOU ARE A GIFT FROM GOD YOU ARE A GREAT PERSON THAT DESERVES LOVE AND HAPPINESS NOT PAIN AND SUFFERING AS THEY DID TO YOU BUT THEY WILL PAY FOR IT YOU ARE TRULY A GREAT FRIEND SARA; I WILL SEE YOU IN THE MORNING AT THE COURTHOUSE AFTER ANDREA SAID THAT SARA WALKED INTO HER HOUSE AND ANDREA AND RANDY TOOK OFF AND WENT HOME ON THEIR WAY HOME ANDREA TOLD RANDY WILL IT LOOKED LIKE THINGS WERE GOING TO FINALLY GO MY WAY AND I WILL GET MY LIFE BACK, YES, YOU ARE BLESSED TO HAVE SO MANY PEOPLE TO CARE ABOUT YOU AND LOVE YOU AS WE ALL DO, THANK YOU RANDY FOR GIVING ME YOUR LIFE AND BEING A PART OF MY LIFE IT IS TO GO TO THE HOUSE AND GO TO BED WE HAVE TO BE READY EARLY TO GO TO THE COURT HOUSE YES ANDREA WILL **WE HAVE MADE IT HOME SO LET'S EAT SOMETHING RIGHT QUICK** AND THEN WE WILL GO TO SLEEP OK RANDY, AS RANDY AND ANDREA SIT THERE AND HAVE THEIR DINNER THEY ARE ONLY CONCERNED ABOUT GETTING TO COURT ON TIME AS THEY FINISH DINNER RANDY LOOKS AT ANDREA AS **HE SAYS** GOOD NIGHT MY LOVE AS THEY SAID THEIR GOOD NIGHTS, THEY WERE BOTH IN A STATE OF GLADNESS AND WORRY AS THEY SLEPT, THEY BOTH WERE THINKING ABOUT THE FOLLOWING DAY WE WILL SEE HOW THE FIRST DAY OF LOTS OF DAYS WILL BE SPENT IN THE COURTROOM **LET'S SEE WHERE** TOMORROW LEADS US, MORNING WILL ARRIVE SOON ANDREA WILL SOON WAKE UP WHAT WILL

HAPPEN NEXT, GOOD MORNING RANDY GOOD **MORNING ANDREA LET'S GET READY TO** GO WE WILLPICK UP SOMETHING TO EAT ON THE WAY WE HAVE TO BE THERE EARLY, WILL ANDREA THIS IS THE DAY YOU HAVE BEEN WAITING FOR ALL OF YOUR LIFE, THE DAY WHEN **YOU'RE HEALING AND** HAPPINESS STARTED, RANDY THE DAY MY HAPPINESS STARTED A LONG TIME AGO AND THAT IS THE DAY YOU CAME INTO MY LIFE, YOU HAVE ALWAYS BEEN THERE WITH ME AND BY MY SIDE, AND NO MATTER WHAT HAPPENS IN COURT TODAY I ALREADY WON THIS BATTLE CAUSE IT DOES**N'T MATTER WHAT THEY DID TO ME** OR HOW THEY ABUSED ME, THEY NEVER COULD BREAK ME, YES, I WAS HEARTBROKEN BUT NOT BROKEN UP TO THE POINT OF NO RETURN, YES ANDREA YOU STAYED STRONG THREW THIS WHOLE ORDEAL I LOVE YOU AND I AM VERY PROUD OF YOU, THE STEPS YOU ARE TAKING FOR JUSTICE OK, WE MADE IT TO THE COURT HOUSE ARE YOU READY TO GO IN, LOOKING AT RANDY WITH A **BIG SMILE ON HER FACE YES, I AM READY LET'S GO DO THIS THEY** BOTH WALK INTO THE BUILDING AND WALK TOWARDS THE COURTROOM SHE SAW THE COPS TAKING HER PARENTS INTO THE COURTROOM IN THEIR ORANGE JAIL CLOTHES AND HANDCUFFS, AND SHE JUST SMILED AND SAID NOW YOU SEE HOW IT FEELS TO BE IN LOCKDOWN AND WITH NO ONE TO HELP YOU ANDREA MOM SPOKE TO HER, ANDREA HOW COULD YOU DO THIS TO YOUR MOM AND DAD, WE LOVE YOU WHY ARE YOU DOING THIS, YOU LOVE ME, YOU LOVE ME HOW DARE YOU SAY THAT AFTER ALL YOU BOTH HAD DONE TO ME, I'M IN TEARS AND HURT HOW COULD YOU DO THIS AND ALLOW ANOTHER MAN TO COME TO MY ROOM, MOM I WAS ONLY 12 YEARS OLD YOU ALLOWED YOUR HUSBAND TO HAVE HIS WAY WITH ME YOU BOTH ARE VERY SICK AND YOU

BOTH WILL GET WHAT YALL HAVE COMING TO YALL, COME ON RANDY LET'S GO INSIDE WILL MR. AND MRS. GARCIA I HAVE YOU KNOW SHE DESPISES THE BOTH OF YOU AND HATES I HOPE YOU BOTH GET WHAT YOU BOTH HAVE COMING TO YALL, AS WE GO INTO THE COURTROOM THERE IS NO SOUND IN THERE IT IS QUIET AS COULD BE ANDREA SAY'S WOW IT IS SILENT IN HERE. ANDREA LET'S GRAB A SEAT THERE IN THE FRONT ROW, OK RANDY THAT IS A GOOD SEAT I SEE THE JUDGE IS WALKING IN ALL RISE THE DISTRICT COURT IS NOW IN SESSION AND THE HONORABLE JUDGE WRIGHT PRESIDING YOU MAY BE SEATED, AS WE SIT DOWN THE JUDGE LOOKS AT ANDREA'S CASE SHAKES HIS HEAD, AND LOOKS AT ANDREA'S PARENTS WITH DISBELIEF AND A MEAN LOOK AND THE JUDGE SPEAKS SAYING MR AND MRS GRACIA YOU BOTH ARE CHARGE WITH ENDANGERMENT TO A CHILD, ALONG WITH ABUSE AND INAPPROPRIATE BEHAVIOR CAUSING THE LOST OF HER INNOCENCE IN THE HANDS OF HER DAD HOW DO YOU BOTH PLEAD, THEIR ATTORNEY SPEAKS AND SAYS NOT GUILTY WHEN HE SAID THAT HE SAW THE LOOK ON ANDREAS'S FACE SHE WANTED TO SPEAK AND I TOLD HER NO DON'T JUST WAIT AND YOU WILL SEE BE OK SO SAY NOTHING YOU WILL GET YOUR CHANCE TO SPEAK I PROMISE, THEN THE JUDGE SAID BAIL WILL BE SET THEN HE SAID NO THERE IS NO BAIL THIS WILL BE GOING TO TRIAL BY JURY, TAKE THEM AWAY THE BAILIFF CAME UP AND TOOK THEM BOTH AWAY AS THEY WERE LEAVING YOU COULD SEE THE RELIEF ON ANDREA'S FACE AS HER PARENTS WENT BACK TO THEIR CELL AS THEY WERE LEAVING THE ATTORNEY WENT UP TO THE JUDGE AND INFORMED HIM THAT THERE WAS ANOTHER GIRL THAT THEY HAD KIDNAPPED AS HE WAS TELLING THE JUDGE

ABOUT THE OTHER GIRL WHOM THEY HAD KIDNAPED THE JUDGE STOPPED HIM AND ASKED HOW OLD WAS SHE THE ATTORNEY LOOKED DOWN AND SAID SHE WAS ONLY 12 YEARS OLD, HE HAD A LOOK OF ANGER AND SAID WE WILL BRING IT IS UP FOR TRIAL ALONG WITH WHAT IS ALREADY AT HAND IN THIS CASE, HAVE ALL YOUR DOCUMENTS IN ORDER WE DO NOT WANT A MISTRIAL AND THEY ARE SET FREE, NO YOUR HONOR I WILL MAKE SURE THEY WILL GO TO JAIL MY DOCUMENTS WILL BE IN ORDER AND THE PEOPLE WILL BE READY WE ALSO HAVE WITNESSES AND LETTERS TO PROVE MY CLIENT STATEMENT GOOD, WE NEED ALL THE EVIDENCE YOU HAVE ON THESE TWO THAT IS ALL, FOR NOW, COURT WILL RESUME IN THE MORNING YES, YOUR HONOR AS THE ATTORNEY LEFT, HE WENT STRAIGHT TO ANDREA AND SAID GOOD NEWS THE JUDGE IS ALSO GOING TO CHARGE THEM FOR KIDNAPPING THE OTHER GIRL I HAVE TO GO TO HER HOUSE AND SEE IF HER PARENTS LET HER TESTIFY, I WILL GO WITH YOU AND TALK TO HER THESE TWO MONSTERS TOOK ADVANTAGE OF A LOT OF PEOPLE AND HURT LOTS OF PEOPLE OK ANDREA YOU AND RANDY CAN GO WITH ME TO HER HOUSE THIS WILL BE A BIG HELP AND WE NEED ALL THE HELP WE CAN GET LOOK SHE LIVES DOWN THE STREET, ANDREA YOU GO INSIDE WITH ME TO TALK TO HER AND HER PARENTS, OK I WILL DO ANYTHING NEEDED TO BE DONE TO GET HER TO GO AND TESTIFY, THE ATTORNEY KNOCKS ON THE DOOR HER PARENTS ANSWER HELLO HOW CAN I HELP YOU, HELLO MY NAME IS WAIT WE KNOW WHO YOU ARE AND WE KNOW YOU ALSO ANDREA, COME IN PLEASE NOW WHAT CAN WE DO FOR YOU, WE NEED YOUR DAUGHTER JUDY TO TESTIFY AT THE TRIAL, I DON'T THINK THAT WILL BE A GOOD SHE IS STILL TRAUMATIZED FROM WHAT HAPPENED SHE IS NOT HERSELF

SHE WAKES UP AT NIGHT CRYING AND SCARED OF THE THINGS THAT WERE DONE TO HER, HOW LONG WAS SHE GONE HOW LONG DID THEY HAVE HER, SHE WENT THREW TORTURE FOR 6 MONTHS, ANDREA LOOKS UP AND SAYS TRY 4 YEARS OF TORTURE ABUSE AND ANYTHING AND EVERYTHING YOU CAN IMAGINE IT STARTED WHEN I WAS A VERY YOUNG AGE IT STARTED WHEN I TURNED 9 YEARS OLD ALL THE WAY TIL I WAS 12 CAN I GO TALK TO HER WHERE IS JUDY, SHE IS IN HER ROOM AND WE ARE DEEPLY SORRY FOR ALL THE PAIN IN SUFFERING THAT YOU WENT THREW, EXCUSE ME I AM GOING TO TALK TO JUDY, ANDREA KNOCKS ON JUDY'S DOOR SHE SPEAKS AND SAYS WHO IS IT HI IT IS ME ANDREA I WOULD LIKE TO COME IN AND SIT WITH YOU FOR A WHILE AND TALK TO YOU ANDREA WHAT ARE YOU DOING HERE AT MY HOUSE, WE BOTH HAVE THE SAME PROBLEM OPENING THE DOOR LET ME COME IN AND TALK TO YOU, JUDY STAYS SILENT FOR A BIT THEN FINALLY OPENS THE DOOR, HEY JUDY HOW ARE YOU DOING, STILL IN SHOCK, AND I STILL HAVE DREAMS FROM THAT TIME IN MY PAST YES ME TOO IT SEEMS TO HAPPEN EVERY NIGHT IN MY DREAMS AS ANDREA SITTING THERE LOOKING AT JUDY ROOM, **SHE SAY'S** WOW YOU HAVE A NICE ROOM IT SAYS YOU HAVE LOTS OF LOVE IN THIS HOUSE YOU KNOW IN MY OLD ROOM BACK IN MY OLD HOUSE THERE WAS NOTHING BUT PAIN AND SUFFERING, MY DAD ALL OF HIS FRIENDS WOULD HAVE THEIR WAY WITH ME, AND MY MOM WOULD JUST LAUGH AT ME I NEVER KNEW WHAT A FATHER AND MOTHER LOVE WAS I WAS NEVER ABLE TO EXPERIENCE THAT A LIFE OF HAPPINESS, THE KIND OF STUFFED I EXPERIENCED SHOULD NOT HAPPENED TO A 12-YEAR-OLD LITTLE GIRL I SHOULD NOT HAVE EXPERIENCED IT, I WAS JUST 12 TRUST ME I KNOW EXACTLY HOW YOU

FELT AND HOW YOU FEEL NOW FROM WHAT THEY DID TO YOU, AND IT IS NOT YOUR FAULT THIS HAPPENED TO YOU IT IS ALL THEIR FAULT, WHICH IS WHY I NEED YOU TO COME TO COURT WITH ME AND HELP PUT THEM AWAY, WILL YOU JOIN ME IN THIS FIGHT FOR JUSTICE YES ANDREA I WILL GO WITH YOU TO COURT, AND WE WILL WIN THIS FIGHT, GREAT JUDY I WILL INFORM YOUR PARENTS YOU ARE GOING TO TESTIFY AND I WILL SEE YOU SOON THANK YOU FOR STANDING UP FOR US IN THE MORNING AT THE DISTRICT COURT, ANDREA, THANK YOU, FOR WHAT EVERYTHING YOU ARE GOING TO DO AND YOU ARE LETTING ME BE A PART OF THE VICTORY, JUDY THANK YOU FOR COMING TOMORROW SEE YOU THEN AS I WALK BACK TO THE FRONT, I HEAR THE ATTORNEY TALKING TO HER PARENTS AS I WALK INTO THE ROOM, THEY LOOK AT EACH OTHER AND THEN STAY QUIET FOR A LITTLE BIT THEN IN A LOW VOICE I I LOOKED INTO THEIR EYES AND THEY BOTH SPOKE AT THE SAME TIME AND ASKED ME WHAT HAPPENED WE HAD A LONG TALK AND SHE AGREED SHE WOULD TESTIFY; SHE SAID IT HURT MORE TO SIT IN HER ROOM AND NOT DO ANYTHING SHE IS GOING TO THE COURTHOUSE IN THE MORNING AFTER I SAID THAT BOTH HER PARENTS STAYED QUIET AND JUST LOOKED AT EACH OTHERS SAID OK WE WILL BE THERE EARLY IN THE MORNING AND WE ALREADY KNOW HOW THIS IS GOING TO TURN OUT, I JUST HAVE ONE THING TO SA WHAT IS THAT MR. TORRES JUDY YOU ARE VERY SPECIAL TO ME, ANDREA I AM SO PROUD OF BOTH OF YOU FOR TAKING A STAND AGAINST THESE EVIL PEOPLE WE WILL SEE YOU IN THE MORNING, AS THEY LEFT JUDY HOUSE, THEY JUST LOOKED AT EACH OTHER WITH A SMILE OF VICTORY, THE REST OF THE NIGHT WAS THEIR BEST NIGHT EVER SINCE ALL THIS HAD BEGAN THIS WAS THE FIRST NIGHT THAT

ANDREA WAS, ABLE TO SLEEP IN PEACE, THE ATTORNEY SAID HIS GOODNIGHT TO ANDREA AND RANDY ANDREA YOU DID IT I WILL SEE YOU BOTH IN THE MORNING GOODNIGHT MR. MARTINEZ, AND GOOD NIGHT TO BOTH OF YALL, AS THEY WALKED THE FEW BLOCKS TO THEIR HOUSE THEY DID NOT SAY A WORD, BUT THERE WAS LOTS OF JOY IN THEIR HEARTS ANDREA KNEW THE BATTLE JUST STARTED BUT SHE ALREADY SAW VICTORY, AS SOON AS THEY GOT TO THEIR HOUSE THEY WENT RIGHT TO BED, THEY WANTED TO MAKE SURE THEY WOKE UP ON TIME THEY KISSED AND SAID THEIR GOODNIGHTS, MORNING HAS COME AND THE TIME HAS COME FOR EVERYONE TO GO TO COURT, THEY RUSH TO GET READY AS RANDY STARTS SPEAKING, ANDREA IT IS ALMOST TIME TO GO ARE YOU READY YES, I AM READY TO GO **LET'S GO I CAN NOT WAIT TO GET** TO COURT AND GET THIS OVER WITH, I HOPE JUDY ARRIVES ON TIME, OK MY LOVE I WILL GET THE STUFF READY AND I WILL MEET YOU OUTSIDE, OK HERE I COME AS THEY LEFT THE HOUSE AND HEADED TOWARDS THE COURTHOUSE, THEY SAW TIM COMING DOWN THE ROAD HE STOPPED AND ASKED THEM ARE YOU ALL HEADING TO THE COURTHOUSE YES, WE ARE ON OUR WAY RIGHT **NOW COME ON LET'S GO I WILL TAKE YALL THERE, WHY ARE YOU** HERE WHAT HAPPENED NOTHING I JUST KNEW I NEEDED TO BE HERE FOR BOTH OF YALL, WE WERE PLEASED THAT TIM CAME BACK AS WE GOT TO AT THE COURTHOUSE WE SEE JUDY AND HER PARENTS WERE OUTSIDE TALKING TO THE ATTORNEY, WE PARKED AND RUSHED TO WHERE THEY WERE, ANDREA, YOU MADE IT ON TIME SO THIS IS HOW IT IS GOING TO GO, FIRST YOUR PARENTS WILL BE CALLED TO THE STAND AND AFTER WE QUESTION THEM, I WILL HAVE YOU CALLED TO THE STAND, AND WHEN YOU TESTIFY I WILL MENTION THE LETTERS

ONE AT A TIME AND YOU WILL EXPLAIN TO THE COURT EXACTLY WHAT HAPPENED IN THE LETTER I KNOW IT IS GOING TO BE HARD ON YOU BUT YOU HAVE TO DO IT, OK I WILL I AM READY FOR THIS I SAID BEFORE I WOULD DO ANYTHING AND EVERYTHING, I HAVE TO DO TO GET JUSTICE FOR WHAT HAPPENED TO ME, OK GOOD, AND AS FOR YOU JUDY, I MIGHT CALL YOU TO THE STAND TODAY OR TOMORROW JUST BE READY FOR WHEN I DO AND ANOTHER THING, DOES RANDY KNOW EVERYTHING THAT HAPPENED NO NOT EVERYTHING JUST WHAT I TOLD HIM AND HE WAS THERE FOR ME WHEN I ALMOST DIED AND HE OVERHEARD MY PARENTS WHEN THEY SAID THEY WISHED I HAD DIED, RANDY WILL YOU TAKE THE STAND AND TESTIFY WHAT YOU SAW AND HEARD YES, I WILL, I WILL TELL EVERYTHING I KNOW GREAT WILL LET US GO INSIDE, AS WE WALKED INTO THE COURTROOM, I SEE MY PARENTS SITTING THERE WITH SMILE ON THEIR FACES I WAS CONFUSED AS TO WHY THEY WERE SMILING, THEY SAT THERE IN THE SAME PLACE AS WE DID THE DAY BEFORE OK HERE COMES THE JUDGE, ALL RISE COURT IN SESSION THE HONORABLE JUDGE WRIGHT PRESIDING, ALLMAY BE SEATED, MR. MARTINEZ IS YOUR CLIENT READY YES, YOUR HONOR SHE IS, AND MR. SANCHEZ ARE YOUR CLIENTS READY YES, YOUR HONOR, THEY ARE, MR. SANCHEZ MAY WE HAVE YOUR OPENING STATEMENT, YES, YOUR HONOR LADIES AND GENTLEMAN OF THE JURY THIS IS NOT AN EASY CASE TO JUDGE AND THERE WILL BE DISTURBING EVIDENCE BROUGHT IN LIGHT OF HOW MY CLIENT'S PARENTS PURPOSELY CAUSED BODY HARM AND MADE HER SUFFER STARTING AT THE AGE OF 10 YEARS OLD UNTIL SHE WAS 12 YEARS OLD THE ATTORNEY STAYED SILENT THE JUDGE ASKED THE ATTORNEY T0 CONTINUE, HE LOOKED UP AND SAID THE WORST PART OF

THIS WAS HER DAD AND HIS FRIENDS ABUSED HER, SHE WAS SOLD TO THESE MEN FOR DRUG MONEY LOOK AT HER PARENTS LOOK AT THEM THEY ARE SUPPOSED TO LOVE HER, AND SHE WAS SUPPOSED TO FEEL SAFE AND PROTECTED IN HER OWN HOME HER DAD WAS SUPPOSED TO PROTECT HER FROM MEN INSTEAD, HE INVITED THEM INTO HIS HOUSE TO HAVE HER AS THEY PLEASE, AND THE OTHER PART HERE MOM ALLOWED THIS TO HAPPEN, BUT INSTEAD OF STOPPING THEN SHE LAUGHED AT HER AND SAID GET WHAT YOU DESERVE, I ASKED FOR THE JURY TO RETURN THE VERDICT TO THE DAD FOR CHILD ENDANGERMENT AND ABUSE FOR WHAT HE DID TO HIS DAUGHTER, AND FOR THE MOM RETURNED THE VERDICT OF ACCESSORY TO CHILD ENDANGERMENT FOR ABUSING HER AND BEING A PART OF THIS BRUTAL ABUSE, THAT IS ALL I HAVE TO SAY ABOUT THIS AT THIS POINT, AS THE ATTORNEY FINISHES, HE WIPES THE TEARS FROM HIS EYES I LOOK OVER AT THE JUDGE AND HE HAD TEARS IN HIS EYES AS WELL, AS THE ATTORNEY SAT DOWN THE JUDGE SAID OK MR. SANCHEZ DO YOU HAVE AN OPENING STATEMENT, YES, YOUR HONOR HE WALKS TOWARDS THE JURY WOW THAT IS A WILD OPENING STATEMENT, PUTTING THE BLAME ON HER PARENTS WHEN ALL THEY DID WAS LOVE AND TRIED TO RAISE HER THE RIGHT WAY SHE WAS OUT OF CONTROL SNEAKING OFF WITH BOYS AT ALL TIMES OF THE NIGHT, SHE GOT CAUGHT SO SHE MADE UP THIS STORY SO SHE WOULD NOT GET IN TROUBLE WITH HER PARENTS, LADIES, AND GENTLEMEN OF THE JURY I ASK THAT YOU ALL BRING BACK THE VERDICT OF NOT GUILTY FOR THE MOM AND DAD ARE TWO GREAT PARENTS, AS THE ATTORNEY RETURNS TO HIS SEAT NEXT TO HER PARENTS, THE JUDGE TURNS TO ANDREA'S ATTORNEY AND SAYS MR. MARTINEZ PROVED YOUR CASE AND CALLED

YOUR FIRST WITNESS LOOKED AT RANDY AND SAID I CALL RANDY GONZALES THE STAND AS HE CALLED RANDY TO THE STAND, HE HAD A SURPRISED LOOK ON HIS FACE TO BE CALLED SO EARLY IN THE TRIAL, AS HE GOT TO THE STAND THE BAILIFF CAME TO RANDY WITH A BIBLE IN HIS HAND RAISE YOUR RIGHT HAND AND PUT YOUR OTHER HAND ON THE BIBLE, DO YOU SWEAR TO TELL THE TRUTH THE WHOLE TRUTH, AND NOTHING BUT THE TRUTH SO HELP YOU, GOD I DO YOU MAY BE SEATED, CAN YOU STATE YOUR NAME FOR THE COURT MY NAME IS RANDY GARCIA AND HOW DO YOU KNOW ANDREA GARCIA SHE IS MY GIRLFRIEND HOW LONG HAVE YOU KNOWN HER, I HAVE KNOWN ANDREA EVER SINCE THE 6TH GRADE, AND WHEN WE GOT TO THE 8TH GRADE, SHE? BECAME MY GIRLFRIEND, WOULD YOU SAY THAT ANDREA HAS ALWAYS BEEN HONEST, WOULD ALWAYS TELL THE TRUTH, AS FAR AS I KNOW, SHE HAS NEVER LIED TO ME OR ANYONE ELSE, DO YOU FIND ANY REASON THAT SHE WOULD LIE ABOUT WHAT HAPPENED TO HER, RANDY LOOKED AT ANDREA SAID NO SHE WOULD NEVER LIE ABOUT SOMETHING LIKE THAT, I HAD SEEN HOW SHE WAS IN SCHOOL HOW SHE ALMOST KILLED HERSELF HOW SHE CRIED OUT FOR HELP AND THERE WAS NO ONE THERE TO ANSWER HER CRY, HOW DO YOU SEE THE RELATIONSHIP BETWEEN HER AND HER DAD RANDY LOOKED AT HER DAD AND SAID HATE TORTURE, WHAT DO YOU MEAN HER DAD HATED ANDREA FOR NO REASON AND HER MOM WAS NO BETTER THEY DID NOT LOVE HER OBJECTION YOUR HONOR HOW DO WE KNOW IF WHAT HE IS SAYING IS THE TRUTH OR IS NOT THE TRUTH ARGUMENTATIVE, OVER RUDE CONTINUE AS YOU WERE SAYING RANDY WHAT DO YOU MEAN BY SAYING HER MOM WAS NO BETTER, HER MOM WOULD HIT HER FOR NO REASON, AND THEN THEY BOTH WOULD LAUGH

AT HER AS SHE SAT THERE IN PAIN CRYING AND HOW LONG HAS THIS BEEN GOING ON FOR, SHE WAS BEING ABUSE FOR 2 YEARS, THANK YOU RANDY NO FURTHER QUESTIONS AS THE ATTORNEY SITS DOWN THE JUDGE ASKS THE OTHER ATTORNEY WOULD YOU LIKE TO CROSS-EXAMINATION YES, YOUR HONOR I WOULD AS HE WALKED TOWARDS RANDY AS RANDY LOOKED AT ANDREA HE SAW SHE WAS IN TEARS LOOKING AT WHAT WAS HAPPENING, SO RANDY YOU ARE ANDREA BOYFRIEND YES, I AM HOW LONG HAVE YOU AND HER BEEN TOGETHER FOR LIKE 7 YEARS THAT IS A LONG TIME SO HAVE YOU AND HER HAD INTIMATE LOVE OBJECTION YOUR HONOR SPECULATIVE LEADING THE WITNESS THEIR RELATIONSHIP IS NOT ON TRIAL HERE SUSTAIN YOUR HONOR I AM TRYING TO PROVE A POINT THAT ANDREA WAS ALREADY ACTIVE SHE CLAIMS THAT HER DAD TOOK HER INNOCENT WHEN IT WAS ALREADY TAKEN BY RANDY SO WHAT HAPPENED TO HER, DID NOT HAPPEN BY HER DAD OVERRULE CONTINUE WITH A NEW LINE OF QUESTIONS, RANDY DID YOU EVER SEE ANDREA WITH OTHER BOYS' OBJECTION YOUR HONOR ARGUMENTATIVE SUSTAIN I GAVE YOU ONE WARNING TO MAINTAIN YOUR QUESTIONS ABOUT THE MATTER AT HAND, RANDY DID YOU EVER SEE HER PARENTS HIT HER OR DO ANYTHING TO HER NO, I DID NOT I NEVER WAS AT TO HER HOUSE, WHEN ALL OF THIS WAS HAPPENING SO YOU DO NOT KNOW EXACTLY WHAT HAPPENED, HOW CAN YOU BELIEVE SOMETHING YOU HAVE NEVER SEEN FOR YOURSELF, RANDY STAYED SILENT AND ASKED THE ATTORNEY CAN I ASK YOU A QUESTION, OK WHAT IS IT DO YOU HAVE KIDS YES, I DO AND DO YOU BELIEVE IN THEM YES, I DO SO IF YOUR SON CAME HOME AND SAY TO YOU I GOT IN A FIGHT IN SCHOOL TODAY BUT SAW NO BRUISE ON HIM WOULD YOU BELIEVE HIM THE

ATTORNEY STOPPED IN HIS TRACKS AND SAID YES, I WOULD BELIEVE HIM, IF YOU WERE NOT THERE HOW DO YOU KNOW IF YOUR SON WAS TELLING THE TRUTH, CAUSE MY SON DOES NOT LIE; YOU SEE ANDREA HAS NEVER LIE TO ME BEFORE THAT IS WHY I BELIEVE HER AFTER THE ATTORNEY SAID NO MORE QUESTIONS THE ATTORNEY WALKED AWAY THE JUDGE SAID YOU MAY STEP DOWN RANDY, AS HE WALKED BACK TO SIT BEHIND ANDREA, HE WHISPERED TO HER I LOVE YOU, ANDREA JUST SMILED AND SAID I LOVE YOU TOO, THE JUDGE ASK TO CALL YOUR NEXT WITNESS, I CALL MR GARCIA TO THE STAND, AS ANDREA'S DAD WALKS TO THE STAND SHE GIVES HIM A LOOK OF HATRED HE JUST LOOKS AT HER AND SMILE AS HE SITS DOWN AT THE STAND DO YOU SWEAR TO TELL THE TRUTH THE WHOLE TRUTH, AND NOTHING BUT THE TRUTH, I DO YOU MAY BE SEATED, MR GARCIA ARE YOU ANDREA'S BIOLOGICAL FATHER NO, I AM NOT HER REAL FATHER BUT SHE IS MY BEAUTIFUL DAUGHTER, I LOVE HER AND IS MRS. GARCIA HER BIOLOGICAL MOTHER, AFTER THE ATTORNEY ASKED THIS QUESTION, HE STAYED SILENT AND JUST LOOKED DOWN TO THE FLOOR THEN THE JUDGE TURNED AND SAID TO ANSWER THE QUESTION IS ANDREA'S MOTHER HER BIOLOGICAL MOTHER, HE CLEARED HIS THROAT AND SAID YES SHE IS AND SHE IS ALSO ANDREA OLDER SISTER WHEN HE SAID THIS THE COURTROOM WAS IN SHOCK THEY DID NOT KNOW WHAT TO BELIEVE AT THIS POINT EVERYONE WAS CAUGHT OFF GUARD THIS CASE WAS GETTING MORE EMOTIONAL ANDREA'S EYES FILLED UP WITH TEARS, SO HOW IS IT POSSIBLE THAT SHE IS ANDREA'S OLDER SISTER WILL YOU SEE MY FIRST WIFE COULD NOT HAVE KIDS AND I WANTED A FAMILY; I WAS NEVER THIS MEAN AND EVIL I LOVED AND CARED FOR EVERYONE AND SHOWED THEM HAPPINESS AND RESPECT,

THEN WHAT HAPPENED WHY DID YOU TURN LIKE THIS, YOU SEE MY FIRST WIFE TRIED AND TRIED TO HAVE KIDS WE COULD NOT, SO I LEFT HER AND FOUND ANOTHER LADY I COULD HAVE KIDS WITH AND I GOT TOGETHER WITH HER, WE STARTED TO HAVE KIDS FIRST THE BABY WE HAD WAS ANDREA OLDER SISTER SO WE NAMED HER ANGIE, HOW DID YOU END UP GETTING TOGETHER WITH YOUR DAUGHTER THIS IS DISTURBING HER OLDER SISTER AFTER WE HAD ANGIE I WANTED ANOTHER BABY YEARS LATER BUT SHE COULD NOT HAVE KIDS SO I STAYED WITH HER FOR A WHILE BY THIS TIME, IT WAS GETTING CLOSE FOR ANDREA OLDER SISTER BIRTHDAY AND SHE WAS TURNING 15 YEARS OLD AND I CAME HOME ONE NIGHT AND MY WIFE HAD LEFT FOR THE STORE SHE WAS NOT THERE I ACCIDENTALLY WALKED INTO ANGIE ROOM FORGETTING THAT SHE WAS MY DAUGHTER AND JUST STOOD THERE AND LOOKED AT HER AND I SAW HER WITH NO CLOTHES, ON AND I WALKED IN CLOSED THE DOOR AND SAID TO HER TONIGHT, YOU WILL BE WITH ME, AND THAT NIGHT, I GOT HER PREGNANT, AFTER THAT DAY WE HAD NO CHOICE BUT TO STAY TOGETHER I LET MY WIFE AND ME AND ANGIE KEPT IT A SECRET A FEW YEARS WHEN ANGIE TURNED 17 YEARS OLD, I MARRIED SHE IS ANDREA'S MOM ANGIE IS ANDREA BIOLOGICAL MOM, I ASSURE YOU WE NEVER MEANT TO HURT HER WE DID NOT INTEND FOR IT TO GO THIS FAR IT ALL STARTED WHEN WE STARTED DOING DRUGS THEN STARTED OTHER BAD THINGS AND WHEN ANDREA TURNED 9 YEARS OLD, THAT WHEN IT GOT WORSE, WE WERE SO LOST WITHOUT HOPE WE GOT INTO DRUGS AND ALCOHOL DEEPER TRYING TO DROWN THE PAIN WE PUT PEOPLE THREW WE FOUND OURSELVES ALWAYS BROKE AND ALWAYS RUNNING OUT OF MONEY THEN ONE DAY I SAW ANDREA PLAYING AND I WAS

DRAWN TO HER, DID YOU AND MRS. GARCIA ABUSED ANDREA, NO WE DID NOT WE TRIED TO DISCIPLINE HER AND TEACH HER RIGHT FROM WRONG, WE WERE NOT THE BEST PARENTS WE TRIED TO BE GOOD PARENTS OK MR GARCIA NO FURTHER QUESTIONS MR. MARTINEZ WOULD YOU LIKE TO ASK QUESTIONS YES, I WOULD YOUR HONOR, AS THE ATTORNEY STOOD UP, HE LOOKED AT ANDREA AND HE LOOKED AT HER PARENTS WITHOUT A CARE IN THE WORLD, HE WAS SHOCKED AT HOW CAN THESE TWO HAVE NO HEART FOR THEIR CHILD AS THE ATTORNEY WALKED TOWARD ANDREA'S DAD, HE LOOKED CONFUSED AT HIM SHAKING HIS HEAD IN CONFUSION I CAN NOT BELIEVE WHAT I HEAR WE KNEW THE TRUTH WAS ABOUT TO COME OUT, THE ATTORNEY WE HAVE IS A GREAT ATTORNEY NOW MR. GARCIA, YOU SAY YOU WERE TRYING DISCIPLINE AND SHOW HER RIGHT FROM WRONG, YES THAT IS RIGHT WE TRY TO SHOW HER RIGHT FROM WRONG, HOW CAN YOU TEACH A **PERSON TO BE GOOD IF YOU ARE EVIL AND DON'T KNOW** THE RIGHT FROM WRONG IF YOU DO NOT KNOW HOW TO LIVE YOUR LIFE RIGHT TELL ME HOW IS THAT POSSIBLE YOU ARE HER DAD HOW COULD YOU EVEN THINK OF DOING THIS, I AM SHOCKED AT WHAT YOU HAVE PUT HER THREW I PROMIS YOU AND YOUR WIFE WILL NOT WALK OUT OF THIS COURTROOM; I HAVE NO MORE FOR THIS MONSTER, EXCUSE ME I MEAN THIS PERSON YOU MAY STEP DOWN WE WILL BREAK FOR AN HOUR FOR LUNCH AND **BE BACK AT 3 O'CLOCK THE ATTORNEY SAID LET'S GO** WE GOT UP AN LEFT THE COURTROOM, ANDREA WAS STARTING TO SEE THE LIGHT AND SHE KNEW IN HER HEART IT WOULD BE JUST A MATTER OF TIME BEFORE IT WOULD ALL BE OVER WITH AND, ON OUR WAY, OUT ANDREA RAN INTO SARA HEY SARA ANDREA I HAVE BEEN TRYING TO GET AWAY I

AM SORRY I AM LATE NO MY FRIEND YOU ARE NOT LATE YOU **ARE ON TIME LET'S GO** TALK TO MY ATTORNEY AND TELL HIM YOU WANT TO TESTIFY ON MY BEHALF THAT YOU HAVE INFORMATION ON THIS CASE I AM HERE NOW I HAVE ALL THE LETTERS YOU WROTE ROBERT, AND I AM READY TO STAND AND TESTIFY FOR YOU TALKED TO ROBERT AND HE SAID IF YOU NEED HIM TO, HE WILL COME AND STAND BY YOUR SIDE AND TESTIFY FOR YOU HE SAYS HE KNOWS YOU AND RANDY ARE IN A SERIOUS RELATIONSHIP AND ALL HE IS HERE TO DO THIS TO MAKE SURE YOU GET YOUR JUSTICE SARA, WOULD YOU LIKE TO JOIN US FOR LUNCH WE NEED TO GO OVER LOTS OF STUFF WE HAVE LITTLE TIME THERE IS A LOT WE HAVE TO GO OVER TO GET YOU READY TO TESTIFY, JUDY IS COMING WITH US SO, WE NEED TO TALK FILL ME IN IF IT IS OKAY WITH YOUR PARENTS YES, IT IS FINE WITH THEM YES, THAT IS FINE SHE CAN GO WITH YALL TO PREPARE HER FOR HER TESTIMONY, SHE IS A GOOD PERSON SARA I WILL BE CALLING YOU TO THE STAND NEXT IS IT THE RIGHT TIME FOR ME TO GO ON THE STAND LOOK THEY ARE WORRIED IT IS THE PERFECT TIME FOR YOU TO TAKE THE STAND WE HAVE THEM AT THE POINT WE WANT THEM AND YOUR TESTIMONY WILL FOR SURE PU THEM AWAY FOR GOOD I KNOW THAT YOU WILL BE STRONG ON THE STAND THE DAD IS CLAIMING HE IS A GREAT PERSON WE ARE GOING TO PROVE THAT HE IS NOTHING BUT LIES AND HE WILL LOSE ALL CREDIBILITY WITH THE JURY, OK THEN I AM READY FOR WHAT I MUST DO TO PREPARE FOR THIS I WILL DO ANYTHING FOR ANDREA, I WILL RUN YOU THREW YOUR DEFENSE, ANDREA AND RANDY GET A TABLE AND LET ME TALK TO SARA AND FILL HER IN ON EVERYTHING THAT HAPPENED SHE WAS NOT THERE FOR THE TRIAL OK ATTORNEY MARTINEZ WILL DO, COME WITH US

JUDY LET'S SIT HERE AT THIS TABLE WILL THEY CALL RANDY TO TESTIFY FIRST RANDY MADE THE OTHER ATTORNEY LOOK REALLY STUPID THEN THEY CALLED MY DAD AND HE GOT PUT TO SHAME HE TRIED TO TALK HIS WAY OUT AND PLAY THE NOBLE PERSON MR. GOOD FATHER BUT THE JURY DID NOT BYE IT AND NOW WITH JUDY'S TESTIMONY THEY WILL LOSE EVERYTHING AND FOR GOOD, ANDREA YES RANDY ARE YOU GOING TO ALLOW YOUR EX-BOYFRIEND TO COME TO THE COURTHOUSE TO TESTIFY RANDY MY LOVE I WILL DO WHATEVER I HAVE TO DO TO MAKE SURE GET MY JUSTICE I DESERVE THIS JUSTICE, I TOLD YOU THIS BEFORE REMEMBER YOU SAID YOU WOULD STAND BY MY SIDE AND SUPPORT ME I LOVE YOU RANDY BE WITH ME EVERY STEP OF THE WAY I AM WITH YOU MY LOVE AND YOU ARE RIGHT I AM SORRY I BROUGHT IT UP HERE COMES THE ATTORNEY AND THEY BOTH LOOK HAPPY OK ANDREA SARA IS READY YES MY FRIEND I AM READY TO TAKE THE STAND SARA YOU WILL BE TAKING THE STAND THE FOLLOWING DAY BE READY FOR TOMORROW AND MAKE SURE YOU ARE READY I WILL BE PRESENTING A FEW OF THE LETTERS DURING THE TIME, THEY WILL BE IN YOUR TESTIMONY YES, THAT IS FINE YOU HAVE A PLAN I AM READY TO DO ANYTHING FOR MY CLOSEST FRIEND LET'S START HEADING BACK TO THE COURTROOM, THEY WILL NOT SEE WHAT IS ABOUT TO HAPPEN THEY HAVE NO CLUE, AND THEY WILL BE SURPRISED. AS WE GOT TO THE COURTHOUSE ANDREA LOOKED UP AND WAS CAUGHT BY SURPRISE HER AUNT AND GRANDMA WAS THERE ON THE STEPS WAITING FOR HER, GRANDMA, WHAT ARE YOU AND GRANDMA DOING HERE? MIJA, WE KNEW WE NEEDED TO BE HERE WITH YOU AND STND BY YOUR SIDE AND SUPPORT YOU, I LOVE YOU GRANDMA AND AUNT SUSIE. GRANDMA THIS IS

MY BOYFRIEND RANDY AND RANDY THIS IS MY VERY BEAUTIFUL GRANDMA AND MY AUNT SUSIE WERE THE ONES I WAS STAYING WITH GRANDMA RANDY WILL BE GOING BACK WITH ME TO STAY WITH YOU, WILL RANDY WE ARE VERY HAPPY TO FINALLY MEET YOU ANDREA HAS TOLD US SO MUCH ABOUT YOU, AND WE FEEL THAT WE HAVE KNOWN YOU FOR A VERY LONG TIME WELCOME TO THE FAMILY, THANK YOU, MRS. GARCIA, I LOVE ANDREA VERY MUCH WILL **LET'S** GO INSIDE THE COURTROOM, MOM AND DAD WILL BE SURPRISED TO SEE YOU BOTH YES, I BET THEY WILL BE, HOW IS THE CASE GOING, FROM THE WAY THINGS LOOK IT IS GOING VERY WELL, AND IT IS FIXING TO GET VERY INTERESTING WHAT DO YOU MEAN, YOU WILL SEE GRANDMAS, WE WALK INTO THE COURTROOM ANDREA'S PARENTS LOOK AT ANDREA GRANDMA AND AUNT WITH A LOOK OF CONFUSION AND FEAR, FOR SOME REASON ANDREA'S PARENTS WERE SCARED OF HER GRANDMA AND AUNT, AS THEY SIT DOWN ANDREA'S DAD SAID WHAT ARE YOU BOTH DOING HERE LEAVE YOU NEED TO LEAVE WE ARE HERE TO SEE YOU BOTH GET WHAT YOU BOTH DESERVE FOR HURTING THIS POOR GIRL SO, SON, THIS IS ONE PLACE YOU CAN NOT KICK US OUT OF SO SIT THERE WITH YOUR DAUGHTER AND TAKE YOUR PAIN AND SUFFERING AND GET YOUR PUNISHMENT AS YOU BOTH GAVE IT OUT SO FREELY AND YOU BOTH WILL FEEL THE PAIN ANDREA WENT THROUGH IN YOUR HANDS, I STILL DO NOT UNDERSTAND HOW YOU BOTH CAN DO THIS TO YOUR DAUGHTER ALL SHE WANTED WAS A CHANCE TO FEEL LOVE AND HAPPINESS BUT THANKS TO THE BOTH OF YOU HER LIFE IS NOW DESTROYED FROM THE INSIDE OUT, REMEMBER THIS DAY, AND MARK MY WORDS YOU BOTH WILL GET WHAT YOU DESERVE WHEN YOU GO TO PRISON REMEMBER THEY HATE PEOPLE

LIKE YALL IN THERE AND NO ONE WILL HELP YOU OUT I SHOULD BE MAD AT BOTH OF YALL BUT I FEEL SORRY FOR YOU AND YOUR DAUGHTER AND THE PAIN AND SUFFERING THAT YALL ARE GOING TO EXPERIENCE I WISH THAT ON NO ONE NOT EVEN MY WORST ENEMIE BUT YOU SHOULD KNOW THAT THE UGLY YOU PUT OUT INTO THE WORLD COMES BACK TO YOU TWICE AS BAD AND NOW THE REALITY OF WHAT YOU DID AND THE TRUE EVIL PEOPLE YOU BOTH ARE WILL BE BROUGHT TO LIGHT I WILL PRAY FOR YOU BOTH AS ANDREAS'S GRANDMA TELLS HER DAD THIS HE HAS NOTHING TO SAY HE JUST SITS THEIR SPEECHLESS AS IF HE IS LOST AT THE FACT THAT HIS LIFE WILL SOON BE OVER AND THERE IS NOTHING NO ONE CAN

CHAPTER 8   PRAYERS BEEN ANSWERED

OR WILL DO TO HELP YOU AS YOU BOTH LAUGH AT ANDREA'S PAIN AND SUFFERING THEY WILL ALSO LAUGH AT YOUR PAIN THEY WILL HAVE THEIR WAY WITH BOTH OF YOU AND YOUR WIFE SO GET READY FOR THE BEGINNING OF THE END OF YOUR SO-CALLED DISGUSTING LIFE MAY GOD HELP YOU CAUSE NO ONE ELSE WILL

AFTER ANDREA'S AUNT TOLD HER PARENTS
THIS, SHE JUST SAT THERE WITH A LOOK OF
HATRED TOWARD THE BOTH OF THEM AT THIS
POINT, THE JUDGE WAS WALKING IN ALL RISE
THE HONORABLE JUDGE WRIGHT PRESIDING
YOU MAY BE SEATED, MR MARTINEZ CALLED
YOUR WITNESS I CALL JUDY RAMIREZ TO THE
STAND, AS SHE WAS CALLED MR. MARTINEZ
SAYS OBJECTION YOUR HONOR WE KNOW
NOTHING ABOUT THIS WITNESS I HAVE NOT
HAD TIME TO SEE HOW SHE IS OF ANY
CONCERN TO THIS TRIAL, OVER RUDE I'M
ALLOWING THIS WITNESS, JUDY MAY YOU TAKE
THE STAND, DO YOU SWEAR, TO TELL THE
TRUTH, THE WHOLE TRUTH, AND NOTHING BUT
THE TRUTH SO HELP YOU, GOD, I DO YOU MAY
BE SEATED AS THE ATTORNEY WALKS TOWARD
JUDY SHE IS FILLED WITH TEARS AND FEAR IN
HER EYES, AS SHE LOOKS AT ANDREA'S DAD
FAIL FROM HER EYES THE ATTORNEY ASKS
WHY ARE YOU CRYING AND SHE WHISPERS I
AM SCARED, SCARE OF WHAT I AM SCARED OF
THAT DIRTY MAN AND LADY THERE, LOOKING
AT ME JUDY I PROMISE YOU THAT YOU ARE
SAFE THEY CAN NOT HURT YOU NO MORE SO
TELL THE COURT EVERYTHING THAT
HAPPENED NOW JUDY DO YOU KNOW ANDREA
GARCIA, NO I DON'T TELL ME IN YOUR OWN
WORDS WHY ARE YOU HERE AND WHAT
HAPPENED TO YOU, WILL IT HAPPEN LIKE THIS
LAST YEAR I WAS AT THE PLAYGROUND IN
FRONT OF MY HOUSE AND THESE TWO PEOPLE
CALLED ME TO THEIR CAR ASKING IF I HAD
SEEN THEIR DOG, I SAID NO I HAVE NOT AS I
TURNED TO WALK AWAY THE MAN GOT OUT OF
THE CAR AND FORCED ME TO GET INTO THE
CAR WITH THEM THE LADY LAUGHED AND SAID
SINCE OUR DAUGHTER IS NOT HERE YOU WILL
TAKE HER PLACE YOU ARE GOING TO MAKE
MONEY FOR US AT FIRST, I DID NOT KNOW
WHAT SHE WAS TALKING ABOUT WHEN WE GOT

TO THEIR HOUSE, I WAS BLINDFOLDED THEY TOOK ME INTO WHAT I BELIEVE TO BE ANDREA'S ROOM, THEY MADE ME SHOWER, THEN WHEN I GOT OUT OF THE SHOWER IT STARTED, WHAT STARTED JUDY WHAT HAPPENED TELL US, AS JUDY SAT ON THE WITNESS CHAIR SHE WAS FULL OF TEARS AND THEN SHE SPOKE ABOUT WHAT HAPPENED, THEY TOOK ME TO ANDREA'S ROOM THE LADY WALKED OUT AND THE MAN SAID I GOT TO SEE HOW GOOD YOU ARE GET ON THE BED I TOLD HIM NO DO NOT DO THAT TO ME I PLEADED WITH HIM, BUT HE WOULD NOT STOP I YELLED FOR HELP NO ONE HEARD ME, MOMMY, I TOLD HIM TO STOP HURTING ME WHY DID HE NOT LISTEN THEY JUST LAUGHED AT ME, HOW OLD WERE YOU WHEN THIS HAPPENED, I WAS ONLY 12 YEARS OLD, BUT THAT IS NOT THE WORST PART, THE WORST PART WAS WHEN HE STARTED CALLING HIS FRIENDS AND THEY CAME OVER AND DESTROYED ME, THEY ALL TOOK TURNS ON ME SLAPPING ME AND CALLING ME ALL KINDS OF NAMES I HAD NO FURTHER QUESTIONS WHEN THE ATTORNEY TURNED THE WHOLE COURT ROOM EVEN THE JUDGE WAS IN TEARS, ATTORNEY SANCHEZ WOULD YOU LIKE TO CROSS-EXAMINE NO QUESTIONS YOUR HONOR YOU CAN STEP DOWN YOU WERE BRAVE WE WILL PICK UP TOMORROW, COURT ADJOURN ALL RISE AS THE JUDGE LEAVES THE ROOM YALL ARE FREE TO LEAVE AS ANDREA AND EVERYONE WALKED OUT ANDREA WENT UP TO JUDY GAVE HER A BIG HUG AND TOLD HER I KNOW IT WAS HARD TO TALK ABOUT IT, I JUST HOPE I AM AS STRONG AS YOU WERE WHEN I AM CALLED TO THE STAND, AS ANDREA SAID THAT THE ATTORNEY SAID WE WILL FIND OUT TOMORROW BECAUSE YOU WILL BE CALLED TO THE STAND TOMORROW, BE READY YOUR TESTIMONY IS THE MOST IMPORTANT ONE IT IS

YOUR TIME TO SHINE YES, MY LOVE THE MOMENT YOU HAVE BEEN WAITING FOR ALL OF YOUR LIFE HAS FINALLY ARRIVED, AND YOUR DAY TO SHINE WILL BE TOMORROW, I KNOW YOU WILL BE GREAT ON THAT STAND AS THE DAY CAME TO AN END ALL ANDREA COULD DO WAS THINK ABOUT THE DAY TO COME, SHE STAYED UP MOST OF THE NIGHT LOCKED HERSELF IN THE ROOM DID NOT WANT TO BE BOTHERED BY NO ONE RANDY KNOCKED ON THE DOOR ASKING HER IF SHE WAS HUNGRY SHE RESPONDED NO I AM OK I JUST WANT TO BE LEFT ALONE I HAVE A LOT TO THINK ABOUT I NEED TO BE READY FOR TOMORROW, AS RANDY WALKED AWAY FROM HER ROOM ALL HE COULD DO WAS THINK ABOUT ANDREA HOW EVERYTHING HAS BEEN GOING HOW EMOTIONAL THE TRAIL HAS BEEN AND STARTING TOMORROW IT IS GOING TO BE MORE HEART-BREAKING ANDREA IS GOING TO LET THE WHOLE WORLD KNOW EVERYTHING THAT HER PARENTS AND THOSE MEN DID TO HER, RANDY JUST SAT AT THE TABLE AND TEARS FELL FROM HIS EYES THEY WERE THE KIND OF TEARS THAT NO ONE CAN EXPLAIN SO MANY EMOTIONS WERE RACING THREW HIS HEAD HE NEVER THOUGHT THAT HE WOULD BE INVOLVED IN A RELATIONSHIP LIKE THIS, AS RANDY CLOSES HIS EYES HE FALLS INTO A DEEP SLEEP MORNING IS NEAR, AS ANDREA LOOKS OUT THE WINDOW, SHE MAKES A WISH UPON THE BRIGHTEST STAR WISHING THAT ALL OF THIS WILL SOON BE OVER, THE ATTORNEY SPENT THE REST OF THE NIGHT PREPARING THE LETTERS FOR TOMORROW'S TRAIL THESE LETTERS ARE A VITAL PART OF THE TRAIL AND THE ONE THAT IS GOING TO BE HURT MORE THAN ANYONE ELSE IS ANDREA AS SHE READ'S THE LETTERS SHE MUST EXPLAIN IN DETAIL EXACTLY WHAT HAPPENED THE NIGHT IN QUESTION IN THE LETTERS, FINALLY,

AT MIDNIGHT THE ATTORNEY FELL ASLEEP THE WHOLE WORLD SLEPT ONLY ANDREA COULD NOT SLEEP WELL, SHE TOSSED AND TURNED ALL NIGHT; MORNING IS HERE **LET'S LOOK ON AS ANDREA AND RANDY PREPARE** TO GO TO THE COURTHOUSE ANDREA RECEIVED A PHONE CALL, RANDY ANSWERED THE PHONE HELLO WHO SPEAKING HELLO RANDY IT IS ME JUDY MAY I SPEAK TO ANDREA MY LOVE IT IS JUDY SHE WANTS TO TALK TO YOU OK TELL HER TO GIVE ME A SECOND I'M GETTING READY JUDY ANDREA SAID GIVE HER A SECOND SHE IS GETTING READY, OH WAIT HERE SHE COMES HELLO JUDY WHATS ON YOUR MIND, WILL IT IS MY DAD WHATS GOING ON WITH YOUR DAD, I OVERHEARD HIM LAST NIGHT TALKING TO MY MOM SAYING HE WAS GOING TO KILL YOUR DAD OH NO JUDY YOU AND YOUR MOM NEED TO STOP HIM WE DO NOT NEED HIM GETTING IN TROUBLE THE LAW IS HANDLING THE CASE I KNOW WE TRIED TALKING TO HIM BUT HE IS NOT LISTENING TO US I WILL KEEP A CLOSE EYE ON HIM MAKING SURE HE DOES NOT DO NOTHING CRAZY, OK THANKS SEE YALL IN COURT WE ARE GETTING READY TO GO OK WE WILL SEE YOU THEIR SOON AS RANDY WALKS IN AND SAW HER HE ASKS HER WHAT IS WRONG IT IS JUDY'S DAD HE WANTS TO KILL MY DAD FOR WHAT HE DID TO HER, NO HE CAN'T DO THAT I WILL KEEP AN EYE ON HIM MAKING SURE HE DOES NOT THROW HIS LIFE AWAY THANKS RANDY, WE DO NOT NEED TO BE GOING TO ANOTHER MURDER TRIAL, ARE YOU READY YES, I AM **LET'S** GO I AM SURE THE ATTORNEY IS WAITING FOR US AT THE COURTHOUSE AS WE LEFT ALL WE COULD DO WAS JUST THINK ABOUT WHAT JUDY TOLD ME ABOUT HER DAD THIS WAS GOING TO BE A VERY INTERESTING DAY, WE ARE ALREADY 2 MONTHS INTO THE TRAIL IT IS GOING IN OUR FAVOR WE DO NOT NEED THIS TO INTERFERE WITH WHAT IS

GOING ON, RANDY, DO YOU THINK WE SHOULD TELL THE ATTORNEY WHAT JUDY TOLD ME YES, YOU NEED TO TELL HIM **BECAUSE IF YOU DON'T THEN IF HE DOES KILL HIM AND WE DID** NOT SAY ANYTHING WE CAN BE CHARGED AS ACCOMPLISHED TO THE MURDER AND YOUR CASE WILL BE LOST YES, YOU ARE RIGHT WE MUST TELL THE ATTORNEY AS WE GET TO THE COURTHOUSE, WE SEE THE ATTORNEY AT THE FRONT DOOR LOOKING AT SOME PAPERS GOOD MORNING MR MARTINEZ GOOD MORNING ANDREA AND RANDY, LOOK MR MARTINEZ I NEED TO TELL YOU SOMETHING VERY IMPORTANT WHAT IS GOING ON **COME HERE LET'S SIT DOWN WILL I TALK TO JUDY THIS** MORNING, SHE TOLD ME THAT HER DAD SAID HE WAS GOING TO KILL MY DAD HE WAS VERY MAD AND HURT AT THE FACT OF WHAT MY DAD DID TO JUDY, OH NO WE CAN NOT ALLOW THAT I WILL LET THE COURT KNOW THEY WILL STAND GUARD TO MAKE SURE, THIS DOES NOT HAPPEN SO ANDREA ARE YOU READY TO GO IN THIS IS YOUR BIG DAY YES, I **AM READY LET'S DO THIS AS WE** START WALKING IN, WE SEE JUDY AND HER PARENTS INSIDE ALREADY I WENT TO TALK TO JUDY AND TOLD HER THAT THE ATTORNEY KNEW HER DAD PLAN TO KILL MY DAD, JUDY THE COURTS KNOW THAT MR. LOPEZ WANTS TO KILL MY DAD I KNOW HE DESERVES IT WE HAVE TO LET JUSTICE BE SERVED THE RIGHT WAY YES ANDREA I AGREE WITH YOU JUSTICE WILL BE SERVED THE RIGHT WAY JUDY AND RANDY SAT BEHIND ANDREA AND ANDREA AND MR. MARTINEZ TOOK THEIR SEAT IN FRONT OF THE JUDGE, ALL RISE COURT WAS IN SESSION THE HONORABLE JUDGE WRIGHT PRESIDING ALL MAY BE SEATED GOODMORNIG COURT MR. MARTINEZ CALL YOUR FIRST WITNESS I CALL ANDREA GARCIA TO THE STAND DO YOU SWAR TO TELL THE WHOLE TRUTH AND NOTHING

BUT THE TRUTH, I DO YOU MAY BE SEATED AS ANDREA SITS DOWN THE COURTROOM DOOR OPENS SLOWLY ANDREA AND EVERYONE LOOK TO SEE WHO IT IS JUDY'S DAD WALKS IN AND GOES STRAIGHT TO ANDREA DAD AND PULLS OUT A GUN AND SPEAKS YOU WILL NEVER HURT ANOTHER CHILD BEFORE HE HAD A CHANCE TO PULL THE TRIGGER ANDREA YELLED NO STOP DO KILL HIM PLEASE JUSTICE WILL BE SERVED FOR YOUR DAUGHTER AND ME AND ALL THE KIDS HE HURT DO IT FOR YOUR DAUGHTER, SHE NEEDS YOU HERE WITH HER NOT IN PRISON AS ANDREA SAID THIS JUDY'S DAD DROPPED THE GUN AND DROPPED TO HIS KNEES IN TEARS AND SAID YOUR RIGHT, I'M SORRY AS THE COPS WERE TAKING HIM AWAY THE JUDGE SPOKE NO LET HIM GO, SIR, YOU MAY TAKE YOUR SEAT THANK YOU YOUR HONOR JUDY GOT UP FROM HER SEAT WALKED TOWARDS HER DAD GRABBED HIS HAND AND SAID COME ON DAD LET'S GO

SIT DOWN JUSTICE WILL BE SERVE AS THEY WERE SITTING DOWN ATTORNEY MARTINEZ STARTED TALKING TO ANDREA. CAN YOU STATE YOUR NAME FOR THE COURT, MY NAME IS ANDREA GARCIA, ANDREA DID YOUR PARENTS ABUSE YOU, OBEJECTON YOUR HONOR LEADING THE WITNESS, SUSTAIN MR. MARTINEZ MAKES THE QUESTION CLEARER ANDREA CAN YOU TELL THE COURT WHY YOU ARE HERE TODAY, I AM HERE TO GET JUSTICE, JUSTICE FOR WHAT PLEASE BE SPECIFIC ABOUT THE ABUSE AND ASSAULT MY PARENTS CAUSED ME ALL THE YEARS OF MY CHILDHOOD, STARTING WHEN I WAS ONLY 9 YRS OLD, ANDREA I HAVE HERE IN MY HANDS LETTERS THAT YOU WROTE TO ROBERT I AM GOING TO GIVE YOU THE LETTERS ONE AT A TIME AND EXPLAIN WHAT HAPPEN ON THOSE DAYS IN QUESTION, OBJECTION YOUR HONOR

HOW DO WE KNOW THOSE LETTERS ARE TRUE IF THAT DID HAPPEN AS IT IS WRITTEN IN THE LETTERS, YOUR HONOR I ALSO HAVE THE MEDICAL RECORDS FROM THE HOSPITAL THAT WILL BACK UP THIS TESTIMONY ALL THE FACTS ARE HERE OVERRULE BEGAN MR. MARTINEZ YES, YOUR HONOR OK ANDREA ARE YOU PREPARED FOR THE FIRST LETTER YES, I AM ANDREA'S HAND WAS SHAKING AS THE ATTORNEY WAS GIVING HER THE LETTER, AND SHE GRABBED THE LETTER IN HER HAND ANDREA STAYED QUITE FOR A FEW SECONDS THEN SHE OPENED THE LETTER AS SHE SAW THE WORDS ON THAT LETTER TEARS FLOWED FROM HER EYES AND THE ATTORNEY ASKED ANDREA TO EXPLAIN THE LETTER SHE WROTE, OK THIS LETTER IS DATED OCTOBER 12, 1977, HELLO ROBERT: HOW ARE YOU DOING AS FOR ME, I DON'T KNOW I AM IN PAIN DOWN THERE MY DADDY WAS PLAYING WITH ME ROUGH HE SAID WE ARE GOING TO PLAY A GAME THAT DADDY AND DAUGHTERS PLAY IT IS OUR GAME OUR SECRET DON'T TELL NO ONE, SO, I SAID OK DADDY WON'T TELL WE ARE GOING TO PLAYHOUSE AND YOU ARE MY PRETEND WIFE YOU WILL HAVE FUN IN THE GAME OK DADDY HOW YOU PLAY THE FIRST THING A WIFE DOES IS MAKE HER HUSBAND HAPPY YOU WANT TO MAKE DADDY HAPPY RIGHT YES, DADDY OK DO WHAT DADDY SAYS AND YOU WILL MAKE ME HAPPY THEN HE GOT ON TOP OF ME AND HE HURT ME I SAW SOMETHING RED, AND IT HURTS TO WALK WHY DID DADDY HURT ME TALK TO YOU TOMORROW BYE, THIS IS THE FIRST LETTER I WROTE TO ROBERT, ANDREA IN YOUR OWN WORDS TELL US EXACTLY HOW AND WHAT HAPPENED THAT DAY, WILL I WAS IN THE KITCHEN WITH MOM, AND HE HAD JUST GOT HOME FROM WORK, HE CAME TO ME AND PICKED ME UP AND KISSED ME ON MY LIPS AND SQUEEZED MY BOTTOM, LATER ON, THAT NIGHT WHEN MY MOM FELL

ASLEEP, HE CAME INTO MY ROOM AND ABUSED ME, I WAS ONLY 10 YEARS OLD AND ANDREA LOOKED AT HER PARENTS AND SAID HOW COULD YOU BOTH DO THIS TO ME I WAS JUST A KID 10 YEARS OLD, YOU BOTH ARE EVIL PEOPLE AND YOU BOTH WILL GET WHAT YOU ALL DESERVE, I HAVE NO FURTHER QUESTIONS, MR. SANCHEZ WOULD YOU LIKE TO CROSS-EXAMINE, YES, YOUR HONOR I WOULD THE ATTORNEY TOOK A MOMENT TO GET UP AND THE JUDGE ASKED HIM AGAIN MR. SANCHEZ WOULD YOU LIKE TO SPEAK TO THE WITNESS YES, YOUR HONOR, AS HE GETS UP TO GO QUESTION ANDREA, HE IS SMIRKING WOW I HEARD SOME STORIES IN THE PASS BUT THIS IS THE BEST, WHY WOULD YOUR DAD DO THAT TO YOU ON HIS CHILD, YOU HAVE AN IMAGINATION, HOW MANY MORE STORIES ARE YOU GOING TO TELL, OBJECTION YOUR HONOR SPECULATING IS THEIR A QUESTION HERE, SUSTAIN MR. SANCHEZ WHAT IS THE QUESTION ANDREA IS IT TRUE THAT YOU WERE ALWAYS

GETTING IN TROUBLE AS YOU WERE GROWING UP AND YOUR PARENTS TRY TO GIVE YOU A GOOD LIFE AND ACTUALLY, YOU ARE THE ONE THAT REJECTED THEM AFTER EVERYTHING THEY DID FOR YOU, THE WAY, YOU PAY THEM BACK IS BY TRYING TO HAVE THEM SENT TO PRISON FOR THE REST OF THERE LIVES, NO YOU ARE WRONG MR. SANCHEZ YOU WERE NOT THERE WHEN ALL OF THIS WAS HAPPENING TO ME YOU WERE NOT THERE WHEN I WOULD WAKE UP AT NIGHT IN A DEEP SWEAT CRYING AND HUGGING MY PILLOW SCARED EVERY TIME THE DOOR OPENED THINKING IT WAS MY DAD OR MY MOM OR ANOTHER MAN TAKING ADVANTAGE OF ME OR HITTING ME, **SO DON'T YOU** SIT THERE IN YOUR THRIFT STORE SUIT YOU KNOW NOTHING THE ONLY THING YOU KNOW IS WHAT THOSE TWO MONSTERS TOLD

YOU BUT YOU WILL SEE ALL THE TRUTH IS COMING OUT AFTER ANDREA SAID THIS THE ATTORNEY SAID NO MORE QUESTIONS YOU MAY STEP DOWN AS ANDREA WALKED BACK TO HER SEAT, SHE LOOKED AT HER PARENTS WITH SO MUCH HATE ANDREA YOU DID GREAT UP THERE I WILL BE CALLING YOU BACK TO THE STAND LATER ON, I AM READY FOR ALL OF THIS TO BE OVER WITH HOW MUCH LONGER IS ALL OF THIS GOING TO LAST WILL THE WAY, IT LOOKS I FEEL IT WILL BE OVER SOONER THEN YOU THINK JUST KEEP YOUR HEAD UP AND YOU WILL SEE ALL WILL COME TO PASS; MY LOVE YOU WERE WONDERFUL UP THERE I KNOW IT WAS HARD FOR YOU TO TALK ABOUT YOUR PASS AND WHEN THIS IS OVER YOU WILL NEVER HAVE TO DEAL WITH THEM AGAIN, MY LOVE SOON IT WILL BE OVER I PROMISE, AS RANDY SPOKE TO ANDREA ALL SHE COULD DO WAS THINK THAT IT WOULD ALL BE OVER SOON, AS ANDREA GRABBED HER SEAT THE JUDGE SAID, " MR SANCHEZ CALL YOUR FIRST WITNESS, I CALL MRS. GARCIA

ANDREA'S MOM GETS UP TO TAKE THE STAND LOOKS TOWARD ANDREA AND JUST SMILES DO YOU SWEAR TO TELL THE TRUTH THE WHOLE TRUTH AND NOTHING BUT THE TRUTH SO HELP YOU GOD, I DO, I DO, YOU MAY BE SEATED, CAN YOU TELL ME IN YOUR OWN WORDS EVERYTHING THAT WENT ON IN YOUR HOUSE, EVERY DETAIL WILL THE LIES STARTED WHEN SHE WAS ABOUT 9 YEARS OLD WHEN SHE DID NOT GET HER WAY SHE WOULD LIE AND SAY THAT WE ABUSED HER THE LIES CONTINUED ALL HER LIFE, WE TRIED TO BE GOOD PARENTS BUT HOW CAN YOU BE A GOOD PARENT TO A CHILD WHO IS REBELLIOUS TOWARDS HER PARENTS AND NOT WANTING TO DO AS WE ASK HER, WE WERE GOOD TO OUR CHILD ANDREA, I DO NOT KNOW WHY SHE IS DOING THIS I KNOW

IT IS THAT BOY THAT SHE IS WITH WHO IS PUTTING HER UP TO THIS SHE WAS A GOOD GIRL UNTIL SHE MET HIM OBJECTION YOUR HONOR SPECULATIVE IT IS HER OWN OPINION THERE IS NO EVIDENCE TO BACK UP HER STATEMENT, OVERRULE MR. SANCHEZ WARNED YOUR CLIENT TO STICK TO THE FACTS, YES, YOUR HONOR, SO MRS. GARCIA WHEN DID YOU NOTICE A CHANGE IN ATTITUDE, I NOTICED THAT THE FOLLOWING DAY AFTER I LET HER GO STAY THE NIGHT AT HER FRIEND'S HOUSE, SHE STARTED ACTING UP THANK YOU MRS. GARCIA NO FURTHER QUESTIONS MR. MARTINEZ WOULD YOU LIKE TO CROSS YES, I WOULD YOUR HONOR, I WOULD LIKE TO ASK HER QUESTIONS, MRS. GARCIA YOU STATED THAT ANDREA'S ATTITUDE CHANGED, DO YOU REMEMBER EXACTLY WHAT DAY THAT WAS AND REMEMBER YOUR UNDER-OATH NO I DO NOT RECALL IT HAS BEEN SUCH A LONG TIME AGO MAYBE I CAN REFRESH YOUR MEMORY IT WAS OCTOBER 12, 1977, THE FIRST TIME THAT YOUR HUSBAND ABUSE HER THAT IS WHY SHE WANTED TO LEAVE SHE NEEDED TO GO TO THE HOSPITAL AND INSTEAD OF HELPING HER YALL ABUSED HER, WILL SHE DID GO TO THE HOSPITAL HER FRIEND'S MOM TOOK HER AND I HAVE THE DR. REPORT HERE IN MY HAND SHOULD I READ IT TO THE COURT, OR ARE YOU GOING TO COME CLEAN AND TELL US THE TRUTH, OK I WILL READ THE REPORT MEDICAL RECORDS FOR ANDREA GARCIA DATED OCTOBER 13, 1977 ANDREA WAS ADMITTED TO THE HOSPITAL, AND SEEN BY DR. MORALES ANDREA COMPLAINED OF INTERNAL PAIN IN HER STOMACH, AND HER PRIVATE PART AFTER FUTURE TESTS ANDREA WAS DIAGNOSED AND THE RESULT OF THE EXAMINATION, THAT ANDREA SUFFERED FROM BEING MOLESTED BY A FAMILY MEMBER, OBJECTION YOUR HONOR, IS MR. MARTINEZ

SPEAKING FACTS OR ASSUMING THAT WAS THE MEDICAL CAUSE, YOUR HONOR I HAVE THE HOSPITAL REPORT HERE IN MY HAND, NOW MRS. GARCIA YOU KNOW WHAT HAPPENED THAT NIGHT AND INSTEAD OF HELPING YOUR CHILD, YOU TRY TO COVER UP FOR YOUR HUSBAND, AS MRS GARCIA SITS THERE SHE HAS NOTHING TO SAY THEN THE ATTORNEY SAID I HAVE NO FURTHER QUESTIONS YOU MAY STEP DOWN MRS. GARCIA. AS ANDREA MOM STEPS DOWN EVERYONE WAS JUST LOOKING AT HER WITH SO MUCH HATE THEN THE JUDGE SAID MR. MARTINEZ CALL YOUR NEXT WITNESS, YOUR HONOR MY WITNESS HAS NOT MADE IT HERE CAN WE GET A CONTINUES, THE COURT ADJOURNED TIL 9 IN THE MORNING, ALL RISE AS THE HONORABLE JUDGE LEAVES, AND THE COURTROOM IS DISMISSED AS EVERYONE LEAVES THE COURTROOM RANDY STAYS QUIET AND ANDREA LOOKED AT RANDY SAYING RANDY WHAT IS ON YOUR MIND YOU HAVE NOT SAID ANYTHING ALL DAY WHAT ARE YOU THINKING ABOUTI WAS JUST THINKING ABOUT YOUR BROTHER, WHAT ABOUT MY **BROTHER THAT'S IT YOU HAVE NOT SEEN HIM SINCE WHEN** I HAVE NOT SEEN MY BROTHER WAS 9 YEARS OLD, THE LAST TIME I SAW HIM SO HE IS ABOUT 13 YEARS OLD RIGHT NOW I WISH I COULD SEE HIM NO TELLING WHERE HE IS, ONLY GOD KNOWS MY **LOVE LET'S JUST PRAY THAT HE RETURNS SOON, AND THEN YOU** WILL GET ALL THE ANSWERS THAT YOU HAVE BEEN SEARCHING FOR, AS FOR NOW WE NEED TO HAVE A MEETING WITH THE ATTORNEY AND SEE WHAT IS THE PLAN FOR TOMORROW, AS WE WENT AND TALKED TO THE ATTORNEY, ALL WE COULD DO WAS THINK ABOUT WHERE ANDREA'S BROTHER WAS, AND HOW HE WAS DOING.MR. SANCHEZ WHAT IS THE PLAN FOR TOMORROW, YOU KNOW WE HAVE BEEN GOING TO COURT ON THE MATTER FOR ALMOST A

YEAR ALREADY TOMORROW COULD BE THE LAST DAY IF THINGS GO AS PLANNED, SO TOMORROW WE WILL LAY EVERYTHING ON THE TABLE, THE TRAIL IS GOING IN OUR FAVOR, YOU HAVE NOTHING TO WORRY ABOUT ANDREA YOU HAVE THIS CASE WON, AND NOW WITH YOUR BROTHER TESTIMONY TOMORROW WILL PUT THE FINISHING TOUCHES ON THE TRAIL, I WILL GET WITH HIM EARLY IN THE MORNING AND GIVE HIM A RUN DOWN OF WHAT TO EXPECT WHEN HE GOES ON THE STAND SINCE HE IS STILL A MINOR, I WOULD NEED THE JUDGE'S APPROVAL FOR YOUR BROTHER TO TESTIFY, I AM SURE I WILL GET IT SO WE HAVE NO WORRY THERE NOW ANDREA, I WILL CALL YOU FIRST TO THE STAND MY BROTHER HOW DO YOU KNOW MY BROTHER WHERE HE IS YOU FOUND HIM I NEED TO TALK TO HIM, YES ANDREA HE REACHED OUT TO ME THE OTHER DAY IT WAS GOING TO BE A SURPRISE WHEN HE CAME BACK TO TOWN AND I TOLD HIM TO WAIT FOR TOMORROW TO SEE YOU WE WANTED

THIS DAY TO BE A DAY TO REMEMBER NOW AFTER YOUR TESTIMONY, I WILL CALL YOUR BROTHER TO THE STAND, AFTER THAT THE CASE SHOULD COME TO AN END WILL THEY BE SENDING MY PARENTS TO PRISON YES ANDREA YOUR PARENTS WILL GO TO PRISON FOR HOW LONG ONLY THE JUDGE KNOWS OK MR. SANCHEZ I WILL SEE YOU TOMORROW I AM GOING TO GO TALK TO MY BROTHER TOMORROW WE HAVE A LOT OF CATCHING UP TO DO, HAVE A GOOD NIGHT AND I WILL SPEAK TO YOU IN THE MORNING, YES GOOD NIGHT MR. SANCHEZ SEE YOU IN THE MORNING AS WE STARTED TO GO BACK TO THE HOUSE ALL ANDEREA COULD DO WAS THINK ABOUT WHERE HER BROTHER HAD BEEN ALL THESE YEARS AS I LOOK AT ANDREA, I SEE TEARS COMING OUT OF HER EYES ANDREA WHY ARE YOU

CRYING, YOU KNOW RANDY I HONESTLY THOUGHT THAT I WOULD NEVER SEE MY BROTHER AGAIN AND HOW DID HE KNOW TO COME TO THE COURTHOUSE AT THE RIGHT TIME WHEN I NEEDED SOMEONE BY MY SIDE WHO WAS THERE WITH ME AND SAW ALL THE ABUSE, I WAS EXPERIENCING THANK YOU, JESUS CHRIST, FOR ANSWERING MY PRAYERS AND HELPING ME FIND FREEDOM FROM ALL THE PAIN, WILL ANDREA I GUESS WE WILL SOON FIND OUT HOW YOUR BROTHER KNOWS ABOUT THIS AND WHAT ELSE HE KNOWS, I DO NOT HAVE NO MEMORIES HAPPY MEMORIES OF US GROWING UP, I WAS ALWAYS LEFT IN THE DARK ABOUT EVERYTHING, MY PARENTS TREATED ME LIKE TRASH AND TREATED THEM WITH LOVE, BUT NOW ALL OF THAT HAS COME TO AN END I WILL NEVER GET THOSE DAYSBACK NO ANDREA YOU WILL NOT GET THE PASS BACK BUT YOU CAN HAVE A NEW START WITH YOUR BROTHER YES, RANDY I CAN NOT WAIT TO SEE **HIM TOMORROW AND TALK TO HIM OK WE ARE HOME LET'S GO** TO BED I AM TIRED YES, MY LOVE I AM TIRED TO GOOD NIGHT AND TOMORROW WHEN YOU SEE HIM YOU WILL THEN START A NEW LIFE WITH YOUR BROTHER THAT YOU HAVE NOT SEEN AND CREATE HAPPY MEMORIES OF YOU AND HIM, AS ANDREA LAY IN HER BED THINKING BOUT HER BROTHER AND WHERE HE HAS BEEN AND HOW HE HAS BEEN THE WHOLE TIME HE WAS GONE I KNOW IT IS GOING TO BE AN EMOTIONAL MOMENT FOR BOTH OF YALL SO JUST TAKE YOUR TIME AND SPEND QUALITY TIME WITH HIM ASK HIM ALL KINDS OF QUESTIONS ESPECIALLY ABOUT THE TIME HE WAS THERE AT THE HOUSE WITH YOU, OK RANDY I WILL IT IS **ALMOST MORNING TIME LET'S GET SOME REST** WE HAVE TO BE AT THE COURTHOUSE EARLY I AM SURE MY BROTHER WILL BE ONE OF **THE FIRST ONE'S THERE HE LIKES**

TO BE EARLY FOR EVERYTHING SO LET US REST AND WE WILL TALK IN THE MORNING AS ANDREA FINALLY FELL ASLEEP, SHE COULD NOT SLEEP ALL SHE COULD DO WAS THINK ABOUT HER BROTHER WHOM SHE HAD NOT SEEN IN A FEW YEARS AS THEY WAKE UP WE WILL SEE HOW THE DAY GOES NOW THAT HER BROTHER IS BACK IN HER LIFE SHE FEELS HER LIFE IS ALMOST COMPLETE **GOOD MORNING RANDY GOOD MORNING ANDREA LET'S GET** READY WE HAVE TO BE IN THE COURT REAL SOON I AM READY I AM JUST WAITING ON YOU I AM READY TO GO AS ANDREA AND RANDY HEAD TOWARDS THE COURTHOUSE ANDREA IS QUIET JUST THINKING ABOUT FINALLY BEING ABLE TO SEE HER BROTHER WILL RANDY HERE WE ARE AT THE COURTHOUSE YES, WE ARE AND LOOK OVER THERE, WHERE ANDREA RIGHT THERE WITH THE ATTORNEY, I BELIEVE THAT IS YOUR BROTHER ANDREA COULD NOT MOVE GO AND TALK TO HIM IT WILL BE OK ANDY AND ANDREA, COULD NOT TAKE THEIR EYES OFF EACH OTHER THEY STAYED THERE FOR A GOOD BIT JUST THEY LOOK AT EACH OTHER FOR A BIT THEN THEY START GETTING TEARS IN THEIR EYES AND THEY HUG EACH OTHER, ANDREA ASKED HER BROTHER ANDY WHERE DID YOU GO, ANDREA IT HURT ME TO LEAVE YOU IN ALL OF THAT PAIN AND ABUSE, I WAS JUST LITTLE KID, I COULD NOT DO ANYTHING TO HELP YOU, AND EVERY TIME THEY DID THINGS TO YOU I WAS SCARED AND I WOULD HIDE UNDER MY BLANKETS AND CRY FOR SOMEONE TO COME AND HELP YOU, ANDY, YOU LEFT ME THERE WITH THOSE MONSTERS WHERE DID YOU GO AFTER I LEFT THE HOUSE; I DID NOT KNOW WHAT I WAS GOING TO DO AFTER ALL I WAS JUST A LITTLE KID I WAS WALKING DOWN OUR STREET IN FEAR NOT KNOWING WHERE I WAS GOING AND I ENDED UP AT MY BEST FRIEND'S HOUSE I SAT ON HIS FRONT PORCH IN TEARS

AS I WAS CRYING MY EYES OUT HIS MOM CAME OUT AND SAID OH NO WHAT IS WRONG COME INSIDE WHAT HAPPENED, I CAN NOT TAKE IT MY PARENTS ABUSE ANDREA EVERY DAY FOR NO REASON AND I AM SCARED THEY ARE GOING TO ABUSE ME TOPLEASE LET ME STAY WITH YALL DON'T MAKE ME GO BACK TO THE HOUSE OF TORTURE OK YOU CAN STAY HERE, SO THAT IS WHERE I BEEN FOR THE PAST FEW YEARS, WHY DIDN'T YOU EVER COME BACK FOR ME, WHY DID YOU LET ME SUFFER NO ANDREA I COULD NOT DO ANYTHING BUT I AM HERE NOW I KNOW IT'S LATE BUT I AM HERE FOR YOU NOW, AND I AM SO SORRY I LEFT YOU THE WAYI DID IT IS OK BROTHER THE IMPORTANT THING IS THAT YOU ARE BACK AND WE CAN START A NEW LIFE TOGETHER YOUR MY LITTLE BROTHERI LOVE YOU YES SISTER, I LOVE YOU AND WOW YOU STIR THINGS UP I'VE NEVER SEEN ANYONE AS MUCH TROUBLE AS MOM AND DAD ARE SO WHAT DID THE ATTORNEY SAY ABOUT HOW MUCH TIME THEY ARE GETTING IN PRISON; HE IS LOOKING AT 50 YEARS FOR DAD AND 30 YEARS FOR MOM, BUT WE WILL WAIT AND SEE WHAT THE JUDGE DECIDES ANYWAY IT IS GETTING LATE TIME TO GO INSIDE THE COURTHOUSE ATTORNEY IS GOING TO TALK TO YOU AND LET YOU KNOW ABOUT THE TRIAL AND THE QUESTIONS HE IS GOING TO ASK YOU AS YOU TAKE THE STAND ARE YOU READY FOR THIS YOU TESTIMONY IS GOING TO BE AS IMPORTANT AS MIND IS SO MAKE SURE YOU TELL THE WHOLE TRUTH WE DO NOT NEED A MISTRAIL AND LET THOSES TWO MONSTERS ESCAPE THE ATTORNEY SAID I HAVE THIS CASE WON SO LET US STAND TOGETHER AND FINISH THIS THAT WAS STARTED CLOSE TO AN YEAR AGO WOW ANDREA THIS HAS BEEN GOING ON FOR ALMOST A YEAR YES ANDY IT HAS AND AGAIN A AM GLAD YOU ARE HERE LIKE I SAID I MISS YOU SO MUCH SO, TALK TO THE

ATTORNEY AND HE WILL LET YOU KNOW EVERYTHING HE IS GOING TO QUESTION YOU ON AND I JUST WANT THIS TO BE OVER WITH I AM READY TO PUT THIS BEHIND ME AND START MY LIFE FREE AND HAPPY WITH THE PEOPLE THAT I LOVE AND THAT TRULY LOVE ME YES SISTER THAT IS WHY I CAME BACK SO I COULD BE WITH YOU AND WE START OUR LIFE TOGETHER I WANT A HAPPY LIFE WITH MY SISTER YOU WILL WIN THIS AND THEN AFTERWARDS WE WILL GO BACK TO YOUR GRANDMA HOUSE AND WE WILL BE HAPPY AND FREE YES

CHAPTER 9   THE FINAL VERDICT

BROTHER WE WILL AND I KNW IT WILL TURN OUT GREAT THE ATTORNEY SAID THAT AFTER TODAY IT MIGHT BE OVER WITH AND WE WILL SEE WHAT IS GOING TO HAPPEN TODAY AFTER MY TESTIMONY AND YOUR TESTIMONY THAT WILL BE ALL THE COURT NEEDS TO PUT THE MONSTERS AWAY FOR GOOD YES, SISTER THIS IS TRUE WILL IT IS GETTING LATE TIME TO GET INSIDE THE COURTROOM I AM SURE EVERYONE IS ALREADY IN THERE WAITING FOR US I AM READY JUST MAKE SURE YOU AND RANDY ARE READY TO DO WHAT WE NEED TO DO THAT WE MAY HAVE VICTORY ALL ANDREA COULD DO WAS JUST THINK ABOUT WHAT WAS GOING TO

HAPPEN WHICH WILL BE THE MOST IMPORTANT PART OF THE TRAIL AS THE WHOLE WORLD LOOKS ON IN THE COURTROOM ANDREA'S BROTHER IS SITTING THERE AS HE SPEAKS HURTFUL WORDS, I CAN NOT BELIEVE I STOOD BACK AND LET MY PARENTS CAUSE ALL THAT PAIN AND SUFFERING TO MY SISTER ANDREA DID NOT DESERVE THIS SHE IS A GOOD PERSON WITH A BEAUTIFUL HEART AND I WILL MAKE SURE THEY GET WHAT THEY HAVE COMING TO THEM, ONLY IF I WAS A LITTLE OLDER BACK THEN I COULD HAVE HELPED HER I PRAY SHE FORGIVES ME AS ANDY SITS THERE IN TEARS ANDREA GOES TO HIM ANDY, I FORGIVE YOU IT WAS NOT YOUR FAULT YOU WERE JUST A YOUNG BOY; YOU WERE SCARED AND DID NOT KNOW WHAT TO DO, THE PAST IS OVER WITH NOW WE MUST FOCUS ON THE FUTURE AND GETTING TO KNOW EACH OTHER AGAIN, I FORGOT TO TELL YOU WHEN WE ARE DONE HERE WITH THE COURT AND RANDY IS WITH ME WE ARE GOING TO GO STAY WITH OUR AUNT AND GRANDMA, YOU HAVE NOT MEET THEM I

TELL YOU BROTHER THEY ARE WONDERFUL PEOPLE FULL OF LOVE AND HAPPINESS, WOULD YOU LIKE TO COME AND LIVE WITH US THERE WITH THEM YES, THAT WILL BE GREAT, OK **ANDREA LET'S GO TALK TO THE ATTORNEY AND SEE WHAT HE** HAS PLANNED FOR THIS IMPORTANT DAY THIS IS IMPORTANT DAY IN COURT, YES, IT IS HELLO MR MARTINEZ ANDREA AND THIS MUST BE ANDY YES SIR IT IS ME HOW ARETHINGS GOING EVERYTHING GOING AS PLANNED AND WITH YOUR TESTIMONY THIS WILL BE THE LAST DAD IN COURT AND ANDREA WILL GET HER VICTORY AS ANDREA AND ANDY ARE TALKING RANDY RECEIVES A PHONE CALL AT THE COURTHOUSE RANDY YOU HAVE A CALL WAITING FOR YOU IN THE LOBBY ANDREA I WILL BE RIGHT BACK I HAVE A CALL WAITING

FOR ME AND I DO NOT KNOW WHO IT COULD BE
I WILL BE RIGHT BACK AS RANDY WALKS DOWN
THE HALL WONDERING WHO COULD BE
CALLING HIM AT THE COURTHOUSE HE GET'S TO
THE PHONE AND PICKS IT UP NOT SAYING A WORD
THEN FINALLY HE SPEAKS IN A LOW VOICE
HELLO THIS IS RANDY HOW ARE YOU DOING
RANDY IM DETECTIVE SMITH, I JUST CALLED TO
INFORM YOU THAT YOUR TRIAL WILL BE IN TWO
WEEKS JUST MAKE SURE YOU ARE PREPARED
AND I NEED YOUR GIRLFRIEND ANDREA THERE
WITH YOU I WILL BE THERE HAVE TO GO I IM IN
COURT RIGHT NOW WITH ANDREA THIS SHOULD
BE THE LAST DAY IN COURT, AS RANDY HANGS
UP THE PHONE HIS HAND STAY'S ON THE PHONE AND
STARTED TO THINK ABOUT THE UP COMING DAY'S
WHEN HE WILL HAVE TO GO TO COURT THEN HE
SAY'S IT STARTING ALL OVER AGAIN AS HE STARTS
WALING DOWN THE HALL AND GOES TO TALK
TO ANDREA ABOUT THE PHONE CALL THE
ATTORNEY INSTRUCTS THEM TO GO INSIDE
ANDREA LOOKS ON IN THE COURTROOM LOOK
RANDY MY CASE IS JUST STARTING, I HOPE
THAT ALL OF THIS WILL BE OVER SOON,
ANDREA I AM HERE BY YOUR SIDE AS ANDY
TALKS TO THE ATTORNEY, ONCE AGAIN BEFORE
THEY GO INTO THE COURTROOM ANDREA
TELLS RANDY, YOU KNOW YOU SAVED MY LIFE I
WILL ALWAYS LOVE YOU, AND LIKE THE WIND I
KNOW THAT YOU WILL ALWAYS BE THERE FOR
ME AND WITH ME YES ANDREA YOU ARE
MYEVERYTHING, I AM BLESSED TO HAVE YOU
AS WE WALK INTO THE COURTROOM, I SEE MY
PARENTS SITTING THERE AND FOR THE FIRST
TIME I SEE THEM IN TEARS AS I SMILE AND
WALK AWAY THEY LOOK AT ME AND SAID TO
ME, WE ARE SORRY FOR ALL THE PAIN AND
ABUSE WE PUT YOU THREW I JUST LOOKED AT
THEM SMILED AND DID NOT SAY A WORD, THEN
WHEN THEY SAW ANDY WALK IN MY MOM
STARTED CRYING OUT LOUD AND SAID MY SON

YOU ARE HERE TO HELP DEFEND YOUR MOM AND DAD HE SMILE AND SAID NO MOM I AM HERE FOR ANDREA ALL THE PAIN YOU BOTH CAUSE HER FOR NO REASON WAS NOT RIGHT AND NOW YOU BOTH WILL PAY FOR THE PAIN YALL CAUSED ANDREA AND THE OTHER KIDS AFTER ANDY SAID THIS, HE WENT TO SIT DOWN BEHIND ANDREA, AS THE JUDGE WALKS IN ALL RISE COURT IN SESSION THE HONORABLE JUDGE WRIGHT PRESIDING ALL MAY BE SEATED, GOOD MORNING COURT GOOD MORNING JUDGE, MR. MARTINEZ IS YOUR WITNESS READY YES, YOUR HONOR CALL YOUR FIRST WITNESS, I CALL ANDREA TO THE STAND, AS ANDREA STARTS WALKING TOWARDS THE STAND THE OTHER ATTORNEY SPEAKS OBJECTION YOUR HONOR THIS WITNESS ALREADY HAD THEIR TIME ON THE STAND I SEE NO NEED FOR THIS WITNESS TO BE CALLED AGAIN, OVERRULE, ANDREA YOU MAY TAKE THE STAND AND REMEMBER YOU ARE STILL UNDER OATH YES, YOUR HONOR, ANDREA I HAVE IN MY HAND A SECOND LETTER YOU WROTE TO ROBERT CAN YOU

PLEASE READ IT TO THE COURT AND EXPLAIN THE EXPERIENCE THAT YOU WENT THROUGH THE DAY IN QUESTION THIS LETTER IS DATED JULY 23, 1978, HELLO ROBERT I AM HERE IN MY ROOM IN PAIN TRYING TO STOP THE BLEEDING IT HURTS SO MUCH TO WALK MY DAD OVER DID IT THIS TIME, I GOT HOME A LITTLE LATE FROM SCHOOL AND MY MOM SLAPPED ME WHEN I WALKED IN AND SAID YOUR WORTHLESS, AND YOU ARE LATE GO TO YOUR ROOM AND GET READY FOR WHAT YOU HAVE COMING TO YOU, AS I WAS WALKING TO MY ROOM, I SAW MY DAD AND HIS TWO FRIENDS LOOKING AT ME FROM HEAD TO TOE LICKING THEIR LIPS I GOT SCARED, I WENT INTO MY ROOM AND I STARTED CRYING, THEN THEY CAME IN ONE AT A TIME

ROBERT THEY HURT ME, I BEGGED THEM TO STOP AND THEY ALL JUST LAUGHED AT ME, THE WORST PART WAS WHEN THEY FINISHED MY DAD CAME IN AND DID THE SAME THING AND MY MOM JUST LAUGH SAYING THAT IS WHAT YOU GET NOW WE HAVE ENOUGH MONEY TO BUY OUR DRUGS AND ALCOHOL IF I DO NOT SHOW UP TO SCHOOL TOMORROW THEN I KILLED MYSELF I CAN NOT TAKE THIS ANYMORE PLEASE SOMEONE HELP ME GET ME OUT OF THIS TORTURE HELP ME, LORD, IS THAT THE END ANDREA YES, IT IS HOW YOU FEEL AND WHAT WAS GOING THREW YOUR MIND WHEN ALL OF THIS WAS GOING ON LIKE IT WAS ALL MY FAULT, AND I WAS THINKING ABOUT HOW COULD MY PARENTS ALLOW THIS TO HAPPEN TO ME AND HOW COULD MY DAD DO THIS TO ME I NEVER THOUGHT A DAD COULD DO THAT TO HIS DAUGHTER BUT IT HAPPENED TO ME, I PRAY THAT THIS KIND OF ABUSE NEVER HAPPENS TO ANOTHER GIRL, I HAVE NO MORE QUESTIONS, MR SANCHEZ WOULD YOU LIKE TO CROSSEXAMINE YES, YOUR HONOR I WOULD, ANDREA HOW YOU ARE FEELING I AM OK I JUST WANT THIS TO BE OVER WITH YES, I KNOW YOU DO SO LET ME ASK YOU THIS HOW DID YOU DRESS IN FRONT OF YOUR DAD, OBJECTION YOUR HONOR HER WARDROBE IS NOT ON TRIAL HERE, YOUR HONOR, THE WAY SHE DRESSED COULD OF TRIGGER HOW HER DAD LOOKED AT HER SUSTAIN CHANGE THE QUESTION MR SANCHEZ, YES, YOUR HONOR DID YOU EVER GIVE YOUR DAD ANY REASON TO DO THIS TO YOU, NO I DID NOT THEY ARE JUST MOSTERS THAT NEED TO BE PUT AWAY NO FURTHER QUSTIONS YOU CAN STEP DOWN ANDREA MR. MARTINEZ CALL YOUR NEXT WITNESS I CALL ANDY GARCIA TO THE STAND, ANDY DO YOU SWEAR TO TELL THE TRUTH THE WHOLE TRUTH AND NOTHING BUT THE TRUTH I DO YOU MAY BE SEATED ANDY CAN YOU TELL

ME IN YOUR OWN WORDS WHAT HAPPENED TO YOUR SISTER AND WHAT YOU HEAR OR SAW, WILL THAT NIGHT I HEARD HER CRY AND SCREAM I GOT SCARE SO I WENT TO HER ROOM TO SEE WHAT HAD HAPPENED AND I SAW MY DAD WALKING OUT OF HER ROOM AND I SAW HER ON THE BED HOLDING HER STOMACH AND THE BED WAS FULL OF BLOOD I WAS SCARED WHEN I SAW THAT I WENT TO TELL MY MOM WHAT I SAW AND SHE JUST LOOKED AT ME AND SAID IS ANDREA DEAD I SAID NO BUT SHE IS BLEEDING A LOT GET OUT OF MY ROOM I AM NOT WORRIED ABOUT HER NOW GO BACK TO BED AND LEAVE ME ALONE, AFTER I WENT BACK TO ANDREA'S ROOM AND TRIED TO HELP HER AS MUCH AS I COULD HOW OLD WERE YOU I WAS ONLY 9 YEARS OLD, AND ANDREA WAS ONLY 11 YEARS OLD AND WHEN SHE TURNED 12 YEARS OLD THINGS GOT WORSE HOW ANDY TELL ME WHAT MADE IT WORSE MY PARENTS STARTED DRINKING MORE AND MORE AND DOING MORE DRUGS THAN BEFORE THEY HAD ALL KINDS OF MAN COME OVER TO THE HOUSE AND GO INTO

ANDREA'S ROOM, I COULD NOT TAKE IT ANYMORE EVERY DAY WAS DIFFERENT MAN, ONE DAY I TRIED TO STOP THEM BUT MY DAD SLAPPED **ME AND SAID DON'T YOU DARE INTERFERE WITH** OUR MONEY NOW GO TO YOUR ROOM AND DO NOT COME OUT UNTIL WE TELL YOU TO, I SAT IN MY ROOM AND I COULD JUST HEAR MY SISTER CRY AND PLEAD FOR THEM TO STOP BUT THEY NEVER DID, THANK YOU ANDY I HAVE NO FURTHER QUESTIONS MR. SANCHEZ WOULD YOU LIKE TO CROSS-EXAMINE, YES, YOUR HONOR WILL ANDY THAT IS A GOOD STORY, HOW OLD DO YOU SAY YOU WERE WHEN THIS WAS GOING ON I SAID I WAS 9 YEARS OLD, HOW CAN YOU REMEMBER SOMETHING THAT HAPPENED WHEN YOU WERE ONLY 9 YEARS

OLD, ARE YOU SURE YOU ARE NOT MAKING THIS UP, TO GET BACK AT YOUR PARENTS FOR SOMETHING ELSE, MR. SANCHEZ LET ME ASK YOU A QUESTION DO YOU REMEMBER YOUR CHILDHOOD, OBJECTION YOUR HONOR I DO NOT SEE WHAT MY CHILDHOOD HAS TO DO WITH THIS CASE OVERRULE ANSWER THE QUESTION, YES, I REMEMBER MY CHILDHOOD HOW FAR BACK DO YOU REMEMBER I REMEMBER BACK TO WHEN I WAS 7 YEARS OLD SO HOW IS IT FAIR TO SAY THAT YOU CAN REMEMBER YOUR CHILDHOOD BUT I CAN NOT KNOW WHAT I SAW AND HEARD AND WITNESSED AND YOU SAY THIS IS A PAYBACK YES, IT IS THEY MUST PAY FOR WHAT THEY DID TO MY SISTER, ATTORNEY SANCHEZ STAYED QUIET THEN HE SAID NO MORE QUESTIONS YOU CAN STEP DOWN ANDY AS HE WENT TO HIS SEAT THE JUDGE SPOKE ANY MORE WITNESS MR. MARTINEZ NO YOUR HONOR PLANTIFF REST MR. SANCHEZ NO, YOUR HONOR THE DEFENSE REST, MR. MARTINEZ WOULD YOU LIKE TO PRESENT YOUR CLOSING ARGUMENT YES, YOUR HONOR, LADIES AND GENTLEMEN OF THE JURY AS THE TRIAL WENT ON ALL THESE

MONTHS YOU ALL HAVE WITNESSED HOW THESE TWO PEOPLE DESTROYED THE LIVES OF MANY PEOPLE INCLUDING THE LIFE OF ANDREA THEIR DAUGHTER, A DAUGHTER THEY WERE SUPPOSED TO LOVE AND PROTECT BUT THEY DID NOT THEY SPENT HOURS AND DAYS TORTURING HER AND ABUSING HER AND CHILD TRAFFICKING IMAGINE THIS BEING YOUR DAUGHTER THEN THEY HAD THE NERVE TO KIDNAP ANOTHER KID TO CONTINUE THEIR DRUG USE I ASK THE JURY TO COME BACK WITH THE VERDICT OF GUILT FOR CHILD ABUSE THE VERDICT OF GUILTY FOR CHILD TRAFFICKING, A VERDICT OF ASSAULT CAUSING BODILY INJURY, AND FOR THE MOM THE VERDICT OF

ACCESSORY TO ALL CHARGES THANK YOU, LADIES, AND GENTLEMAN OF THE JURY, MR. SANCHEZ WOULD YOU LIKE TO PRESENT YOUR CLOSING ARGUMENT NO YOUR HONOR, VERY WELL JURORS YOU MAY LEAVE THE COURTROOM AND GO TO THE JURY ROOM AND BEGIN YOUR DELIBERATIONS AS THE JURY LEFT THE COURTROOM EVERYONE WAS ON THEIR TOES HOPING FOR A GOOD VERDICT, LET US GO ANDREA NO I AM GOING TO WAIT HERE IN THE COURTROOM UNTIL THE JURY RETURNS I WILL WAIT HERE WITH YOU; THIS IS FINALLY THE MOMENT YOU HAVE BEEN WAITING FOR WHEN THAT DOOR OPENS YOUR HAPPINESS WILL START AND YOUR FREEDOM, THE JURY DID NOT TAKE THAT LONG THEY WERE BACK IN THE COURTROOM WITHIN 1 HOUR, ANDREA SAT IN THE FRONT ROW SHE SEES THE JUDGE WALK BACK INTO THE COURTROOM RANDY LOOKS AT THE JUDGE AND SEES HE IS BACK YES, I WILL BE BACK I WILL BE BACK ANDREA I AM GOING TO CALLEVERYONE TO COME BACK INTO THE COURTROOM, AS EVERYONE RETURNS TO THE

COURTROOM THE JUDGE ASKS THE JURY HAVE THE JURY REACH A VERDICT YES, WE HAVE YOUR HONOR, PLEASE READ THE OUTCOME, ON THE CHARGE OF CHILD ABUSE WE FIND THE DEFENDANTS GUILTY, ON THE CHARGE OF CHILD ENDANGERMENT WE FIND THE DEFENDANTS GUILTY ON THE CHARGE OF CHILD TRAFFICKING, WE FIND THE DEFENDANTS GUILTY THANK YOU LADIES AND GENTLEMEN OF THE JURY YOU ALL ARE DISMISSED WILL THE DEFENDANTS STAND FOR SENTENCING, MR. GARCIA I AM SHOCKED ATHOW YOU WERE WITH YOUR DAUGHTER, ALL MY YEARS AS A JUDGE I NEVER HEARD A CASE MORE DISTURBING, I HOPE YOU REALIZE ONE DAY THAT WHAT YOU DID WAS NOT NORMAL,

AND MAY GOD HELP YOU; MR. GARCIA I SENTENCE YOU TO LIFE IN PRISON WITHOUT THE POSSIBILITY OF PAROLE, WHEN THE JUDGE GAVE ANDREA DAD, SHE DROPPED TO HER KNEES AND CRIED HAPPY TEARS WE DID IT HE IS GONE FOR GOOD YES MY LOVE LET SHE WHAT YOUR MOM IS GOING TO GET MRS GARCIA I AM HEARTBROKEN THAT YOU ALLOW THIS TO HAPPEN TO YOUR CHILD AND OTHER CHILDREN, MRS. GARCIA I SENTENCE YOU TO 40 YEARS IN PRISON WITHOUT THE POSSIBILITY OF PAROLE, AS ANDREA SEE HER PARENTS TAKEN AWAY SHE IS IN SO MUCH TEARS BUT HAPPY TEARS AND SHE TELLS HER PARENTS WELCOME TO YOUR HELL IN PRISON NOW IT IS TIME FOR YOU TO EXPERIENCE YOUR PAIN AND SUFFERING AND NO ONE THERE TO HELP YOU THE BAILIFF TAKES THE PRISONERS AWAY, THE COURT ADJOURNS, EVERYONE STANDS AS THE HONORABLE JUDGE LEAVES, AS THE JUDGE LEAVES THE COURTROOM ANDREA'S EYES ARE FILLED WITH TEARS, OF HAPPINESS, AS SHE TELLS RANDY WILL IT IS FINALLY OVER THEY WILL NEVER HURT ANOTHER KID, YES, MY LOVE THEY ARE GONE FOR GOOD, AS ANDREA AND RANDY REJOICE OVER THE FINAL VERDICT **JUDY'S** DAD STILL HAD A LOT OF ANGER THE ONLY THOUGHT GOING THREW HIS HEAD WAS HAVING ANDREA'S DAD KILLED, AND HE SWORE NOT TO REST UNTIL HE IS DEAD, NO ONE KNOWS WHAT HE HAS PLANNED, WILL RANDY LET US GO HOME AND CELEBRATE OUR VICTORY, AS THEY GOT TO THEIR HOUSE THE DETECTIVE WAS THERE WAITING FOR RANDY,HELLO DETECTIVE HOW MAY I HELP YOU, WILL RANDY I CAME TO INFORM YOU THAT YOU WILL NOT NEED TO GO TO COURT NEXT **WEEK WHY DON'T TELL ME THEY RELEASE JOEY,** WILL JOEY BE GONE BUT NOT BECAUSE HE WAS RELEASED, THEN WHAT HAPPENED THE OTHER NIGHT THERE WAS A RIOT IN THE JAIL AND

JOEY ENGAGED IN THE RIOT HE GOT STABBED 21 TIMES IN THE CHEST, HE DID NOT MAKE IT TO THE HOSPITAL, AS THE DETECTIVE SAID BOTH ANDREA AND RANDY WERE SHOCKED THEY HAD NO WORDS TO SAY AS THE DETECTIVE WAS LEAVING RANDY SAID THANK YOU RANDY LOOKED AT ANDREA AND SAID I AM SORRY HE IS DEAD, WHY ARE YOU SORRY HE TRIED TO KILL YOU YES, I KNOW BUT TWO WRONGS DO NOT MAKE IT RIGHT I WANTED JUSTICE THE RIGHT WAY NOT LIKE THIS, MAY GOD FORGIVE HIM FOR ALL HE HAS DONE WRONG, AS RANDY AND ANDREA WERE TALKING ABOUT THIS JUDY'S DAD WAS TRYING TO FIND OUT WHICH PRISON ANDREA DAD WAS GOING HE WAITED PATIENTLY UNTIL HE WAS ABLE TO GET THE INFORMATION, HE NEEDED TO HAVE HIM KILLED ON THE INSIDE OF THOSE PRISON WALLS, WHAT THEY DID NOT KNOW MR. TORRES HAD LOTS OF CONNECTIONS ON THE INSIDE, SO HE WILL BE SEEKING JUSTICE IN HIS WAY BACK AT ANDREA HOUSE ANDREA WAS LOOKING AT RANDY AS THEY BOTH SAT THERE NOT SAYING A WORD JUST THINKING ABOUTWHAT THEY FOUND OUT, AND AS THEY LOOKED AT EACH OTHER RANDY SAID TO ANDREA WILL MY LOVE IT LOOKLIKE I WILL NOT HAVE TO GO TO COURT AFTER ALL, NOW WHAT IS OUR NEXT MOVE WHAT DO WE DO NOW, ANDREA STAYED QUIET, THEN SAID WILL RANDY I ACCOMPLISHED WHAT I WAS SEEKING THERE IS ONLY ONE THING LEFT TO DO AND THAT IS TO MOVE BACK TO MY AUNT AND GRANDMA HOUSE, AND REGISTER TO GO BACK TO SCHOOL I HAVE ONE YEAR LEFT I MUST FINISH SCHOOL AND THEN ENROLL IN COLLAGE YES, YOU ARE RIGHT I NEED TO FINISH SCHOOL TOO, **LET'S TELL ANDY WHAT OUR PLANS ARE** ANDY YES SIS COME IN HERE WE NEED TO TALK TO YOU, WHAT IS IT WE AREDONE HERE AND WE ARE MOVING BACK TO

GRANDMA HOUSE ARE YOU COMING WITH US YES, ANDREA I WILL BE GOING BACK WITH YALL, AS THEY WERE MAKING THEIR FUTURE PLANS THE PHONE RANG ANDREA ANSWERED THE PHONE HELLO WHO SPEAKING HELLO IT IS JUDY DAD HOW YOU ARE DOING MR. TORRES, IS THERE SOMETHING THAT YOU NEED YES, I WOULD LIKE TO KNOW WHAT PRISON YOUR DAD IS IN, HMMM WHY WOULD YOU LIKE TO KNOW THAT WHAT ARE YOUR PLANS NO PLANS I AM JUST MAKING SURE HE IS IN A WILL SECURE PRISON SO HE CAN NOT ESCAPE AND HURT ANYONE ELSE OK, HE IS IN RAMSEY 3 NEAR HOUSTON TX. OK ANDREA THANKS A LOT BYE, YES BYE SIR AS THEY HUNG UP THE PHONE ANDREA STAYED SILENT AS SHE WALKED BACK INTO THE ROOM WHO WAS IT ON THE PHONE IT WAS JUDY DAD WHAT DID HE WANT HE WANTED INFORMATION ON WHAT PRISON MY DAD WAS AT AND DID YOU TELL HIM YES, I DID DO YOU THINK HE WILL TRY TO GET HIM KILLED HE WAS MAD AT THE COURTHOUSE BUT WE WILL WAIT AND SEE WHAT HAPPENS YOU KNOW RANDY IT HAS BEEN A YEAR SINCE I LEFT GRANDMA HOUSE, RANDY STAYED QUIET AND DID NOT SAY A WORD, THEN HE SAID ANDREA I HAVE TO TELL YOU SOMETHING, WHAT IS IT RANDY SAID WHEN I WAS YOUNGER I TRIED A NEW DRUG THAT CAME TO TOWN AND IT WAS THE BEST THING THAT HAS HAPPENED I LOVED IT MORE THAN MY OWN LIFE, YES, EVERYONE WAS DOING IT SO I DECIDED TO TRY IT, THE NAME OF THE DRUG WAS CRACK COCAINE, AND AFTER THE FIRST HIT I GOT HOOKED I STAYED ON THAT DRUG FOR OVER 6 MONTHS, I HATED IT BUT COULD NOT LEAVE THE DRUG ALONE MATTER HOW I TRIED I LOST EVERYTHING WHAT DID YOU LOSE I LOST EVERYONE RESPECT LOST THEIR TRUST, AND NO ONE TRUSTED ME IN THEIR HOUSE EVERY TIME,

THEY SAW ME COMING THEY WOULD SAY HERE COMES RANDY HIDE YOUR STUFF HE LIKESTOSTEAL FOR HIS DRUGS BUT MOST OF ALL I LOST MY SELF RESPECT I DID THAT SO I COULD GET A 10-DOLLAR ROCK THE HIGH ONLYLASTED 10 MINUTES I WAS THROWING MY LIFE AWAY AND DID NOT CARE ALL I CARED ABOUT WAS WHERE MY NEXT HIGH WAS COMING FROM, I ALMOST OVERDOSED 3 TIMES BUT THAT DID NOT STOP ME UNTIL THE SADDEST DAY OF MY LIFE HAPPENED MY GRANDMA PASSED AWAY, AS I WAS AT HER FUNERAL I SAT THERE IN TEARS THINKING ABOUT ALL THE PAIN AND SUFFERING I CAUSED MY FAMILY A FAMILY THAT LOVED ME I TURNED MY BACK ON THEM AND WENT THE OTHER WAY IN THE DEADLY WORLD OF DRUGS SO THAT DAY I MADE A PROMISE AT MY GRANDMA'S FUNERAL I WOULD NEVER DO DRUGS AGAIN AND SINCE THAT DAY I STOPPED IT TOOK A LONG TIME TO GET EVERONE TRUST AND RESPECT BACK BUT SLOWLY I GOT EVERYONE TO TRUST ME AND RESPECT ME AGAIN I AM HERE TO TELL YOU THE WORLD OF DRUGS IS NO GOOD IT WILL KILL YOU TEAR YOU DOWN AND HURT THE PEOPLE THAT LOVE YOU AND CARE FOR YOU I AM BLESSED I LEFT THE DRUGS WHEN I DID I LOVE YOU RANDY AND THANK YOU FOR TELLING ME, I LOVE YOU TOO AS RANDY AND ANDREA WHERE THERE TALKING IT WAS DIFFERENT FOR HER DAD AS HE SAT IN HIS PRISON CELL, HE GOT A VISIT FROM ANOTHER INMATE SO YOU ARE ANDREA DAD, THE FATHER OF THAT POOR DEFENSELESS LITTLE GIRL THAT COULD NOT PROTECT HE SELF YOU TORTURE, ABUSE, AND RAPE HER DUDE SHE WAS YOUR DAUGHTER AND ONLY 12 YEARS OLD I SHOULD KILL YOU RIGHT NOW BUT I AM NOT WE ARE GOING TO MAKE YOU SUFFER THE WAY YOU AND THOSE MAN MADE ANDREA AND JUDY SUFFER JUDY TORRES WAS

ONLY A 12-YEAR-OLD GIRL SHE WAS ENJOYING HER DAY AT THE PARK UNTIL YOU INTERFERE WITH HER LIFE AND MADE HER LIFE A LIVING HELL SO I SAY TO YOU WELCOME TO HELL EVERYDAY THAT YOU ARE HERE WE ARE GOING TO MAKE YOUR LIFE A LIVING HELL, AS THE INMATE WAS LEAVING HIS CELL, HE GRABBED HIM BY HIS THROAT AND SAID ONCE AGAIN WELCOME TO HELL, THE FOLLOWING MORNING THE TORTURE STARTED TWO INMATES WENT INTO MR. GARCIA CELL AND SAID TO HIM " LET'S SEE HOW GOOD YOU ARE GOING TO MAKE DADDY HAPPY HE TRIED TO FIGHT THEM OFF BUT THEY OVERPOWERED HIM, THEY TOOK TURNS ON HIM, AND TEARS STARTED COMING OUT OF HIS EYES HE BEGGED THEM TO STOP THEY JUST LAUGHED AT HIM AND SAID REMEMBER MAKE YOUR DADDY HAPPY WHEN THEY SAID THAT HE WAS REMINDED OF WHAT HE WOULD TELL ANDREA AND JUDY THIS WENT ON FOR ABOUT A WEEK HE WOULD GET TORTURED 6 TIMES A DAY AS THE WEEK CAME TO AN END THE FIRST INMATE CAME INTO THE CELL AND SAID THIS IS YOUR LAST DAY WITH US IT IS TIME FOR YOU TO LEAVE WHERE AM I GOING TO HELL THIS IS FROM JUDY DAD AND HE STABS HIM TO DEATH. AFTER HE STABBED ANDREA'S DAD, HE STOOD OVER THE BODY AND JUST LOOKED AT HIS DEAD BODY LAYING ON THE PRISON FLOOR I CAN NOT BELIEVE YOU DID THIS TO YOUR DAUGHTER I ALWAYS WANTED KIDS BUT WAS NOT BLESSED TO HAVE ANY AND YOU WERE BLESSED TO HAVE KIDS AND INSTEAD OF LOVING YOUR DAUGHTER, YOU HURT HER AND MADE HER LIFE A LIVING HELL YOU WILL NOT HURT ANY MORE KIDS NOW YOU WILL SUFFER FOR ETERNITY AFTER HE SAID THIS, HE WAS WALKING OUT OF THE CELL AT THAT POINT HE SAW THE PRISON GUARD WAS WALKING TOWARDS HIM AND LOOK INTO THE CELL AND

SAW ANDREA DAD LAYING THERE AND THE OTHER INMATE FULL OF BLOOD ON HIS HANDS AND SHIRT AND THE ALL OVER THE CELL ANDREA DAD WAS IN AS THE INMATE STANDS OVER ANDREA DAD HE STILL CAN NOT BELIEVE THAT SOMEONE WAS SO HATEFUL AND HAD SO MUCH OF A BLACK HEART THAT THEY WOULD HURT THEIR OWN DAUGHTER BUT HE WILL NEVER HURT NO ONE AGAIN HIS LIFE IS OVER WITH NOW HE WILL PAY THE PRICE FOR ALL THE PAIN AND SUFFERING HE HAS CAUSE SO MANY PEOPLE AND THERE IS NO ONE TO HELP HIM HE IS GONE FOR GOOD AT THIS POINT AS HE STANDS THEIR HE TURNS AND LOOKS AT ALL THE BLOOD ALL OVER THE CELL AND AS HE THINKS ABOUT ALL THE KIDS ANDREA DAD HAS HURT AND DESTROYED THEIR LIVE'S HE IS GLAD OF WHAT HE DID HE KNOWS IT WAS WRONG IN GOD'S EYES TO KILL HIM BUT HE ALSO NEW THAT THIS PERSON WAS FULL OF HATRED AND EVIL AND HE NEEDED TO BE PUT OUT OF THIS WORLD SO AS HE LOOKS OUT THE WINDOW AND AS HE STIRS DOWN AS IF HE COULD NOT BELIEVE WHAT HAD JUST HAPPEN AS HE STANDS THERE WITH BLOOD ON HIS HANDS HE TURNS AND LOOKS AROUND FOR A MIN HE FEELS LOST AND DID NOT KNOW WHAT WAS GOING TO HAPPEN NEXT, HE NEW THAT WHEN THE GUARD FINDS OUT HE KILLED ANOTHER INMATE HE WOULD NEVER GET OUT SO HE IS STANDING OVER ANDREA DAD STILL HOLDING THE KNIFE IN HIS HANDS AND AS HE LOOKS UP, HE SEE THE GUARD AND THE GUARD SEE HIM

CHAPTER 10   FREEDOM AT LAST

STANDING OVER **ANDREA'S DAD DEAD BODY** HE SAY'S **IN A LOVE VOICE** YOU ARE FULL OF EVIL AND HATE YOU HAD A CHANCE TO BE A GOOD DAD TO YOUR DAUGHTER A GIFT FROM GOD BUT INSTEAD YOU DESTROYED THAT GIFT NOW YOUR LIFE IS OVER AND DESTROYED NOW YOU WILL WITNESS AND FEEL WHAT IT IS TO ASK FOR HELP AND NO ONE AROUND TO HELP YOU, LIFE FOR YOU WILL BE A LIVING HELL AS HE FINISH SPEAKING THE INMATE TURNS AND SEE THE GUARD STANDING THERE THE INMATE TELLS THE GUARD I COULD NOT HOLD BACK ANYMORE SO YES, I KILLED HIM, NOW WHAT WILL HAPPEN TO ME THE GUARD LOOKS AND HIM AND **SAY'S WHAT ARE YOU TALKING ABOUT I DO NOT SEE**

NOTHING THE INMATE JUST SMILED AND WENT BACK TO HIS CELL, AS HE THOUGHT THIS MAN MADE ANDREA SUFFER NOW HE WILL SUFFER WHEREVER HE GOES I JUST HOPE THAT POOR GIRL IS DOING OK NOW I KNOW SHE HAS BEEN THREW A LOT BACK AT ANDREA HOUSE, THEY WERE GETTING READY FOR DINNER, AS THEY SAT THERE; THEY WERE JUST THINKING ABOUT WHAT HAPPENED TO JOEY THIS WAS THE FIRST TIME THAT NO ONE SAID A WORD DURING DINNER, THEY JUST SAT THERE AND FINISHED THEIR DINNER WHEN THEY WERE DONE, THEY HEARD A KNOCK ON THE DOOR, HELLO DETECTIVE WHY ARE YOU HERE WHAT

HAPPENED NOW, AS ANDREA LOOKED AT THE DETECTIVE SHE KNEW SOMETHING WAS WRONG, THE DETECTIVE SAID TO ANDREA, LOOKED I AM SORRY TO HAVE TO BE THE ONE TO TELL YOU THIS BUT YOUR DAD GOT KILLED EARLY THIS MORNING HE WAS STABBED TO DEATH, ANDREA HAD SO MUCH HATE FOR HER PARENTS SHE DID NOT EVEN CARE ALL SHE SAID WAS OK THAT'S GREAT ANYTHING ELSE I CAN HELP YOU WITH SHE DID NOT CARE SHE KNEW WHO SENT THE HIT ON HER DAD BUT DID NOT SAY A WORD, WOW MY LOVE JUDY DAD DID IT AND HAD HIM KILLED YES, HE DID WILL LET'S TELL ANDY, OK ANDY COME IN HERE WE NEED TO TELL YOU SOMETHING YES, WHAT IS IT ANDREA, WE JUST FOUND OUT THAT OUR DAD GOT STABBED TO DEATH THIS MORNING, OK WILL HE GET WHAT HE DESERVES, NOW WHEN ARE WE LEAVING THIS TOWN, I AM READY TO GET OUT OF HERE, WE WILL BE LEAVING IN THE MORNING, IT IS A 4-HOUR BUS RIDE SOUNDS GREAT, WHERE DID YOU SAY GRANDMA LIVES AGAIN, SHE STAYS IN AUSTIN TEXAS OK SIS I'M GOING TO GET MY THINGS TOGETHER AND I WILL SEE YOU FIRST THING IN THE MORNING, YES, ANDY HAVE A GOOD NIGHT'S REST SEE YOU IN THE MORNING WILL RANDY THIS IS OUR LAST NIGHT HERE TOMORROW WE WILL BE LEAVING THIS TOWN FOR GOOD AND GOING TO A BETTER PLACE YES, ANDREA FINALLY WE ARE GOING TO BE OUT OF THIS TERRIBLE PLACE THAT HAS BROUGHT NOTHING BUT PAIN AND SUFFERING FOR THE BOTH OF US WILL GOOD NIGHT TIL MORNING COMES LET US REST AS ANDREA AND RANDY FELL FAST ASLEEP ALL THEY COULD THINK ABOUT WAS HOW THEIR LIVES HAD BEEN A LIVING HELL IN THE HANDS OF ANDREA'S PARENTS' HANDS EVEN THOUGH ANDREA PARENTS ARE BOTH IN PRISON THE PAIN THEY CAUSE HER WILL ALWAYS BE A PART OF HER LIFE THAT SHE WILL NEVER FORGET AS

MORNING COMES ANDREA SAYS TO RANDY YOU KNOW I NEED TO MAKE ONE STOP BEFORE WE LEAVE THIS TOWN AND WHERE IS THAT I AM GOING TO GO VISIT MY MOM IN PRISON, WHY WOULD YOU DO THAT AFTER ALL THE PAIN, SHE CAUSED YOU AND ALLOW ALL THOSE MEN TO HAVE THEIR WAY WITH YOU, THAT IS EXACTLY WHY I AM GOING TO VISIT HER TO LET HER KNOW THAT EVERYTHING THEY DID TO ME THEY NEVER BROKE ME ALL THEY DID WAS MAKE ME STRONGER, OK LET'S GO THEN AND SEE YOUR MOM FOR THE LAST TIME AS ANDREA GETS TO THE PRISON, SHE STOPS AT THE GATE SHE WALKS IN AND ARE YOU OK WHY DID YOU STOP, I WAS JUST THINKING OF ALL THE EVIL PEOPLE IN THIS PRISON, AND IT KINDA OF SCARED ME BUT I AM OK, AS THEY GET TO THE VISITATION ROOM ANDREA MOM IS ALREADY THERE WAITING FOR HER AND AS SHE LOOKS AT HER SHE SAYS ANDREA WOW WHAT ARE YOU DOING HERE, I AM HERE BECAUSE THERE IS SOMETHING YOU MUST KNOW SO SIT THERE AND LISTEN AND DO NOT SAY ONE WORD UNTIL I AM DONE OK AND YOU KNOW IT HAS BEEN OVER AN YEAR SINCE I CAME TO PRISON SO WHAT DO YOU NEED TO TELL ME, I JUST WANTED TO LET YOU KNOW THAT YOU AND DAD NEVER BROKE ME DOWN, I JUST HAVE ONE QUESTION HOW COULD YOU DO THIS TO ME ON YOUR OWN DAUGHTER AND CAUSE ME ALL THAT PAIN AND SUFFERING AND THEN LET THOSE MAN HAVE THEIR WAY WITH ME WHAT WAS WRONG WITH YOU AND DAD I AM SORRY ANDREA WILL IT IS LATE FOR THAT, LISTEN ANDREA WE WERE LOST IN THE WORLD OF DRUGS WE WERE ADDICTED BADLY, AND WE DID WHATEVER WE NEEDED TO DO TO GET OUR NEXT HIGH, BUT I AM PAYING FOR IT EVERY DAY IN HERE WHY WHAT GOING ON WELL SINCE I HAVE BEEN HERE, I HAVE GOT BEATEN UP RAPED, AND ABUSED, AND AS THEY WOULD

DO THIS TO ME, THEY WOULD SAY LAUGH AS YOU LAUGH WHEN YOUR DAUGHTER ANDREA AND JUDY WERE GETTING RAPED ANDREA STARTED GETTING TEARS IN HER EYES AND HER MOM ASKED HER WHAT WAS WRONG AND WHY SHE WAS CRYING, HEARING HER SAY THAT I WAS REMINDED OF HOW THINGS WERE FOR ME AS YOU AND DAD DID THE SAME TO ME SO ALL I CAN SAY IS NOW IS YOUR TURN TO EXPERIENCE THE PAIN AND SUFFERING YOU BOTH HAVE BEEN PUTTING ME THREW YES ANDREA YOU ARE RIGHT OK WILL I HAVE TO GO THIS WILL BE THE LAST TIME YOU SEE ME I ALMOST FORGOT TO TELL YOU DAD GOT KILLED YESTERDAY MORNING HE WAS STABBED TO DEATH BYE, MOM, YOU WILL NEVER SEE ME AGAIN YOU WILL SPEND THE REST OF YOUR LIFE ALONE AS YOU DESERVE YOU HURT A LOT OF PEOPLE NOW IT IS TIME FOR YOU TO LIVE IN THE SOLITARY OF YOUR LIFE, AS ANDREA GOT UP AND WALKED AWAY HER MOM SAT THERE IN TEARS THINKING OF ALL THE PAIN SHE CAUSE HER DAUGHTER BECAUSE SHE DECIDED TO LIVE HER LIFE IN THE DRUG WORLD AS SHE GOT UP AND WALKED BACK TO HER CELL SHE DECIDED TO DO THE MOST UNBELIEVABLE THING AS SHE WALKED INTO HER CELL, SHE WHISPERED TO HERSELF I WAS A TERRIBLE MOM I DESERVE ALL THAT IS HAPPENING TO ME I CAN NOT GO ON WITH THIS GUILT IN MY LIFE SO I SAY BYE TO THE WORLD THEN SHE GOT A ROPE AND HUNG HERSELF IN THE CELL, AS ANDREA WALKED OUT OF THE PRISON RANDY WAS THERE WAITING AS SHE WALKS TO HIM ARE YOU OK YES, I AM GREAT LET'S START GOING TO THE BUS STATION THE BUS WILL BE HERE SOON THEY ARE ALL EXCITED TO LEAVE THIS TOWN AND GO TO THEIR AUNT'S HOUSE, BUT LITTLE DOES ANDREA KNOW WHEN SHE GETS AT HER AUNT'S HOUSE SHE WILL RECEIVE THE

MOST HEARTBREAKING NEWS SHE EVER GOT IN HER LIFE, ANDREA WILL FIND OUT THE TRUTH ABOUT HER DAD WHO IS HER REAL DAD HAS COME INTO THE PICTURE AND THE MAN THAT SHE KNEW AS HER DAD WAS HER STEPDAD SHE WILL HEAR ALL THE TRAGIC TRUTH OF HOW HER FATHER LEFT HER WHEN SHE WAS STILL A LITTLE BABY AS THEY BOARD THE BUS RANDY LOOKS AT ANDREA AND SEE TEARS COMING OUT OF HER EYES WHAT IS WRONG WHY ARE YOU ARE CRYING, IT IS JUST THAT I NEVER THOUGHT THIS DAY WOULD COME ALL THE PAIN AND SUFFERING I WAS GOING THREW ALL MY LIFE I THOUGHT IT WOULD NEVER END AND I ALMOST ENDED UP DEAD I HAVE BEEN THREW SO MUCH AND I THINK GOD THAT YOU WERE THERE WITH ME AND BY MY SIDE THE WHOLE TIME AND YOU NEVER ABANDON ME, I AM HAPPY AND AT THE SAME TIME I AM SAD ABOUT WHAT HAS HAPPENED IN MY LIFE YOU KNOW MY LOVE OUR LIFE IS NOT DEFINED BY WHAT HAPPENS IN OUR PAST BUT BY WHAT WE MAKE OF IT IN THE FUTURE, WILL SAID RANDY WE SHOULD BE AT GRANDMA'S HOUSE IN AROUND 4 HOURS, SOUNDS GREAT WILL I AM EXCITED TO BE THERE AND THEN WE WILL GO BACK TO SCHOOL AND PREPARE FOR OUR CAREERS, AS THE BUS LEAVES THE STATION, THEY NOTICE ANDY IS NOT WITH THEM AS THEY BOARD THE BUS TO GET READY TO LEAVE ANDREA LOOKS OUT OF THE WINDOW AS TEARS OF HAPPINESS ROLL DOWN HER CHEEKS, WILL RANDY IN A FEW HOURS WE WILL BE AT MY AUNTS HOUSE, WHERE IS ANDY I THOUGHT HE WAS COMING WITH US, WILL BEFORE WE LEFT THE HOUSE ANDY GAVE ME THIS LETTER AND ASKED ME NOT TO OPEN IT UNTIL I GOT ON THE BUS AND WHAT DOES THE LETTER SAY AS ANDREA OPENS THE LETTER AND STARTS READING IT TEARS START COMING OUT OF HER EYES ANDREA WHAT DID HE SAY

HE WROTE ANDREA MY WONDERFUL AND BEST SISTER IN THE WHOLE WORLD I AM SO SORRY I CAN NOT GO WITH YOU AND RANDY AT OUR AUNT'S HOUSE I MUST FIND MY OWN LIFE AND MAKE MY PATH IN THIS CRAZY WORLD I NEED TO FIND OUT WHO I AM I WILL ALWAYS REMEMBER AND CHERISH THE MOMENTS WE SPENT TOGETHER NOW RANDY IS A GREAT PERSON AND I SEE HE TRULY LOVES YOU WITH ALL HIS HEART, AND AS LONG AS YOU BOTH HAVE EACH OTHER I KNOW YALL WILL ALWAYS BE HAPPY SO, WITH THAT I SAY I AM HAPPY FOR YOU THAT YOU GOT THE JUSTICE THAT YOU BEEN SEARCHING FOR ALL THIS TIME, I LEAVE YOU FOR NOW BUT NOT FOREVER IF YOU EVER NEED ME, YOU KNOW WHERE YOU CAN FIND ME BYE, FOR NOW, SISTER BUT NOT FOREVER, I LOVE YOU THE BEST SISTER IN THE WHOLE WORLD AS ANDREA FINISH READING THE LETTER SHE WAS IN TEARS AND COULD HARDLY SPEAK, WOW MY LOVE ANDY IS NOT COMING WITH US, LOOK RANDY EVEN THO HE IS NOT HERE IN PERSON HIS LOVE WILL ALWAYS BE IN OUR HEARTS THIS IS SAD I WAS HOPING HE WOULD HAVE STAYED WE COULD HAVE BEEN HAPPY FAMILY WILL RANDY THE WAY, I SEE IT WE ARE STILL A HAPPY FAMILY LOOK RANDY WHERE LOOK OUT THE WINDOW YOU SEE THAT, WHERE WHAT ARE YOU TALKING ABOUT, WE ARE GETTING CLOSER TO AUSTIN TX. YOU SEE THOSE MOUNTAINS YES; I DO THEY LOOK SO PEACEFUL WILL THE LAST TIME I SAW THEM I JUST SAW A PLACE TO RUN AND HIDE FROM THE WORLD I WAS RUNNING FROM MY FEARS OF LIFE WHICH IT WAS BACK THEN, AS I SEE THEM, I LOOK AT THEM WITH A DIFFERENT ASPECT OF THIS WORLD NOW I CAN SEE HOW BEAUTIFUL AND PEACEFUL THEY ARE NOW THERE IS NO MORE RUNNING, I JUST WANT TO SPEND THE REST OF MY LIFE WITH YOU AND BE SURROUNDED BY THE PEOPLE I

LOVE AS THEY COME TO THE END OF THERE TRIP, THEY ARE OVERWHELMED BY THE CONVERSATION THEY HAD OF ALL THAT HAS TO HAPPEN AS THEY GET OFF THE BUS, ANDREA IS IN A HURRY TO GET TO HER GRANDMA'S HOUSE IT HAS BEEN A LONG TRIP AN EMOTIONAL TRIP WALKING TOWARDS GRANDMOM'S HOUSE ANDREA HOLDS RANDY HAND AS SHE LOOKS AT HIM AND TELLS HIM SOMETHING IS NOT RIGHT WHAT DO YOU MEAN SOMETHING IS NOT RIGHT THE WAY; I SEE IT EVERYTHING IS GOING RIGHT, WHAT DO YOU FEEL TO MAKE YOU SAY THAT I **DON'T KNOW AT THIS MOMENT BUT I AM SURE I WILL SOON FIND** OUT WHY I AM FEELING LIKE THIS, THERE GOES GRANDMA HOUSE ON THE NEXT BLOCK FINALLY WE MADE IT HERE IT HAS BEEN A LONG TRIP I AM TIRED AND READY TO REST AND GET MYSELF SOME GOOD HOME COOK MEAL YES, RANDY I AM WORN OUT LOOK THERE GOES GRANDMA AND AUNT ON THE PORCH **COME ON LET'S GO AND JOIN THEM** MIJA YOU FINALLY MADE IT BACK YES GRANDMA I AM BACK HOME AND HAPPY TO BE BACK, HELLO MIJO I AM GLAD YOU CAME BACK WITH ANDREA, BUT WAIT WHERE IS ANDY I THOUGHT HE SAID HE WAS COMING BACK

WITH YALL YES GRANDMA HE DID SAY HE WAS GOING BUT AS WE GOT TO THE BUS STATION, HE CHANGED HIS MIND I DO NOT KNOW WHY HE WAS EXCITED TO COME TO YALL HOUSE ALL HE DID WAS TELL ME HE LOVES ME AND HE IS HAPPY FOR ME AND GAVE ME THIS LETTER AND ASKED ME NOT TO OPEN IT UNTIL I GOT ON THE BUS, I KNOW HE WILL BE HAPPY IN WHATEVER HE PLANS ON DOING IN HIS LIFE, WHERE DID TIA JOSIE GO, SHE WENT INSIDE RIGHT QUICK SO ARE YOU BOTH HUNGRY I KNOW IT WAS A LONG TRIP NO GRANDMA I AM NOT HUNGRY RIGHT NOW OK HOW ABOUT YOU RANDY ARE YOU HUNGRY YES GRANDMA I DID NOT HAVE A

GOOD BREAKFAST OK I JUST FINISHED MAKING A POT OF CHICKEN MOLE AND RICH SOUNDS GOOD AS THEY BOTH SAT DOWN AT THE TABLE ANDREA AUNT CAME IN WITH THE SADDEST LOOK ON HER FACE AND LOOK AT ANDREA AND SPOKE ANDREA LETS GO TO THE OTHER ROOM I NEED TO TALK TO YOU AND IT IS GOING TO BREAK MY HEART TO TELL YOU WHAT I NEED TO TELL YOU OK TIA JOSIE WHAT IS IT YOU ARE SCARING ME; I HAVE TO TELL YOU ABOUT YOUR DAD WHAT ABOUT HIM HE IS DEAD NO MIJA **YOU DON'T UNDERSTAND** WHAT DO YOU MEAN I DO NOT UNDERSTAND TELL ME WHAT AM I SUPPOSED TO UNDERSTAND, WILL THAT MAN THAT ABUSED YOU WAS NOT YOUR BIOLOGICAL DAD HE WAS YOUR STEPDAD, WHAT NO WHAT THE HELL ARE YOU TALKING ABOUT, AND HOW THE HELL, HE WAS NOT MY DAD, HE WAS NOT MY TRUE DAD WHO THE HELL IS HE AND WHERE IS MY DAD AT AND WHY DID YOU LIE TO ME THE LAST TIME THAT WE TALK WHY DID YOU NOT TELL ME THE TRUTH I AM SICK AND TIRED OF PEOPLE TELLING ME LIES, I AM SO SORRY I LIED TO YOU I COULD NOT TELL YOU THE TRUTH LAST TIME YIOU WAS GOING THREW SO MUCH I COULD NOT ADD MORE BAD NEWS TO YOUR PAINS AND SUFFERING SO, TELL ME THE TRUTH IS MY MOM, MY MOM SO HOW DID ALL THIS HAPPEN THE TRUTH NO MORE LIES, WILL WHEN YOU WAS BORN YOU DAD LOOKED AT YOU WILL ALL THE LOVE HE HAD TO OFFER YOU HE TRULY LOVED YOU SO MUCH THAT HE SAID YOU WERE A BLESSING THAT IS WHY HE GAVE YOU THE NAME ANDREA, **WHICH WAS HIS MOM'S NAME, BUT A FEW MONTHS PASS AND** YOUR PARENTS WOULD FIGHT A LOT OF THEM WERE ALWAYS LATE ON THEIR RENT AND BILLS NOT A DAY PASSED THAT THEY DID NOT FIGHT, AND THEN ONE DAY YOUR DAD COULD NOT TAKE IT NO MORE SO HE PACKED HIS BAGS AND LEFT BUT BEFORE HE DID, HE

PICKED YOU UP AND HELD YOU IN HIS ARMS AND WITH TEARS IN HIS EYES HE SAID MIJA I LOVE YOU SO MUCH I AM NOT LEAVING YOU I AM LEAVING YOUR MOM; I KNOW YOU ARE TOO YOUNG TO UNDERSTAND WHAT I AM SAYING IS I JUST HOPE WHEN YOU GROW UP YOU FORGIVE ME FOR LEAVING THEN HE KISSED YOU AND LEFT WITH TEARS IN HER EYES AND COULD HARDLY TALK SO YOU ARE TELLING ME THIS WHOLE TIME I HAVE BEEN GETTING RAPED AND ABUSED BY A TOTAL STANGER, AS RANDY WALKS INTO THE ROOM HE SEES ANDREA FULL OF TEARS AND GOES UP TO HER AND HUGS HER AND SAY'S MY LOVE WHAT IS WRONG WHAT HAPPENED I JUST FOUND OUT THAT MY REAL DAD IS ALIVE WAIT WHAT DO YOU MEAN HE IS ALIVEHOW I AM SO CONFUSEDWILL THE MAN WHO HAS BEEN ABUSING ME ALL THIS TIME WAS MY STEPDAD MY REAL DAD LEFT ME WHEN I WAS STILL A BABY WOW SO WHAT IS GOING TO HAPPEN NOW, I AM GOING TO TALK AND MEET WITH MY DAD AND ASK HIM WHAT THE HELL HAPPENED WHY DID HE LEAVE ME; LOOK ANDREA IT'S BEEN A LONG TIME SINCE IT HAPPENED DO YOU THINK IT IS WISE TO BRING UP THE PASS, RANDY MY WHOLE LIFE IT HAS BEEN THE PASS DO YOU KNOW HOW IT FEELS TO LOVE AND NOT BE LOVED BY YOUR PARENTS THIS WHOLE TIME I THOUGHT THE MAN LIVING WITH MY MOM WAS MY REAL DAD, NOW I SEE WHY IT WAS SO EASY FOR HIM TO DO ALL THOSE THINGS TO ME, SO YES, I MUST FIND OUT THE TRUTH OF EVERYTHING, AND AS I REMEMBER YOU ONCE TOLD ME THAT OUR PASS DOES NOT MAKE US WHO WE ARE, IT IS OUR FUTURE THAT DETERMINES OUR LIFE, YES, I DID TELL YOU THAT WILL MY LOVE THAT IS WHY I AM TRYING TO FIND OUT SO I CAN DETERMINE MY LIFE WITH MY REAL DAD, AS ANDREA AND RANDY WERE SPEAKING THE PHONE RANG, AS ANDREA

HEARD THE PHONE RINGING, SHE LOOKED AT RANDY SPEECHLESS THEN SHE SAID OH MY GOD WHAT IF IT IS MY DAD, I DO NOT KNOW WHAT I WOULD SAY TO HIM RIGHT NOW HE IS A TOTAL STRANGER TO ME AND I DO NOT KNOW HOW I WOULD ACT IN FRONT OF HIM, IT IS OK ANDREA YOU WILL BE JUST FINE ONCE YOU TALK TO HIM, AS RANDY TELLS ANDREA THIS HER GRANDMA WALKS INTO THE ROOM AND LOOKS AT ANDREA MIJA IT IS YOUR DAD ON THE PHONE HE WANTS TO TALK TO YOU, OK TELL HIM I WILL BE RIGHT THERE AS ANDREA SLOWLY WALKS INTO THE KITCHEN LOOKING AT THE RECEIVER LYING ON THE TABLE, SHEHESITATE TO PICK IT UP AND FINALLY, SHE DOES, AS SHE HOLDS THE PHONE, SHE DOES NOT SAY ONE WORD, MIJA IS THAT YOU THIS IS YOUR DADDY ANSWER ME PLEASE LOOK I KNOW YOU PROBABLY DO NOT WANT TO TALK TO ME AND I DO NOT BLAME YOU IF YOU HATE ME, I AM SORRY I LEFT BUT I DID NOT LEAVE YOU I LEFT YOUR MOM DREA, I LOVE YOU MIJA HOW COULD YOU SAY THAT YOU WERE NOT FOR THE PASS 16 YEARS OF MY LIFE AND 4 OF THOSE YEARS I WAS ABUSED AND TORTURED BY A MAN I THOUGHT WAS MY DAD YOU ARE MY DAD YOU WERE NOT THERE TO HELP ME I CRIED OUT FOR HELP AND NO ONE WOULD HELP ME I NEEDED YOU AND YOU WERE NOT THERE FOR ME WHEN I NEEDED YOU THE MOST, I ALMOST KILLED MYSELF I HAVE BEEN THREW A LOT AND WHERE WERE YOU, ALL MY LIFE IF I NEW I HAD A REAL DAD SOME ONE THAT WOULD LOVE ME AND CARE FOR ME I WOULD HAVE BEEN LOOKING FOR YOU DO YOU KNOW HOW MUCH PAIN AND TORTURE I WENT THREW IN THE HANDS OF THAT OTHER MAN I SUFFER ALL MY LIFE I NEVER NEW WHAT HAPPINESS WAS HOW IT FELT TO GET A BIRTHDAY PRESENT INSTEAD OF GETTING PRESENTS I GOT ABUSE AND MADE FUN OF

THERE WERE MANY TIMES I WANTED TO END MY LIFE BUT I NEVER DID CAUSE OF RANDY AND I NEW THAT WAS SOMETHING BETTER FOR ME OUT THERE I NEW ONE DAY I WOULD BE FREE BUT DADDY I STILL WANT TO KNOW WHY YOU NEVER CAME LOOKING FOR ME JUST TELL ME DADDY I NEED TO KNOW WHERE WERE HAVE YOU BEEN IT IS A LONG STORY BUT I PROMISE YOU MIJA I WILL TELL YOU REAL SOON THE IMPORTANT THING IS THAT I AM HERE WITH YOU NOW I WISH I WOULD HAVE FOUND YOU EARLY BUT I FOUND YOU NOW SO THAT IS ALL THAT MATTERS I LOVE YOU YES DADDY BUT ANSWER MY QUESTION WHERE WERE YOU ALL THESE YEARS LIKE I SAID DREA WHEN I SEE YOU I WILL TELL YOU EVERYTHING YOU NEED TO KNOW ALL I ASK IS FOR YOU TO BELIEVE ME AND LET ME THE FATHER YOU NEVER HAD, YES YOU ARE RIGHT I NEVER HAD A FATHER IN MY LIFE, I WISH I DID

CHAPTER 11   THE LOVE OF A DAD

 YOU WERE SUPPOSED TO PROTECT ME NOT LEAVE ME, I KNOW ANDREA I AM SO SORRY BUT I DO LOVE YOU AND I MISS YOU SO MUCH I WANTED TO COME BACK TO YOU ALONG TIME AGO BUT I COULD NOT FIND YOU I SEARCHED FOR YOU AND YOU WERE NO WHERE TO BE FOUND HOW COULD YOU SAY I LOVE YOU TO SOMEONE YOU ABANDED PLEASE LET ME GO SEE YOU ANDREA I DO NOT KNOW I GOTTA GO BUT BEFORE I LEAVE AND HANG UP I GOT ONE

THING TO TELL YOU WHAT IS IT MIJA I LOVE YOU, DADDY, I NEEDED YOU AND YOU WERE NOT THERE FOR ME BUT YOU ARE HERE NOW AND YOU HAVE A LOT OF CATCHING UP, DO NOT LET ME DOWN COME BY HERE THIS WEEKEND AND WE WILL GET TO KNOW EACH OTHER I CAN FINALLY KNOW WHAT MY TRUE DAD IS ALL ABOUT AND YOU HAVE 16 YEARS OF PRESENTS YOU OWN ME JUST PLAYING I WILL SEE YOU THIS WEEKEND THANK YOU MIJA FOR GIVING ME A CHANCE TO MAKE IT UP TO YOU AND A CHANCE TO BE A PART OF YOUR LIFE YES, DADDY, I WILL SEE YOU THIS WEEKEND I AM SO HAPPY YOU HAVE COME BACK INTO MY LIFE I AM TOO DREA AS ANDREA AND HER DAD HANG THE PHONE SHE STANDS THERE WITH HER HAND STILL ON THE PHONE AS RANDY WALKS IN HE SEES HER HOLDING ONTO THE PHONE AND HE ASKS HER IS EVERYTHING OK AS SHE TURNS AND LOOKS AT RANDY, SHE HAS TEARS FALLING FROM HER EYES WHAT HAPPENED WHAT DID YOUR DAD SAY HE IS COMING TO SEE ME THIS WEEKEND I HAVE A DADDY WHOLOVES ME AND WANTS TO SEE ME ANDREA DO YOU THINK IT IS A GOOD IDEAL TO SEE HIM **YOU KNOW NOTHING ABOUT HIM I JUST DON'T WANT** YOU TO GET LET DOWN OR HURT AGAIN RANDY THANK YOU FOR WORRYING ABOUT ME AS ANDREA TELLS RANDY THIS, SHE SLOWLY WALKS TOWARDS THE WINDOW AND LOOKS OUT, YOU KNOW WHAT RANDY, WHAT MY LOVE WILL MY WHOLE LIFE I PRAYED TO JESUS TO LET ME KNOW HOW IT FEELS TO HAVE A PARENT THAT LOVES ME AS THEIR DAUGHTER AND WOULD DO ANYTHING AND EVERYTHING TO PROTECT ME AND LOVE ME AND CARE FOR ME I NEVER FELT THAT AS I WAS GROWING UP AND FINALLY, IT IS GOING TO HAPPEN, I WAITED LOTS OF YEARS FOR THIS TO FEEL THE LOVE OF MY TRUE FATHER RANDY I HAVE

A FATHER THAT LOVES ME AND CARES FOR ME YES, HE WAS WRONG TO LEAVE ME WHEN I WAS A BABY, I FORGIVE HIM THE ONLY THING THAT MATTERS KNOW IS THAT HE IS BACK, YES ANDREA I AM SO HAPPY FOR YOU THAT YOU FINALLY HAVE A FATHER THAT LOVES YOU AND CARES FOR YOU I KNOW YOU WENT THREW HELL AND BACK IN THE HANDS OF THE OTHER MAN WE THOUGHT WAS YOUR FATHER AND I KNOW THAT YOU AND YOUR DAD ARE GOING TO BE HAPPY TOGETHER ONCE YOU BOTH GET TO KNOW EACH OTHER BETTER, I CAN NOT WAIT TO MEET IT SOUNDS LIKE HE IS A GOOD DAD HE MUST HAVE MISSED YOU SO MUCH AND FOR HIM TO COME BACK AND LOOK FOR YOU AFTER ALL THESE YEARS SAYS A LOT ABOUT HIM, I JUST WONDER WHY HE WAITED SO LONG TO COME LOOKING FOR YOU I DO NOT KNOW RANDY BUT I WILL FIND OUT WHEN I SEE TOMORROW, **LET'S JUST HOPE HE** HAS A GOOD REASON WHY HE NEVER CAME AROUND BEFORE, WILL RANDY ALL THESE QUESTIONS WILL BE ANSWER TOMORROW BUT IT IS GETTING LATE I AM HUNGRY AND SLEEPY, AS THEY WERE TALKING ANDREA AUNT WAS STANDING IN THE DOORWAY AND HEARING ALL THAT WAS SAID AS SHE WALKS IN, SHE LOOKS AT ANDREA LOOK MIJA I WILL TELL YOU, TELL ME WHAT WHY DID YOUR DAD WAIT SO LONG TO COME LOOKING FOR YOU, OK WHY DID HE WAIT SO LONG TO COME AND SEE ME WILL YOU SEE WHEN YOUR DAD LEFT HE FELT ASHAMED AND EMBARRASSED OF WHAT HE DID AND HE FELT IN HIS HEART DID YOU WOULD NOT WELCOME HIM BACK INTO YOUR LIFE DAD SHOULD HAVE NOT FELT THAT WAY HE IS MY DAD, AND I LOVE HIM, YES MIJA I KNOW THAT BUT HE DID NOT KNOW THAT YOU CAN TELL HIM WHEN YOU SEE HIM, TOMORROW NOW HERE EAT THIS I MADE DINNER FOR THE BOTH OF YALL AND GET YOUR REST TOMORROW IS

GOING TO BE A LONG DAY YES TIA IT WILL BE AS RANDY AND ANDREA EAT THEIR DINNER ALL ANDREA CAN DO IS JUST THINK ABOUT HER DAD AND WHAT WILL IT BE LIKE TO FINALLY MEET HER DAD AFTER SO MANY YEARS OF NOT KNOWING THAT SHE HAD A TRUE FATHER THAT LOVES HER WILL RANDY I AM TIRED I AM GOING TO GO TO BED I AM ALSO GIVE ME A MINUTE I WILL BE IN THERE WITH YOU, OK MY LOVE GOODNIGHT TIA AND GRANDMA GOODNIGHT MIJA SEE YOU IN THE MORNING, AS ANDREA LEAVES THE ROOM RANDY STAYS THERE TALKING TO ANDREA TIA SARA I HAVE TO TALK TO YOU YES WHAT IS IT RANDY, FIRST I WANT TO SAY THANK YOU FOR SHOWING ANDREA MORE LOVE AND HAPPINESS THAT SHE HAS EXPERIENCED ALL OF HER LIFE TO TELL YOU THE TRUTH SHE WAS NEVER HAPPY SHE PRETENDED TO BE BUT WAS NOT SHE HAS BEEN THREW A LOT IN HER LIFE AND I AM ASKING YOU DO YOU THINK IT IS A GOOD IDEAL THAT SHE MEETS UP WITH HER DAD TOMORROW LOOK RANDY I UNDERSTAND WHAT YOU ARE SAYING AND I HAVE THOUGHT ABOUT IT FOR A LONG TIME WAIT WHEN YOU SAY A LONG TIME HOW LONG HAVE YOU KNOWN ABOUT THIS FOR A LITTLE OVER A YEAR THE LAST TIME THAT ANDREA CAME DOWN HER DAD SAW HER BUT DECIDED NOT TO TALK TO AT THAT TIME HE WAS NOT READY TO TALK TO HER HE WAITED AND WE TALKED EVERYDAY AND AFTER A WHILE I CAME TO REALIZE THAT HE IS A GOOD PERSON AND REGRETS LEAVING BUT LIKE HE SAID HE DID NOT LEAVE ANDREA HE LEFT HER MOM SO HOW MUCH DO YOU KNOW HOW IT WAS BETWEEN ANDREA DAD AND HER MOM WILL I KNOW THAT THEY NEVER GOT ALONG THE WERE ALWAYS FIGHTING THE ONLY REASON YOUR DAD STAYED AS LONG AS HE COULD FOR YOU BUT HE COULD NOT TAKE IT NO MORE AND WHAT DROVE HIM AWAY WAS

WHEN HE CAUGHT YOUR MOM CHEATING ON HIM LET ME GUESS SHE CHEATED ON HIM WITH THAT LOOSER SHE WAS WITH YES, YOU ARE RIGHT SHE LEFT A GOOD MAN FOR A MONSTER THAT WAS NO GOOD AND DESTROYED YOUR MOM MORE THEN SHE ALREADY WAS BUT THANK GOD THAT ANDREA IS HERE NOW AND SAFE YES, THANK GOD FOR THAT, WILL TIA IT IS TIME FOR ME TO GO TO BED THANKS FOR THE TALK AND I WILL SEE YOU IN THE MORING, YES RANDY GOODNIGHT AS RANDY AND ANDREA FALL FAST ASLEEP ANDREA DAD IS UP LOOKING AT THE PAPER CLIPPINGS OF THE COURT AND THE MAN THAT HURT HIS DAUGHTER WHEN HE READ THIS, HE WAS FULL OF ANGER AND ALL HE COULD THINK ABOUT WAS GETTING REVENGE FOR WHAT THEY DID TO HIS DAUGHTER AS HE PUT THE PAPER DOWN, HE SPOKE IN A LOW VOICE THEY WILL PAY FOR WHAT THEY DID, WHEN THE TIME IS RIGHT, I WILL ASK MY DAUGHTER IF SHE KNOWS WHO THEY WERE THIS WILL NOT GO WITHOUT JUSTICE IT WILL BE SEVERE ALL THE PAIN THEY CAUSE ANDREA AND THE 2 MEN WILL SUFFER TWICE AS BAD AS ANDREA'S DAD SPOKE THESE WORDS HE LAID DOWN AND WENT FAST ASLEEP, THE WHOLE WORLD IS ASLEEP BUT MORING IS JUST AROUND THE CORNER, THIS WILL BE AN INTERESTING MORNING COMING UP ANDREA IS HAPPY RANDY IS CONFUSED, AND ANDREA'S DAD IS HAPPY TO FINALLY SEE HIS DAUGHTER THAT HE LEFT YEARS AGO AND AT THE SAME TIME, HE IS FULL OF ANGER FOR WHAT HAPPENED TO HER GOOD MORNING RANDY GOOD MORNING MY LOVE HOW WAS YOUR NIGHT; IT WAS OK I WAS JUST IN DEEP THOUGHT ABOUT MY DAD YES, I KNOW I WAS THINKING A LOT ABOUT THIS WHAT WERE YOU THINKING I WAS THINKING THAT I HOPE EVERYTHING GOES WELL BETWEEN YOU AND YOUR DAD I DO NOT WANT TO SEE YOU

GET HURT YOU HAVE ALREADY SUFFERED ENOUGH IN YOUR LIFE YOU DO NOT NEED ANY MORE PAIN, THANKS FOR CARING RANDY BUT I ASSURE YOU EVERYTHING WILL BE GREAT I FEEL IN MY HEART THAT THINGS ARE GOING TO WORK OUT **WILL LET'S GET READY DAD WILL BE HERE SOON** AS ANDREA SAID THOSE WORDS TEARS FELL TO THE FLOOR AS RANDY SAW HER CRYING, HE ASKED ANDREA WHY ARE YOU CRYING IT IS JUST THAT I NEVER THOUGHT THAT I WOULD SAY THOSE WORDS WITH LOVE IN MY HEART AND IT FEELS SPECIAL I HAVE MIXED FEELINGS RIGHT NOW WHAT DO YOU MEAN YOU HAVE MIXED FEELINGS WHAT DO YOU FEEL I AM HAPPY AND GLAD THAT MY DAD CAME LOOKING FOR ME AND CAME BACK INTO MY LIFE AND WE CAN REBUILD THE LIFE TOGETHER THAT WE NEVER HAD A CHANCE TO DO IN THE PAST, AND ALSO, I AM KIND OF SCARED I DO NOT WANT TO LOSE HIM AGAIN, WE BOTH HAVE BEEN THREW SO MUCH THAT I DO NOT KNOW WHO SUFFER MORE ME OR HIM, LOOK AT THE TIME ANDREA, YOU NEED TO GET READY AND I AM SURE THAT YOU WILL NOT LOSE YOUR DAD AGAIN AS RANDY WAS TALKING TO ANDREA THE PHONE RANG ANDREA PAUSE AND SAID THAT IS MY DAD LETTING ME KNOW HE IS ON HIS WAY LET ME HURRY UP AND GET READY OK YOU DO THAT AND I AM GOING TO SEE IF THAT IS YOUR DAD ON THE PHONE AS RANDY WALKS INTO THE KITCHEN ANDREA'S AUNT WAS ON THE PHONE TALKING TO SOMEONE AS SHE HUNG UP, I ASKED ANDREA IF THAT WAS HER DAD IT WAS, AND WHAT HE SAY HE JUST CALLED TO REMIND ANDREA THAT HE WILL BE HERE SOON, AS A MATTER OF FACT, HE IS ON HIS WAY IS ANDREA READY SHE IS GETTING READY RIGHT NOW, I AM KIND OF NERVOUS FOR HER YES, I AM TOO IT HAS BEEN OVER 15 YEARS SINCE THE LAST TIME HER DAD SAW HER, SO I KNOW IT IS GOING TO BE AN

EMOTIONAL ENCOUNTER FOR THE BOTH OF THEM, YES, IT WILL LET ME GO TELL ANDREA HER DAD IS ON THE WAY ANDREA YOUR DAD CALLED HE IS ON HIS WAY HE WILL BE HERE IN A LITTLE BIT ARE YOU READY, YES, I AM READY LET'S GO OUTSIDE AND WAIT FOR HIM OK LET'S GO, AS RANDY AND ANDREA STEP OUTSIDE THEY SEE A CAR PULLING UP ANDREA HEART STOPS RANDY THERE IS MY DAD HE IS HERE AS ANDREA DAD FINALLY GET'S TO THE HOUSE WHERE ANDERA IS STAYING AT, HE DRIVES UP THE DRIVEWAY AND LOOKS AT ANDREA AS SHE STANDS THERE ON THE PORCH WITH A BOY HE DOES NOT KNOW HE SLOWLY OPENS THE DOOR TO HIS CAR STEPS OUT AND JUST STANDS THEIR SPEECHLESS DADDY IS THAT YOU YES ANDREA IT IS YOUR DAD SHE RUNS TO HIM AND HUGS HIM AND SAYS WHERE HAVE YOU BEEN ALL MY LIFE, I NEEDED YOU I AM SORRY DREA I WAS NOT THERE WITH YOU AS I SHOULD HAVE BEEN BUT I PROMISE YOU I WILL NEVER LEAVE YOU AGAIN PLEASE DON'T DADDY, I NEED YOU IN MY LIFE ANDREA LET HER DAD GO, SHE STOOD THERE AND LOOKED AT HIM THEN SAID YOU KNOW DAD ALL MY LIFE I PRAYED AND WISHED FOR A DIFFERENT DAD BUT WE WILL TALK ABOUT THAT LATER WHEN THE TIME IS RIGHT YES ANDREA, WE WILL DEFINITELY DO THAT THERE IS MUCH WE NEED TO TALK ABOUT SO LET ME LOOK AT YOU MIJA YOU HAVE GROWN UP TO BE A STRONG AND VERY BEAUTIFUL YOUNG LADY AND I AM PROUD TO CALL YOU MY DAUGHTER THE BEST PART OF MY LIFE THE PART I WISH I WOULD HAVE NEVER LEFT I AM SO SORRY I WILL TELL YOU A THOUSAND TIMES HOW SORRY I AM I LEFT YOU IT IS OK DAD THE IMPORTANT PART IS THAT YOU ARE BACK WITH ME THAT IS ALL THAT MATTERS SO, WHO IS THAT STANDING ON THE PORCH OH THAT IS MY FIANCE RANDY, FIANCE WHEN DID THIS HAPPEN IT IS A LONG STORY TELL ME I AM NOT

GOING NOWHERE WILL DAD IT HAPPENED WHEN WE WERE IN THE 8TH GRADE, HE CAME UP TO ME AND STARTED TELLING ME HOW MUCH HE LIKES ME AND HAS WANTED TO BE WITH ME FOR THE LONGEST AND I TOLD HIM THE SAME SO SINCE THAT DAY WE HAVE BEEN TOGETHER DADDY HAS BEEN THE BEST BOYFRIEND IN THE WORLD HE HAS BEEN BY MY SIDE THREW ALL MY TRAUMA TAKING CARE OF ME AND MAKING SURE I HAD EVERYTHING I NEEDED HIM EVEN WHEN I WAS IN THE HOSPITAL, HE WAS THERE WITH ME AND NEVER LEFT MY SIDE HE WOULD GO DAYS WITHOUT EATING JUST TO MAKE SURE, THAT HE WAS THERE WITH ME I LOVE HIM SO MUCH DADDY AND HE LOVES ME YES DREA I SEE HE CARES ABOUT YOU A LOT THAT IS GOOD COME ON DADDY LET ME INTRODUCE YOU TO HIM RANDY THIS IS MY DAD RAYMOND REYES HOW ARE YOU DOING MR. REYES I AM RANDY ANDREA BOYFRIEND/FIANCE I KNOW SON, SHE TOLD ME EVERYTHING AND I WANT TO THANK YOU FOR BEING THERE WITH HER WHEN SHE NEEDED SOMEONE WHO LOVES HER AND CARES FOR HER TO BE THERE WITH HER AT THE MOST TERRIBLE MOMENT OF HER LIFE AS ANDREA DAD SAID THIS HIS EYES FILLED WITH TEARS I WISH I COULD HAVE BEEN THERE FOR HER TOO I DID NOT KNOW ALL OF THIS WAS GOING ON IF I HAD KNOWN I WOULD HAVE COME AND GOT HER, FOR REAL YOU WOULD HAVE COME FOR ME IF YOU KNEW I WAS GOING THREW ALL OF THIS YES DREA AS RANDY AND ANDREA LISTENED TO WHAT HER DAD WAS SAYING ANDREA STOP HIM BUT I THOUGHT YOU HAVE BEEN TALKING TO MY AUNT FOR A WHILE ALREADY YES FOR ALMOST 6 MONTHS ALL WE DID WAS TALK ABOUT YOU AND HOW MUCH I MISS YOU AND HOW I WANT TO MAKE UP FOR ALL THE TIME I WAS NOT THERE WITH YOU SO MY AUNT NEVER TOLD YOU ANYTHING ABOUT

ME GETTING ABUSED BY MY PARENTS NO SHE DID NOT AND I GUESS SHE DID NOT TELL ME CAUSE AT THAT TIME SHE DID NOT KNOW EXACTLY WHAT WAS GOING ON IN YOUR OLD HOUSE I KNOW YOUR AUNT CALLED YOUR PARENTS ALWAYS TOLD HER NOT TO WORRY EVERYTHING WAS OK THAT YOU WERE JUST ACTING UP AND BEING A BAD GIRL, THAT IS NOT TRUE I WAS NEVER A BAD GIRL OR A BAD DAUGHTER BUT BAD THINGS HAPPENED TO ME YOUR AUNT LOVES YOU SO MUCH AND THERE IS NOTHING THAT SHE WILL NOT DO FOR YOU SHE WILL GIVE YOU THE WORLD IF SHE KNOWS THAT WILL MAKE YOU HAPPY SO DREA TO TELL YOU THE TRUTH THE ONLY THING THAT MATTERS TO ALL OF US INCLUDING YOUR BOYFRIEND IS YOUR HAPPINESS AND WELL-BEING AS HER DAD TELLS ANDREA THIS SHE TURNS AND LOOKS AT RANDY YES, MY LOVE YOUR DAD IS TELLING THE TRUTH THAT IS ALL WE EVER CARED ABOUT WAS MAKING SURE YOU WERE SAFE AND HAPPY AS RANDY SAYS THIS ANDREA TEARS OF LOVE AND HAPPINESS FALL FROM HER EYES THANK YOU ALL THIS IS THE BEST NEWS I HAVE HEARD IN A VERY LONG TIME SO DAD WHAT ARE WE GOING TO DO NOW, WILL WE ARE GOING TO GET SOMETHING TO EAT AND THEN SEE **OK DADDY WILL LET'S** GO AND GET SOMETHING TO **EAT LET'S** GO TO A RESTAURANT RANDY, WOULD YOU LIKE TO GO WITH US TO EAT I WOULD LOVE **TO BUT THIS IS YALL'S MOMENT TO SPEND TOGETHER** AND GET TO KNOW YOUR DAUGHTER YALL, HAVE A LOT TO TALK ABOUT, AND ANDREA I AM HAPPY FOR YOU THAT YOU FINALLY WITH YOUR DAD GET TO KNOW HIM BETTER AND CATCH UP ON THE TIMES THAT WAS LOST OK MY LOVE WE WILL BE BACK IN A LITTLE WHILE I LOVE YOU DREA, AND I LOVE YOU TOO HAVE FUN, AND MR. REYES IT WAS NICE MEETING YOU SEE YALL

WHEN YALL COME BACK, OK MIJA WHERE WOULD YOU LIKE TO GO EAT AT, WELL, THERE IS THIS NEW RESTAURANT THAT HAS OPENED UP DOWN THE ROAD **OK SOUNDS GOOD LET'S GO THERE** MIJA WHAT IS THE NAME OF THE RESTAURANT ANDREA LAUGHS AND SAYS IT IS **CALLED RAYMOND'S STEAK AND SEAFOOD** IT HAS MY NAME YES, DADDY IT HAS YOUR NAME BUT DON'T GET HAPPY IT IS NOT YOUR RESTAURANT OH I SEE YOU HAVE JOKES AS THEY BOTH ENJOY THEIR TIME TOGETHER AND DRIVE DOWN TO THE RESTAURANT BUT ANDREA DAD ONLY HAD ONE THOUGHT IN HIS HEAD AND THAT WAS TO GET REVENGE FOR WHAT HAPPENED TO HIS DAUGHTER AS THEY GET CLOSE TO THE RESTAURANT OK MIJA IS THIS THE PLACE YES, IT IS **COME ON LET'S GO INSIDE AS** THEY ENTERED ANDREA HAD TEARS IN HER EYES HER DAD ASKED HER WHY IS SHE CRYING OH DADDY I AM JUST SO HAPPY AND EXCITED TO HAVE MY FIRST DINNER AT THIS WONDERFUL PLACE WITH MY DADDY IT BRINGS HAPPINESS TO MY HEART TO KNOW THAT YOU EXIST IN MY LIFE AND TO SEE THAT YOU LOVE ME AND CARE FOR ME I AM SO BLESSED TO HAVE PEOPLE IN MY LIFE THAT CARE FOR ME, AS THEY ARE TALKING THE WAITRESS WALKS UP TO THEM HOW MANY IT IS JUST ME AND MY DADDY SO TWO YES OK COME THIS WAY IS THIS SEAT FINE YES THANK YOU HERE YOU GO AND YOUR SERVER WILL BE RIGHT WITH YOU SO WHAT DO YOU FEEL LIKE HAVING WILL DAD I AM GOING TO HAVE THE STEAK AND FISH COMBO SOUNDS GOOD I AM GOING TO HAVE THE SAME THING GREAT AS THE SERVER WALKS UP TO THE TABLE HI MY NAME IS TONY I WILL BE YOUR SERVER WHAT CAN I GET THE BOTH TO DRINK WE WILL HAVE TWO TEAS GREAT AND ARE YOU READY TO ORDER YES, WE WILL BOTH HAVE THE STEAK AND FISH AND WE

WILL START WITH THE NACHOS DELUXE GREAT I WILL BE RIGHT BACK WITH YOUR APPETIZER AS THE SERVER WALKS AWAY RAYMOND LOOKS AT ANDREA WITH TEARS IN HIS EYES DAD WHY ARE YOU CRYING DREA I AM SO SORRY I LEFT YOU WE NEED TO HAVE A SERIOUS TALK OK DADDY ABOUT WHAT I KNOW YOU WANT TO FORGET ABOUT THE PAST BUT THERE ARE SOME QUESTIONS I NEED TO ASK YOU AS ANDREA'S DAD SAID THIS ANDREA WAS SPEECHLESS THEN SAID OK DAD BUT CAN WE TALK ABOUT THIS AFTER WE EAT YES DREA THAT IS FINE LET'S ENJOY OUR TIME TOGETHER THANKS DADDY SO DREA WHAT ARE YOUR PLANS ARE YOU GOING BACK TO SCHOOL YES, I AM ME AND RANDY TALKED ABOUT IT AND W ARE GOING BACK TO SCHOOL NEXT FALL THEN WE GOING TO COLLEGE FOR CRIMINAL JUSTICE WE WANT TO HELP THE KIDS AND PROTECT THEM SINCE THERE WAS NOBODY THERE TO HELP US AND PROTECT US BUT MOST OF ALL BELIEVE US WE WANTED TO SHOW THE KIDS THAT THEY HAVE SOMEBODY THEY CAN TURN TO AND LISTEN TO AND BELIEVE WHAT THEY HAVE TO SAY AND THEN HELP THEM WE WANT TO GIVE BACK TO OUR COMMUNITY THAT IS GREAT AND I KNOW BOTH YOU AND RANDY WILL BE GREAT PEOPLE TO HELP THESE KIDS THERE ARE SO MANY YOUNG PEOPLE GETTING HURT AND ABUSED THESE DAYS AND THE SAD PART IT IS THEIR PARENTS OR FAMILY MEMBERS HURTING THEM AND NOBODY DOESNOTHING ABOUT IT YOU KNOW JUST LAST YEAR ALONE THERE WAS OVER 2000 CASE OFCHILD ENDANGERMENT CHILD NEGLECT AND WORST OF ALL CHILD ABUSE I KNOW REMEMBER I HAD EXPERIENCED THAT BUT WE WILL TALK ABOUT THAT LATER TODAY SO DAD WHAT HAVE YOU BEEN DOING WHAT KIND OF WORK DID YOU DO WILL AFTER I LEFT YOUR MOM,

I DID NOT KNOW WHAT I WAS GOING TO DO I WAS LOST BECAUSE I DID NOT TAKE YOU WITH ME, I WANTED TO BUT I COULD NOT I WAS IN A BAD PLACE AND DID NOT HAVE A STEADY JOB SO I KNEW I COULD NOT TAKE CARE OF YOU I COULD BEARLY TAKE CARE OF MYSELF THEN ONE NIGHT I SAW THIS COMMERCIAL ON TV SAYING GO BACK TO SCHOOL AND GET THE DEGREE YOU WANT SO ALL NIGHT I SAT THERE AND THOUGHT ABOUT IT AND I THOUGHT ABOUT HOW MY LIFE HAD BEEN I WAS SO ASHAMED OF MYSELF HERE I WAS A 28-YEAR-OLD MAN AND HAD NOTHING TO SHOW SO I DECIDED TO GO BACK TO SCHOOL AND STUDY BUSINESS MANAGEMENT I LEARNED HOW TO RUN A BUSINESS AND EVERYTHING IN THAT FIELD SO I STARTED WORKING FOR THIS COMPANY AND SOON I BECAME GOOD AT WHAT I WAS DOING IN A SHORT TIME I LEARNED A LOT I HAD SAVED UP ALMOST ALL MY MONEY I DECIDED TO OPEN UP MY RESTAURANT THE FIRST ONE I OPENED WAS IN SAN ANTONIO TEXAS THEN A FEW YEARS LATER I OPENED UP A FEW MORE WAIT DAD ARE YOU FOR REAL YOU HAVE A RESTAURANT HOW MANY DO YOU HAVE AND WHAT IS THE NAME OF IT HE JUST SMILED WHEN ANDREA ASKED THIS QUESTION AND SHE SAID ARE YOU TELLING ME THAT THIS IS YOUR RESTAURANT WHEN SHE SAID THIS THE MANAGER OF THE RESTAURANT CAME OVER TO THE TABLE AND SAID HELLO MR REYES SIR NICE TO SEE YOU AGAIN AND THANK YOU FOR THE BONUSES YOU GAVE US THAT WAS VERY GENEROUS OF YOU, IT IS OK YOU ALL DESERVE IT YALL HAVE DONE GREAT WORK FOR ME SO, WHO IS THIS YOUNG LADY **I'M SORRY THIS IS MY DAUGHTER ANDREA HELLO ANDREA NICE** TO FINALLY MEET YOU HOW DO YOU KNOW ABOUT ME YOUR DAD HAS TALK ABOUT YOU SO MUCH ABOUT HE HAD A DAUGHTER AND BEEN WANTING TO MEET HER FOR SO MANY

YEARS BUT NEVER COULD FIND HER BUT I CAN SEE THAT YOU BOTH ARE VERY HAPPY TO FINALLY MEET I HAVE TO GET BACK TO MY STAFF HOPE YOU BOTH ENJOY YALL DAY TOGETHER YES, THANK YOU WE WILL, SO YES ANDREA THIS IS MY RESTAURANT SEE DREA I OPENED RESTAURANTS IN THESE DIFFERENT CITIES HOPING I WOULD FIND YOU SO WAIT YOU DID ALL OF THIS FOR ME, DAD, WHY BECAUSE YOU ARE MY DAUGHTER, I LOVE YOU AND THERE IS NOTHING I WOULD NOT DO TOFIND YOU I SEARCH THE WHOLE WORLD LOOKING FOR YOU AND I DID NOT STOP LOOKING FOR YOU UNTIL I FOUND YOU AND I NEW THE DAY WOULD COME WHERE I WOULD FIND YOU ANDREA YOU MEAN

CHAPTER 12   FOR YOU DADDY

THE WORLD TO ME AND I NEW IN MY HEART THAT I WOULD ONLY BE HAPPY WHEN I FOUND YOU SO YES DREA I NEW I NEEDED TO BRING MY DAUGHTER BACK INTO MY LIFE I NEEDED TO LOCATE WHERE YOU WERE AND I KNEW IT YOU WERE JUST LIKE ME YOU WOULD LOVE FISH AND STEAK; I WAS RIGHT SO I OPENED THIS LOCATION HOPING YOU WOULD BE HERE AND YES, I WAS RIGHT WOW DAD THANK YOU THAT IS SPECIAL TO ME I LOVE YOU, DADDY, I

LOVE YOU DREA, AND HERE GOES OUR MEAL, I HOPE YOU LIKE IT I CREATED THIS PLATE JUST FOR YOU MIJA SO ENJOY AND I HOPE YOU LIKE THIS MEAL I CREATED THIS PLATE JUST FOR YOU WOW DAD THIS TASTES SO GOOD HOW DID YOU LEARN HOW TO MAKE FOOD THAT HAS SO MUCH FLAVOR IN IT, WHAT ARE YOUR PLANS FROM THIS DAY FORWARD WILL DREA I PLAN TO SPEND AS MUCH TIME WITH YOU AS POSSIBLE AND MAKE SURE I KEEP YOU SAFE AND HAPPY AND I PROMISE SO HOW MANY RESTAURANTS DO YOU HAVE AS OF TODAY I HAVE 8 RESTAURANTS ARE YOU GOING TO OPEN ANYMORE NO NEED TO I FOUND WHAT I BEEN LOOKING FOR YOU ALL OF THESE YEARS AND WHAT IS THAT DADDY IT IS YOU I FINALLY FOUND YOU SO NO NEED TO OPEN UP ANY MORE RESTAURANTS I AM SO PROUD OF YOU DADDY AND TO THE QUESTION YOU ASKED ME EARLIER IT ALL STARTED WHEN I HAD JUST TURNED 10 YEARS OLD, I REMEMBER I WAS IN THE LIVING ROOM ON THE FLOOR WATCHING MY FAVORITE TV SHOW THE PERSON, I THOUGHT WAS MY DAD CAME UP TO ME AND SLAP MY BEHIND AND SAID YOUR DADDYS GOOD LITTLE GIRL I THOUGHT NOTHING ABOUT IT I CONTINUED WATCHING TV THEN THAT NIGHT IT STARTED TO AS ANDREA SAID THAT SHE PAUSED AND DID NOT SAY A WORD AND HER DAD ASKED HER WHAT HAPPENED MIJA WILL HE ENTER MY ROOM THAT NIGHT I WAS ON MY BED DRAWING AND HE CAME UP TO ME AND STARTED GRABBING ALL OVER ME I FELT SO UNCOMFORTABLE AND I ASKED HIM NOT TO DO THAT I DID NOT WANT TO PLAY WITH HIM **LIKE THAT AND HE SAID IT IS OK DON'T WORRY FATHERS AND** DAUGHTERS PLAY LIKE THIS AND THEY DO IT ALL THE TIME THIS IS HOW THEY SHOW EACH OTHER HOW MUCH THEY LOVE ONE ANOTHER THIS WENT ON FOR ABOUT A YEAR EVERY NIGHT THE SAME THING THEN

WHEN I TURNED 11 YEARS OLD THAT IS WHEN THE ABUSE AND TORTURE STARTED FIRST, HE WOULD WALK IN ON ME WHEN I WAS CHANGING MY CLOTHES, HE SAW ME A FEW TIMES WHEN NOTHING WAS ON AND HE WOULD JUST SAY GOOD GIRL I WAS SCARED OF HIM I DID NOT KNOW WHAT WAS GOING TO HAPPEN NEXT AND DID YOU TELL YOUR MOM WHAT WAS GOING ON YES, I TOLD HER EVERY TIME AND ALL SHE WOULD SAY WAS JUST MAKE YOUR DAD HAPPY GIVE HIM WHAT HE WANTS AFTER SHE SAID THAT MY WHOLE WORLD WAS TURNED INSIDE OUT AT THAT POINT, I KNEW I WAS IN THIS BY MYSELF THERE WAS NO ONE THAT COULD OR WOULD HELP ME THEN THE MOST TERRIBLE DAY AT LEAST I THOUGHT IT WAS THE MOST TERRIBLE DAY OF MY LIFE HE CAME INTO MY ROOM ONE NIGHT WHEN EVERYONE WAS STILL ASLEEP, I COULD SMELL THE ALCOHOL ON HIM AS I SAW HIM, I PULLED THE COVERS OVER ME AND ASKED HIM WHY ARE YOU IN MY ROOM GO BACK TO HIS ROOM YOU ARE DRUNK WHAT DO YOU WANT HE GAVE ME THE WEIRDEST LOOK I EVER SAW AND HE SAID THE TIME HAS COME WHAT DO YOU MEAN THE TIME HAS COME YES, IT IS TIME FOR YOU TO SHOW DADDY WHAT YOU HAVE AND MAKE ME HAPPY WHEN HE SAID THAT I GOT UP AND TRIED TO RUN OUT OF THE ROOM BUT HE GRABBED ME AND THREW ME BACK ONTO THE BED AND SAID STAY STILL TONIGHT, I TAKE WHAT I WANT FROM YOU AND THERE IS NOTHING YOU OR ANYONE CAN DO ABOUT IT SO **JUST TAKE WHAT YOUR DADDY GOT'S TO GIVE YOU** WHEN IT STARTED, I CRIED AND SCREAMED FOR SOMEONE TO HEAR ME AND HELP ME THEN MY MOM WALKED IN ON US AND I THOUGHT SHE WAS GOING TO HELP ME BUT I WAS WRONG SHE SAID SHUT UP AND LET YOUR DADDY **FINISH YOU'RE** WAKING THE WHOLE HOUSE UP DO NOT ACT LIKE YOU DON'T LIKE IT

THAT NIGHT MY WHOLE LIFE WAS DESTROYED HE TOOK MY INNOCENCE AND DESTROYED ME AND THEN THEY WOULD JUST LAUGH AT MY PAIN AS ANDRIA WAS TELLING HER DAD THIS, HE WAS IN SO MANY TEARS COULD HARDLY SPEAK AND HE SAID TO ANDREA I AM SO SORRY I SHOULD OF BEEN THERE TO HELP YOU DADDY IT IS NOT YOUR FAULT THERE IS MORE TO SAY ABOUT THIS IF YOU WANT TO KNOW THE WHOLE TRUTH, YES, MIJA I DO TELL ME, AFTER THAT DAY I WOULD CONTINUE TO GET ABUSE EVERY DAY I WOULD GET HOME FROM SCHOOL, AND AS SOON AS I WALKED IN MY MOM WOULD SLAP ME AND SAY YOU ARE LATE GO TO YOUR ROOM NO DINNER FOR YOU IF WE HAVE LEFTOVERS, YOU CAN EAT THEM AS A DOG DOES THEY WERE HOOKED ON DRUGS THEN ONE DAY I GOT HOME FROM SCHOOL AND AGAIN MY SLAPPED ME AND SAID GO TO YOUR ROOM AND GET WHAT DO YOU HAVE COMING TO YOU AS I WAS WALKING TO MY ROOM, I SAW MY DAD AND HIS TWO FRIENDS AT THE TABLE LOOKING AT ME UP AND DOWN AS I GOT TO MY ROOM ONE MAN CAME IN AND SAID YOU ARE MINE AND HE GOT ON TOP OF ME THEN THE NEXT MAN CAME IN AND THE SAME THING HAPPENED AT THAT POINT I COULD NOT MOVE WALK OR TALK THEN HE WALKED IN AND SAID NOW MAKE YOUR DADDY HAPPY WHEN HE FINISHES, I JUST WANTED TO KILL ME AND I CRIED OUT PLEASE LORD SEND SOMEONE TO HELP ME AFTER A WHILE THEY FINALLY BROUGHT ME TO MY GRANDMA AND AUNT HOUSE AT THAT POINT THINGS STARTED GETTING BETTER DREA IF YOU WERE TO SEE THOSE OTHER TWO GUYS AGAIN WOULD YOU RECOGNIZE THEM YES, I WOULD NEVER FORGET THE FACE OF A PERSON THAT MADE YOUR LIFE A LIVING HELL, I WOULD KNOW THEM ANYWHERE WHY DO YOU ASK THAT WHAT ARE YOU THINKING ABOUT DOING

NOTHING DREA I WAS JUST ASKING OK DADDY SO WHAT ARE WE GOING TO DO AFTER THIS I AM **THINKING ABOUT THAT I DON'T** KNOW IF WE MIGHT TAKE A SMALL ROAD TRIP TODAY YES AND WHERE ARE WE GOING THAT IS A SURPRISE SO, ARE YOU READY TO GO YES, I AM DONE OK DREA I AM GOING TO TAKE YOU BACK TO YOUR HOME THEN I WILL COME BACK AND PICK YOU UP FOR OUR ROAD TRIP JUST BE READY WHEN I GET BACK I GOTTA GO CHECK ON SOMETHING I WILL NOT BE THAT LONG OK I WILL BE HERE WAITING FOR YOU TO GET BACK AS ANDREA DAD DRIVES OFF, SHE STANDS ON THE PORCH LOOKING AT HIM LEAVE AND STANDS THERE WONDERING WHERE THEY ARE GOING WHEN HE **GET'S BACK TO AS SHE IS STANDING** THEIR RANDY WALKS OUT TOWARDS ANDREA IS EVERYTHING OK YES RANDY EVERYTHING IS JUST GREAT SO HOW WAS YOUR TIME TOGETHER IT IS NOT OVER YET WHAT DO YOU MEAN YES RANDY HE IS COMING BACK TO PICK ME UP WE ARE GOING ON A SHORT ROAD TRIP WHERE ARE YOU AND YOUR DAD GOING, I DO NOT KNOW BUT WE TALKED ABOUT WHAT HAPPENED TO ME IN THE PAST I TOLD HIM EVERYTHING AND THEN HE ASKED ME IF I WAS TO SEE THOSE TWO MEN AGAIN WOULD I KNOW WHO THEY WERE AND I TOLD **HIM YES, I WOULD KNOW THEM DON'T MATTER** WITH HOW MUCH TIME PASSES THAT IS A PART OF MY LIFE I WILL NEVER FORGET THE ONES THAT CAUSE ME SO MUCH PAIN AND SUFFERING AS THEY LEFT THE RESTAURANT; THEY SAID NOTHING ON THEIR DRIVE BACK TO ANDREA HOUSE THEY BOTH STAYED QUIET AS ANDREA SAT THERE AND WONDERED WHY HER DAD ASKED HER IF SHE WOULD REMEMBER THOSE TWO MEN IF SHE WAS TO SEE THEM AGAIN, AND THOUGHT IF HER DAD WAS GOING TO TAKE HER WITH HIM TO GO AND LOOK FOR THOSE TWO MEN AND

KILL THEM WILL DREA HERE WE ARE BACK AT YOUR HOUSE I WILL BE BACK IN A LITTLE BIT I HAVE TO GO PICK SOMETHING UP RIGHT QUICK BE READY WHEN I GET BACK OK DADDY, I WILL BE READY AS SHE GETS OUT OF THE CAR RANDY WALKS OUT OF THE HOUSE AND STANDS THERE ON THE PORCH WAITING FOR ANDREA TO WALK TOWARDS HIM SO HOW WAS YOUR TIME WITH YOUR DAD WILL IT IS NOT OVER HE IS COMING BACK TO PICK ME UP AND WE ARE TAKING A LITTLE ROAD TRIP WHERE TO I DO NOT KNOW, BUT HE WILL LET ME KNOW WHEN WE TAKE OFF GUESS WHAT ELSE I FOUND OUT ABOUT MY DAD WHAT IS THAT HE IS THE OWNER OF THE NEW RESTAURANTS **THAT OPEN YOU MEAN RAYMOND'S** STEAK AND FISH IS HIS BUSINESS YES, IT IS AND HE HAS 8 LOCATIONS ALL TOGETHER, WHY SO MANY WILL HE TOLD ME THAT HE OPEN UP THESE PLACES HOPING THEY WOULD BRING ME TO HIM SINCE I LOVE FISH AS MUCH AS HE DOES THIS IS AMAZING THAT YOUR DAD WOULD GO THREW SO MUCH TO FIND YOU, I SAY TO YOU ANDREA YOU ARE BLESSED TO HAVE A DAD THAT LOVES YOU AND CARES SO MUCH FOR YOU SO DO YOU HAVE ANY IDEA OR CLUE AS TO WHERE YOUR DAD MIGHT BE TAKING YOU, NO **I DON'T KNOW** BUT I HAVE A STRANGE FEELING THAT WE ARE GOING BACK TO OUR HOMETOWN YOU MEAN THE TOWN WE JUST CAME FROM YES BUT WHY WILL DURING LUNCH DAD ASKED ME WHAT HAPPENED AND I TOLD HIM EVERYTHING I SAW THE LOOK ON MY DAD FACE FULL OF HURT AND ANGER SO, I BELIEVE THAT HE WENT TO BUY A GUN AN WHEN HE COMES **BACK, HE GONNA SAY LET'S GO FOR OUR LITTLE TRIP THEN HE** WILL TELL ME WE ARE GOING BACK TO YOUR HOMETOWN TO KILL THOSE MONSTERS THAT HURT YOU, AND WHEN HE TELLS ME THAT I WILL HELP HIM DESTROY THEM THEY DID NOT CARE ABOUT ME WHEN

THEY WERE HURTING ME AND DESTROYING MY CHILDHOOD SO I DO NOT CARE ABOUT THEM SO, YES, I HAVE A STRONG FEELING THAT WE ARE GOING TO GO LOOKING FOR THEM MY DAD WAS SO HURT AND MAD WHEN I TOLD HIM THIS HE HAD THAT LOOK IN HIS EYES OF REVENGE AND ANGER ANDREA, I LOVE YOU PROMISE ME THAT WHATEVER HAPPENS TODAY YOU WILL BE CAREFUL I WILL MY LOVE AND I AM GOING TO BE WITH MY DAD I KNOW HE WILL NOT LET ANYTHING HAPPEN TO ME LOOK THERE HE GOES HE IS PULLING UP AS ANDREA GETS IN THE CAR WITH HER DAD, SHE ASKS HIM WHERE ARE WE GOING HER DAD STAYS QUIET FOR A LITTLE BIT THEN AS THEY GOT DOWN THE ROAD ANDREA ASKED HER DAD AGAIN SO WHERE ARE WE GOING HER DAD LOOKED AT HER WITH THE SADDEST EYES EVER LOOK DREA I WAS NEVER AROUND TO STAND BY YOUR SIDE AND HELP YOU AND SAVE YOU WHEN YOU NEEDED SOMEONE THERE WITH YOU SO I AM GETTING REVENGE FOR WHAT HAPPENED TO YOU DAD ARE YOU TELLING ME WE ARE GOING TO GO LOOK FOR THOSE MAN THAT HURT ME YES, ANDREA WE ARE GOING TO GO LOOK FOR THE MAN THAT HURT YOU I HOPE YOU UNDERSTAND YES DADDY I UNDERSTAND AND I AM WITH YOU ON THIS LET'S GO LOOKING FOR THOSE MEN THAT HURT ME AND GET MY PAYBACK, NOW DREA REMEMBER WHAT I TOLD YOU WHAT IS THAT YOU HAVE TO THINK LIKE THEM WHERE COULD WE FIND THEM WHAT ARE INTERESTED IN, WILL FROM WHAT I KNOW AND EXPERIENCE THEY LIKE YOUNGER GIRLS ARE MONSTERS YES DAD AND REMEMBER I HAD TO DEAL WITH THEM I AM SORRY DREA BUT THIS IS THE DAY THAT YOU GET YOUR PAYBACK FOR WHAT HAPPENED WILL WE ALMOST ON THE FREEWAY AND SOON WE WILL BE BACK TO YOUR HOMETOWN I HAVE A QUESTION DAD YES, WHAT IS IT YOU NEVER

TOLD ME WHERE YOUR HOMETOWN WAS WHERE DID YOU GO AFTER YOU LEFT MOM WILL DREA I DID NOT HAVE A HOMETOWN I MEAN WHEN I LEFT YALL I JUST WONDER AROUND HOPELESS NOT KNOWING WHAT MY NEXT MOVE WAS SO I WAS HOPELESS AND THOUGHT I WOULD NEVER FIND A WAY OUT BUT I THANK GOD I WAS ABLE TO COME AROUND AND PUT MY LOVE FOR YOU FIRST NOTHING ELSE MEANS MORE TO ME THA YOUR HAPPINESS THANK YOU, DADDY, FOR COMING BACK INTO MY LIFE AND THESE TWO MEN ARE THE LAST PART OF MY HAPPINESS WHAT DO YOU MEAN DREA THEY ARE THE LAST PIECE OF YOUR HAPPINESS YES, DADDY AFTER YOU KILL THEM THAT WILL MAKE ME THE HAPPIEST PERSON IN THE WORLD OK DREA WE ARE HERE IN YOUR HOMETOWN TIME TO GO AND LOOK FOR THESE TWO MEN YES, DADDY TIME TO FIND THE MONSTERS AND GET IT OVER WITH I **WAITED SO LONG FOR THIS DAY LET'S GO DOWN THIS STREET.** AS ANDREA AND HER DAD SEARCHED UP AND DOWN THE STREETS OF ROSENBERG, THE ONLY THING ON BOTH OF THEIR MINDS WAS FINDING THESE TWO MEN AND GETTING REVENGE FOR THE PAIN AND SUFFERING THEY HAD CAUSED ANDREA ALONG WITH HER PARENTS SHE HAD SUFFERED A LOT MANY TEENS SUFFER AS ANDREA HAD TO SUFFER AT THE HANDS OF THEIR PARENTS AND THEY HAVE NO ONE TO TURN TO THAT WILL BELIEVE THEN THEY ARE TORN INTO LITTLE PIECES BROKEN UP CRYING AND SCREAMING ON THE INSIDE AND NO ONE HEARS THEIR CRY OUT FOR HELP ANDREA IS A STRONG PERSON AND CAN COME OUT OF THIS THE SCARS AND MEMORIES OF THOSE NIGHTS WILL ALWAYS BE A PART OF HER LIFE LOOK DADDY WHAT AM I AM LOOKING AT THAT HOUSE RIGHT THERE WHAT ABOUT IT THAT IS THE HOUSE THAT USED TO STAY AT AND THAT IS THE HOUSE

WHERE I WAS ABUSED AND IT'S OK ANDREA YOU DON'T HAVE TO SAY ANYTHING ELSE, I KNOW LET'S JUST FIND THESE MAN LOOK ANDREA I HAVE SOMETHING TO TELL YOU WHAT IS IT DADDY WILL WHEN I GOT THESE RESTAURANTS I THOUGHT LONG AND HARD WHO WOULD I LEAVE THEM TO WHEN IT IS MY TIME TO GO, AND DREA WHEN THE TIME COMES YOU WILL BE THE NEW OWNER OF ALL MY RESTAURANTS, NO DADDY I DO NOT WANT THE RESTAURANTS I WANT YOU TO REMEMBER YOU PROMISED YOU WOULD NEVER LEAVE ME I WON'T ANDREA, I LOVE YOU LOOK DADDY THERE THEY GO ARE YOU SURE THAT IS THEM YES THAT'S THEM OK COME ON LET'S GET THEM, OK I AM WITH YOU HEY, YOU WHO ME YES YOU COME HERE I NEED TO TALK TO YOU WHAT ABOUT DO YOU RECOGNIZE THIS GIRL HERE NO I DO NOT WHO IS SHE YOU DO KNOW WHO I AM YOU AND YOUR FRIEND HERE AND MY DAD TORTURED ME WHEN I WAS ONLY 12 YEARS OLD, I BEG YALL TO STOP AND YOU NEVER DID SO NOW IT IS PAYBACK TIME, OH YES ANDREA RIGHT YES, I REMEMBER THAT NIGHT YOU WERE REAL GOOD, AS HE SAID THIS RAYMOND WAS PULLING OUT HIS GUN WHEN THE OTHER MAN SAW THE GUN, HE PULLED OUT HIS GUN THEY BOTH SHOT AND ANDREA DAD FELL TO THE GROUND, AS ANDREA SAW HER DAD FALL, SHE FELL TO HER KNEES AND GRABBED HER DAD'S HAND DADDY GET UP YOU CAN NOT DIE ON ME YOU PROMISED ME YOU WOULD NEVER LEAVE ME PLEASE DAD, I NEED YOU DON'T GO YOU JUST CAME BACK INTO MY LIFE I CAN NOT LOSE YOU A SECOND TIME PLEASE DAD WAKE UP AS ANDREA WAS THERE BY HER DAD HOLDING HIS HAND AND HER CLOTHES WERE FULL OF BLOOD AND TEARS FALLING FROM HER EYES, SHE SAW HER BROTHER AS

HE WALKS UP TO HER, ANDREA WHAT HAPPENED AND WHAT ARE YOU DOING HERE, ANDY, THEY KILLED HIM THEY KILLED OUR DAD HE IS GONE HE PROMISE ME HE WOULD NEVER LEAVE ME LOOK AT HIM ANDY HE IS GONE AND IT'S MY FAULT THEY DID IT ANDY, THEY KILLED HIM WHO KILLED HIM AND WHAT DO YOU MEAN OUR DAD YES THIS IS OUR REAL DAD; ANDY, PLEASE HELP ME WAKE HIM UP HE CAN NOT LEAVE US COME ON SISTER THERE IS NOTHING WE CAN DO FOR HIM LET'S GO CALL THE COP NO ANDY I AM NOT LEAVING HIM HE IS DEAD CAUSE OF ME I AM NOT LEAVING HIM, WHO KILLED HIM THE MONSTERS THAT HURT ME WHEN I WAS YOUNGER, YOU MEAN THEY ARE STILL AROUND YES, THEY ARE, WILL THIS IS FAR FROM OVER DON'T WORRY SIS THEY WILL GET WHAT THEY HAVE COMING TO THEM YOUR RIGHT ANDY THIS IS FAR FROM OVER WITH AS THE AMBULANCE AND COPS GET THERE, THEY SEE ANDREA ON HER KNEES CRYING OVER HER DAD THEY RUSH UP TO HER AND PICK HER UP WHAT HAPPENED HERE THERE WERE THESE TWO GUYS WHO CAME UP TO US AND TRIED TO HURT US AND MY DAD TRIED TO STOP THEM AND THEY SHOT HIM HAVE YOU SEEN THES GUYS BEFORE YES, I HAVE WHO ARE THEY ANDREA STAYED SILENT FOR A MOMENT MAMA WHO ARE THOSE TWO GUYS THEY ARE THE OTHER TWO GUYS THAT HURT ME WHEN I WAS YOUNGER, THEY WERE MY STEPDAD'S FRIENDS WAIT YOUR ANDREA GARCIA YES THAT IS ME OH MY GOD, YOU DO NOT REMEMBER ME DO YOU NO I DON'T WHO ARE YOU I AM DETECTIVE GARCIA I WORKED YOUR CASE WHEN IT ALL STARTED, OH YES, NOW I REMEMBER YOU MR. GARCIA, WE NEED TO GET THESE MONSTERS OFF THE STREET THEY HAVE DESTROYED MY LIFE I STILL HAVE NIGHTMARES FROM WHAT HAPPENED TO ME AND BECAUSE OF THEM I DO

NOT HAVE A NORMAL LIFE, I ASSURE YOU ANDREA WE WILL GET THE MONSTERS YES, I KNOW YOU WILL LOOK WHAT THEY DID TO MY DADDY HE JUST CAME BACK INTO MY LIFE AND I LOST HIM AGAIN CAUSE OF THOSE TWO GUYS **COME ON ANDREA LET'S GO CALL** RANDY I AM SURE HE WANTS TO TALK TO YOU AND IS WORRIED **ABOUT YOU YES AND YOU ARE RIGHT LET'S GO** CALL HIM AS ANDREA LEAVES WITH ANDY SHE STANDS THERE FOR A BIT OVER HER DAD'S BODY AND TEARS FALL FROM HER EYES AND WHISPERS I ASSURE YOU DAD; I WILL GET THEM FOR DOING THIS TO YOU THEY HURT ME FOR THE LAST TIME TAKING YOU OUT OF MY LIFE WILL NOT GO JUST LIKE THAT DADDY, I LOVE YOU AND I WILL ALWAYS CHERISH THE LITTLE TIME WE HAD

TOGETHER AND I WILL NEVER FORGET WHAT YOU DID FOR ME I WILL NEVER FORGET YOU LOVE YOU DADDY REST IN PEACE I WILL TAKE CARE OF THIS MATTER I PROMISE YOU COME ON ANDY LET GO CALL RANDY AS ANDREA AND ANDY LEAVE TO CALL RANDY ANDREA IS SO HURT AND MAD AT WHAT HAS HAPPENED THAT THE ONLY THOUGHT ON HER MIND IS TO GET PAY BACK TO WHAT HAS HAPPENED TO HER DAD ON ANDREA HERE, WE GO THE PHONE AS ANDREA CALLS RANDY SHE IS SHAKING HELLO WHO IS THIS **THERE WAS A SILENT'S ON THE** PHONE ALL RANDY COULD HEAR WAS CRYING ON THE OTHER SIDE ANDREA MY LOVE IS THAT YOU WHAT HAPPENED ARE YOU OK RANDY, THEY KILLED MY DAD, WAIT WHAT DO YOU MEAN THEY KILLED YOUR DAD WHO KILLED HIM THOSE TWO MONSTERS KILLED HIM I NEED YOU TO COME OVER HERE RIGHT NOW ANDY IS HERE WITH ME OK MY LOVE I AM LEAVING RIGHT NOW I SHOULD BE THERE IN A FEW HOURS HURRY UP I NEED YOU HERE

NOW OK I AM LEAVING RIGHT NOW WHERE WILL YOU BE WHEN I GET THERE, I WILL BE WITH ANDY WE WILL BE SITTING ON THE DOORSTEP OF OUR OLD HOUSE WHERE IT ALLSTARTED PLEASE JUST HURRY AND GET HERE OK MY LOVE I AM ON MY WAY BE THERE SOON AS ANDREA HUNG UP WITH RANDY, SHE TURNED TO ANDY AND SAID **YOU HAVE A LOT OF CONNECTIONS HERE DON'T** YOU YES, I KNOW SOME PEOPLE WHY YOU ASKING I NEED YOU TO GET A HOLD OF THEM WE NEED TO GET A GUN NO ANDREA WE CAN NOT DO THIS LIKE THIS LOOK THOSE TWO MEN DESTROYED MY LIFE AND THEY MADE ME TAKE OFF FROM THE HOUSE WHEN I WAS STILL A LITTLE GIRL THE COPS ARE NOT GOING TO DO NOTHING THIS ENDS TONIGHT NOW WILL YOU DO THIS FOR US OR DO I HAVE TO GO OUT AND GET IT MYSELF ANDY, I KNOW YOU ARE SCARED I AM TOO BUT THIS IS THE HAND WE WERE DEALT THIS IS THE WORLD WE LIVE IN EVERYONE THAT WE TRUSTED TO TAKE CARE OF US HURT US AND THE ONE PERSON THAT HAS COME INTO MY LIFE THEY TOOK HIM AWAY FROM ME THIS IS A HEARTLESS WORLD AND WE HAVE TO LIVE WITH IT NOW ARE YOU GOING TO GET THE GUN OR NOW ANDY SAT THERE AND STAYED QUIET AND THEN HE SAID OK ANDREA YOU ARE RIGHT, WE STRUGGLE OUR WHOLE LIVES CAUSE OTHER PEOPLE ARE EVIL STAY **HERE DON'T GO NOWHERE** I SHOULD BE BACK IN A FEW OK ANDY MAKE IT QUICK RANDY WILL BE HERE SOON OK I WILL BE BACK SOON AS ANDY LEAVES ANDRA SITS THERE AND JUST THINKS ABOUT ALL THAT HAS HAPPENED AS RANDY HEADS TOWARDS **ANDRA SHE RUNS AND HOLD'SHIM TIGHT AND SHE SAY'S THEY KILLED MY DADDY THOSES MOSTERS KILLED HIM** I CAN NOT BELIEVE THIS IS HAPPENING TO ANDREA HER DAD IS DEAD I KNOW SHE IS HURTING RIGHT

NOW I JUST NEED TO BE BY HER SIDE AND COMFORT HER AND ASSURE HER THAT EVERYTHING IS GOING TO BE OK I JUST HOPE SHE DOES NOT TRY TO DO ANYTHING THAT SHE WILL REGRET LATER ALL THAT SHE HAS BEEN THREW ANYTHING SHE DOES SHE WILL NOT REGRET AND AT THIS POINT I DO NOT BLAME HER FOR WANTING TO GET REVENGE FOR ALL THE PAIN, THEY CAUSE HER IN HER LIFE WILL THERE GOES THE TURN TO GO BACK TO ROSENBERG TEXAS, I NEVER THOUGHT WE WOULD SEE THIS TOWN AGAIN I GREW UP HERE AND IT WAS A GREAT CHILDHOOD FOR ME BUT NOT FOR HER ANDREA HAS A LOT OF BAD MEMORIES IN THIS TOWN AS RANDY DRIVES TO ANDREA OLD HOUSE ANDY RETURNS TO THE HOUSE WHERE ANDREA IS AT, ANDREA LOOK AT ANDY AND ASK HIM DID YOU GET THE GUN YES, I GOT IT RIGHT HERE LOOK ARE YOU SURE YOU WANT TO DO THIS I KNOW YOU ARE IN A LOT OF PAIN AND YOU ARE SUFFERING RIGHT BECAUSE OF WHAT THEY DID TO DAD, YOU KNOW ANDY WHEN DAD CAME BACK INTO MY LIFE, I SAY THE LOOK IN HIS EYES OF JOY AND LOVE AS IF HE FINALLY FOUND WHAT HE HAD BEEN SEARCHING FOR ALL OF HIS LIFE AND WHEN HE HUGGED ME, I FELT THE LOVE HE HAD FOR ME, AND A MOMENT I WAS AT PEACE BECAUSE I HAD DAD BACK IN MY LIFE AND HE LOOKED ME IN MY EYES AND PROMISED ME THAT HE WOULD NEVER LEAVE ME AND THAT HE WAS GOING TO BE BY MY SIDE FOREVER AND THESE TWO MEN TOOK ALL THAT AWAY FROM ME WITHIN MINUTES ALL OF THAT WAS TAKING AWAY SO YOU ASK IF I WANT TO DO THIS YES ANDY, I AM SO SERIOUS I WANT TO DO THIS BECAUSE IT IS WHAT THEY HAD MADE ME BECOME, I HAVE SO MUCH REMORSE IN ME I AM AT THE POINT WHERE DO NOT CARE ABOUT ANYTHING ELSE JUST GETTING MY PAYBACK FOR WHAT

THEY DID TO MY DAD RANDY MY DAD IS DEAD I KNOW YOU TOLD ME SO I SEE THAT LOOK IN YOUR EYES WHAT ARE YOU PLANNING ON DOING, RANDY IT IS SIMPLE ANDY WENT TO GET A GUN AND WE ARE GOING TO FIND THESE TWO GUYS AND GET PAYBACK FOR ALL THE PAIN AND SUFFERING THEY HAVE BROUGHT INTO MY LIFE SO ARE YOU GOING TO COME WITH US OR ARE YOU GOING TO TRY AND STOP ME YOU SAY YOU LOVE ME THAN STAND BY MY SIDE ON THIS ANDREA, I DO LOVE YOU I LOVE YOU MORE THAN YOU CAN IMAGINE, AND OK IF THIS IS SOMETHING THAT YOU MUST DO THEN I AM HERE FOR YOU, AND I **WILL STAND BY YOUR SIDE ON THIS OK GREAT LET'S GO WHERE** ARE WE GOING TO FIND THEM, I THINK I KNOW WHERE THEY ARE AT COME ON LET'S GO THIS WAY, ANDREA THE LOVE I HAVE FOR YOU IS ENDLESS AND I HAVE NEVER SEEN YOU AT THIS STAGE OF YOUR LIFE ARE YOU GOING TO BE OK, WILL RANDY I WAS ONCE OK BUT I DO NOT KNOW ANYMORE I DO NOT KNOW WHAT BEING OK FEELS LIKE BUT WHEN WE GET REID OF THOSE TWO GUYS THEN I WILL TELL YOU HOW I FEEL LOOK ANDY AND RANDY WHAT ARE WE LOOKING AT RIGHT THERE AT THE PARK THAT IS THEM THEY ARE THE ONES THAT KILLED MY DAD OK WE GOTTA HAVE A PLAN HOW ARE WE GOING TO APPROACH THEM THEY ALL STAYED QUIET THEN ANDREA CAME UP WITH A PLAN THAT WOULD END EVERYTHING LOOK RANDY AND ANDY THEY THINK I AM BY MYSELF SO I AM GOING TO APPROACH THEM AND AS I AM SPEAKING TO THEM THEN YOU BOTH GET THEM OK **SOUNDS GOOD MY LOVE JUST PLEASE BE CAREFUL DON'T WORRY** RANDY, I PROMISE I WILL BE CAREFUL YOU BOTH JUST BE READY WHEN THIS GOES DOWN, I AM READY ANDY ARE YOU READY YES **SIS I AM READY LET'S GET THEM FOR WHAT THEY DID TO YOU YES LET'S GO** AS ANDREA

WALKS TOWARDS THE TWO GUYS SHE IS AS NERVOUS AS COULD BE THEN THEY SEE HER HEY COME OVER HERE YOU FOUND US I GUESS YOU WANT MORE OF WHAT WE GAVE YOU IN THE PAST NO I JUST WANT TO ASK YOU BOTH SOME QUESTIONS **COME HERE LET'S SEE WHAT YOU HAVE** FOR US I WANT TO KNOW WHY YOU BOTH DID WHAT YOU DID TO ME AND WHY YOU KILLED MY DAD HOW COULD YOU BOTH HURT ME I WAS JUST A LITTLE GIRL YES YOU WERE AND WHAT HAPPENED TO YOU WE DID IT AND THERE IS NOTHING YOU CAN DO TO CHANGE THAT JUST REMEMBER THAT WHAT HAPPENED TO YOU AND THERE IS NOTHING ANYBODY CAN DO TO CHANGE THAT YOU KNOW YALL BOTH ARE RIGHT THAT WAS A PART OF MY LIFE THAT I LIVE WITH EVERYDAY AND I CAN NEVER CHANGE WHAT HAPPENED TO ME I CAN ONLY LIVE WITH IT AND TRY AND GO ON WITH LIFE BUT THERE IS ONE THING THAT WILL CHANGE AND WHAT IS THAT FROM THIS DAY FORWARD YOU BOTH WILL NEVER HURT ANOTHER PERSON THE WORLD WILL BE FREE FROM THEY BOTH OF YALL, RANDY SHOWED THEM WHAT I MEAN AS SHE SAID THAT THERE WERE 6 GUNSHOTS AS THEY BOTH FAIL TOO THE GROUND ANDREA SMILED AND SAID FINALLY I GOT MY REVENGE FOR WHAT THEY DID TO ME AND MY DAD BEFORE THEY DIED ANDREA LOOKED AT THEM AND SPOKE AND SAID THIS IS FOR YOU DADDY, I LOVE YOU REST IN PEACE, AND THANK YOU FOR HELPING ME FIND PEACE OF MIND AS THEY WALK AWAY ANDREA STOOD THERE IN SILENCE THEN SHE SPOKE YOU KNOW RANDY AND ANDY I CAN NOT BELIEVE EVERYTHING THAT HAPPENED TONIGHT THERE BEEN A LOT OF BLOODSHED HERE TONIGHT I NEVER THOUGHT IT WOULD END LIKE THIS I HOPE NO OTHER KID GOES THREW WHAT I'VE BEEN THREW I THANK GOD THAT I

MADE IT THIS FAR FOR IT WAS BY HIS GRACE LOVE AND MERCY THAT I AM HERE AND I AM STRONG LORD FORGIVE ME FOR ALL THE WRONG I HAVE DONE I KNOW IT WAS NOT RIGHT TO KILL THESE TWO MEN THEY JUST CAUSED ME SO MUCH PAIN AND SUFFERING I AM ASKING FOR FORGIVENESS WILL RANDY IT IS OVER NOW WE CAN LIVE OUR LIVES AS WE PLAN ANDY ARE YOU COMING BACK TO AUSTIN WITH US, WE NEED YOU THERE YOUR OUR FAMILY YOU NEED TO GET OUT OF THIS TOWN IT IS NO GOOD PLACE FOR YOU TO BE, YOUR RIGHT ANDREA I WILL BE GOING BACK WITH ALL YOU KNOW RANDY IT HAS BEEN A LONG JOURNEY AND LOT'S OF PEOPLE GOT HURT AND KILLED BUT WE SURVIED THREW IT ALL YES, IT HAS BEEN ANDREA AND I AM GLAD AND WE ARE BLESSED THAT WE DID MAKE IT OUT WITHOUT LOOSEN ONE ANOTHER KNOW **WE CAN ALL GO BACK TO YOUR AUNT'S HOUSE** AND START A NEW LIFE WITHOUT A WORRY IN THE WORLD YES, **RANDY WE WILL BE GOING BACK TO MY AUNT'S HOUSE AND YOU** WILL SEE IT IS A MUCH BETTER LIFE THEN HERE SO ARE YOU BOTH READY TO GO YES, ANDREA WE ARE READY TO GO WE GOT A LONG RIDE BACK HOME, I LOVE YOU SO MUCH ANDREA, AND I LOVE YOU TOO RANDY THIS IS ONE DAY I WILL NEVERFORGET I WILL NOT FORGET THIS DAY NITHER YOU KNOW ANDREA THERE HAS BEEN A LOT THAT HAS HAPPEN IN THIS TOWN THNGS THAT WE WILL NEVER FORGET IT WILL ALWAYS BE A PART OF OUR **LIVES DON'T MATTER** HOW MUCH WE TRY WE WILL NOT FORGET IT BUT ONE THING I CAN SAY THAT THREW THE WHOLE TIME THAT WE HAVE BEEN GOING THREW THIS OUR LORD AND SAVIOR HAD HIS **HAND ON OUR LIVE'S** I JUST FEEL SORRY FOR THE MANY PEOPLE THAT GOT HURT AND THEIR LIFE WAS DESTROYED BY YOUR PARENTS I PRAY THAT THEY CAN FIND INNER PEACE AND LIVE THEIR

LIVES WITH NO PAIN FROM WHAT HAPPENED IN THE PASS, YES RANDY THIS IS TRUE IT'S OVER BUT THE MEMORIES OF WHAT HAPPEN WILLALWAYS BE IN MY MIND AND IN MY HEART BUT WE HAVE TO MOVE FORWARD AND MAKE IT A BETTER LIFE WILL NOW ARE WE READY TO GET OUT OF THIS TOWN YOU KNOW ANDREA I WAS JUST THINKING IF YOUR DAD WOULD OF NOT GOT KILLED BY THOSES MAN THEN YOU AND HIM WOULD OF HAVE A GREAT LIFE TOGETHER BUT EVERYTHING HAPPENS FOR A REASON AND LIFE WILL GO ON FOR YOU AND ME AND ANDY AND I KNOW THAT HE IS IN HEAVEN LOOKING DOWN ON US AND HE WILL BE PROUD AND IS PROUD OF THE WONDERFUL AND LOVING PERSON YOU HAVE BECOME NOW LET'S GET READY AND GO HOME YES WE ARE COME ON ANDREA AND ANDY LET'S GET OUT OF THIS TOWN AND GO HOME.

THE END

THIS BOOK WAS WRITTEN AND CREATED BY RANDY FLORES IS FICTIONAL BUT BASE ON TRUE LIFE EVENTS **NAME'S WERE CHANGE**D IN THE BOOK TO PROTECT THE PEOPLE IN THE BOOK THIS BOOK MAY BE FICTIONAL BUT THESE THINGS HAPPEN EVERY DAY TO KIDS AND EVERYONE AS WE GO ON WITH OUR LIFE PAY ATTENTION TO OUR KIDS IF THEY SEEM TO BE UNCOMFORTABLE AND COMPLAIN TO YOU PLEASE LISTEN TO THEM A CHILD NEEDS THEIR PARENTS IN THEIR LIFE TO CARE FOR THEM AND BELIEVE THEM A CHILD IS A GIFT OF GOD AND NEED'S THEIR PARENTS LOVE AND ATTENTION TO BE THERE FOR THEM AND DO NOT TRUST EVERYONE AROUND YOUR CHILDREN NOT EVENONE IS AS GOOD OF A PERSON AS THEY CLAIMED TO BE IF YOUR CHILD IS SCARE OF THAT PERSON THERE IS A REASON FOR THEM BEING SCARE SIT DOWN WITH THEM AND TALK ABOUT THEIR FEARS GOD BLESS YOU ALL UNTIL NEXT TIME

THIS BOOK WAS WRITTEN AND CRATED

BY RANDY FLORES

EMAIL FLORESRANDY003@GMAIL.COM

COPTRIGHT ON 8/29/2023

REGISTERED BY THE STATE OF TEXAS

ON 8/29/2023

Made in the USA
Coppell, TX
28 November 2023